ROCK SPRINGS

Richard Ford was born in Jackson, Mississippi, in 1944, and lives in Montana. His
work has appeared in *Esquire*, *Harper's* and
Granta, and his stories have been reprinted
in several recent anthologies, including
Penguin's *Great Esquire Fiction* and *Writers of
the Purple Sage* (about Western writers).

One of America's finest short-story
writers, Richard Ford is also a highly
acclaimed novelist. His first novel, *A Piece
of My Heart*, was runner-up for the Ernest
Hemingway Award. "This is quality
writing," said *The Times*, "in the highest
American tradition of Faulkner, Hemingway
and Steinbeck." *The Sportswriter* was "the
best novel I read in 1986"

— JONATHAN RABAN

RICHARD FORD

ROCK SPRINGS

STORIES

Flamingo
Published by Fontana Paperbacks

These stories all appeared first in the following magazines:
Going to the Dogs (Triquarterly, 1979); Rock Springs (Esquire, 1982);
Winterkill (*Esquire*, 1983); Fireworks (*Esquire*, 1984);
Communist (*Antaeus*, 1984); Sweethearts (*Esquire*, 1986);
Empire (*Granta*, 1986); Great Falls (*Granta*, 1987);
Children (*New Yorker*, 1987); Optimists (*New Yorker*, 1987).

First published in Great Britain by
Collins Harvill in 1988

This Flamingo edition first published
in 1989 by Fontana Paperbacks,
8 Grafton Street, London W1X 3LA

Flamingo is an imprint of
Fontana Paperbacks, part of
the Collins Publishing Group

Printed and bound in Great Britain by
William Collins Sons & Co. Ltd, Glasgow

Kristina

CONTENTS

ACKNOWLEDGEMENTS

I am grateful to the following publications in which these stories originally appeared: Esquire: *"Rock Springs", "Winterkill", "Fireworks"* and *"Sweethearts";* Anteaeus: *"Communist";* The New Yorker: *"Optimists"* and *"Children";* Granta: *"Empire"* and *"Great Falls";* Tri-Quarterly: *"Going to the Dogs".*

I wish to express my appreciation to the National Endowment for the Arts for its generous support. And I wish, as well, to express my thanks to Gary L. Fisketjon and L. Rust Hills for their editorial advice, and for their indispensable encouragement as I wrote these stories.

RF

ROCK SPRINGS

Edna and I had started down from Kalispell, heading for Tampa-St. Pete where I still had some friends from the old glory days who wouldn't turn me in to the police. I had managed to scrape with the law in Kalispell over several bad checks—which is a prison crime in Montana. And I knew Edna was already looking at her cards and thinking about a move, since it wasn't the first time I'd been in law scrapes in my life. She herself had already had her own troubles, losing her kids and keeping her ex-husband, Danny, from breaking in her house and stealing her things while she was at work, which was really why I had moved in in the first place, that and needing to give my little daughter, Cheryl, a better shake in things.

I don't know what was between Edna and me, just beached by the same tides when you got down to it. Though love has been built on frailer ground than that, as I well know. And when I came in the house that afternoon, I just asked her if she wanted to go to Florida with me, leave things where they sat, and she said, "Why not? My datebook's not that full."

Edna and I had been a pair eight months, more or less man and wife, some of which time I had been out of work, and some when I'd worked at the dog track as a lead-out and could help with the rent and talk sense to Danny when he came around. Danny was afraid of me because Edna had told him I'd been in prison in Florida for killing a man, though that wasn't true. I had once been in jail in Tallahassee for stealing tires and had gotten into a fight on the county farm where a man had lost his eye. But I hadn't done the hurting, and Edna just wanted the story worse than it was so Danny wouldn't act crazy and make her have to take her kids back, since she had made a good adjustment to not having them, and I already had Cheryl with me. I'm not a violent person and would never put a man's eye out, much less kill someone. My former wife, Helen, would come all the way from Waikiki Beach to testify to that. We never had violence, and I believe in crossing the street to stay out of trouble's way. Though Danny didn't know that.

But we were half down through Wyoming, going toward I-80 and feeling good about things, when the oil light flashed on in the car I'd stolen, a sign I knew to be a bad one.

I'd gotten us a good car, a cranberry Mercedes I'd stolen out of an ophthalmologist's lot in Whitefish, Montana. I stole it because I thought it would be comfortable over a long haul, because I thought it got good mileage, which it didn't, and because I'd never had a good car in my life, just old Chevy junkers and used trucks back from when I was a kid swamping citrus with Cubans.

The car made us all high that day. I ran the windows up and down, and Edna told us some jokes and made faces. She could be lively. Her features would light up like a beacon and you could see her beauty, which wasn't ordinary. It all made me giddy, and I drove clear down to Bozeman, then straight on through the park to Jackson Hole. I rented us the bridal suite in the Quality Court in Jackson and left Cheryl and her little dog, Duke, sleeping while Edna and I drove to a rib barn and drank beer and laughed till after midnight.

It felt like a whole new beginning for us, bad memories left behind and a new horizon to build on. I got so worked up, I had a tattoo done on my arm that said FAMOUS TIMES, and Edna bought a Bailey hat with an Indian feather band and a little turquoise-and-silver bracelet for Cheryl, and we made love on the seat of the car in the Quality Court parking lot just as the sun was burning up on the Snake River, and everything seemed then like the end of the rainbow.

It was that very enthusiasm, in fact, that made me keep the car one day longer instead of driving it into the river and stealing another one, like I should've done and *had* done before.

Where the car went bad there wasn't a town in sight or even a house, just some low mountains maybe fifty miles away or maybe a hundred, a barbed-wire fence in both directions, hardpan prairie, and some hawks riding the evening air seizing insects.

I got out to look at the motor, and Edna got out with Cheryl and the dog to let them have a pee by the car. I checked the water and checked the oil stick, and both of them said perfect.

"What's that light mean, Earl?" Edna said. She had come and stood by the car with her hat on. She was just sizing things up for herself.

"We shouldn't run it," I said. "Something's not right in the oil."

She looked around at Cheryl and Little Duke, who were peeing on the hardtop side-by-side like two little dolls, then out at the mountains, which were becoming black and lost in the distance. "What're we doing?" she said. She wasn't worried yet, but she wanted to know what I was thinking about.

"Let me try it again."

"That's a good idea," she said, and we all got back in the car.

When I turned the motor over, it started right away and the red light stayed off and there weren't any noises to make you think something was wrong. I let it idle a minute, then pushed the accelerator down and watched the red bulb. But there wasn't any light on, and I started wondering if maybe I hadn't dreamed I saw it, or that it had been the sun catching an angle off the window chrome, or maybe I was scared of something and didn't know it.

"What's the matter with it, Daddy?" Cheryl said from the backseat. I looked back at her, and she had on her turquoise bracelet and Edna's hat set back on the back of her head and that little black-and-white Heinz dog on her lap. She looked like a little cowgirl in the movies.

"Nothing, honey, everything's fine now," I said.

"Little Duke tinkled where I tinkled," Cheryl said, and laughed.

"You're two of a kind," Edna said, not looking back. Edna was usually good with Cheryl, but I knew she was tired now. We hadn't had much sleep, and she had a tendency to get cranky when she didn't sleep. "We oughta ditch this damn car first chance we get," she said.

"What's the first chance we got?" I asked, because I knew she'd been at the map.

"Rock Springs, Wyoming," Edna said with conviction. "Thirty miles down this road." She pointed out ahead.

I had wanted all along to drive the car into Florida like a big success story. But I knew Edna was right about it, that we shouldn't take crazy chances. I had kept thinking of it as my car and not the ophthalmologist's, and that was how you got caught in these things.

"Then my belief is we ought to go to Rock Springs and negotiate ourselves a new car," I said. I wanted to stay upbeat, like everything was panning out right.

"That's a great idea," Edna said, and she leaned over and kissed me hard on the mouth.

"That's a great idea," Cheryl said. "Let's pull on out of here right now."

The sunset that day I remember as being the prettiest I'd ever seen. Just as it touched the rim of the horizon, it all at once fired the air into jewels and red sequins the precise likes of which I had never seen before and haven't seen since. The West has it all over everywhere for sunsets, even Florida, where it's supposedly flat but where half the time trees block your view.

"It's cocktail hour," Edna said after we'd driven awhile. "We ought to have a drink and celebrate something." She felt better thinking we were going to get rid of the car. It certainly had dark troubles and was something you'd want to put behind you.

Edna had out a whiskey bottle and some plastic cups and was measuring levels on the glove-box lid. She liked drinking, and she liked drinking in the car, which was something you got used to in Montana, where it wasn't against the law, but where, strangely enough, a bad check would land you in Deer Lodge Prison for a year.

"Did I ever tell you I once had a monkey?" Edna said, setting my drink on the dashboard where I could reach it when I was ready. Her spirits were already picked up. She was like that, up one minute and down the next.

"I don't think you ever did tell me that," I said. "Where were you then?"

"Missoula," she said. She put her bare feet on the dash and rested the cup on her breasts. "I was waitressing at the AmVets. This was before I met you. Some guy came in one day with a monkey. A spider monkey. And I said, just to be joking, 'I'll roll you for that monkey.' And the guy said, 'Just one roll?' And I said, 'Sure.' He put the monkey down on the bar, picked up the cup, and rolled out boxcars. I picked it up and rolled out three fives. And I just stood there looking at the guy. He was just some guy passing through, I guess a vet. He got a strange look on his face—I'm sure not as strange as the one I had—but he looked kind of sad and surprised and satisfied all at once. I said, 'We can roll again.' But he said, 'No, I never roll twice for anything.' And he sat and drank a beer and talked about one thing and another for a while, about nuclear war and building a stronghold somewhere up in the Bitterroot, whatever it was, while I just watched the monkey, wondering what I was going to do with it when the guy left. And pretty soon he got up and said, 'Well, good-bye, Chipper'—that was this monkey's name, of course. And then he left before I could say anything. And the monkey just sat on the bar all that night. I don't know what made me think of that, Earl. Just something weird. I'm letting my mind wander."

"That's perfectly fine," I said. I took a drink of my drink. "I'd never own a monkey," I said after a minute. "They're too nasty. I'm sure Cheryl would like a monkey, though, wouldn't you, honey?" Cheryl was down on the seat playing with Little Duke. She used to talk about monkeys all the time then. "What'd you ever do with that monkey?" I said, watching the speedometer. We were having to go slower now because the red light kept fluttering on. And all I could do to keep it off was go slower. We were going maybe thirty-five and it was an hour before dark, and I was hoping Rock Springs wasn't far away.

"You really want to know?" Edna said. She gave me a quick glance, then looked back at the empty desert as if she was brooding over it.

"Sure," I said. I was still upbeat. I figured I could worry about breaking down and let other people be happy for a change.

"I kept it a week." And she seemed gloomy all of a sudden, as if she saw some aspect of the story she had never seen before. "I took it home and back and forth to the AmVets on my shifts. And it didn't cause any trouble. I fixed a chair up for it to sit on, back of the bar, and people liked it. It made a nice little clicking noise. We changed its name to Mary because the bartender figured out it was a girl. Though I was never really comfortable with it at home. I felt like it watched me too much. Then one day a guy came in, some guy who'd been in Vietnam, still wore a fatigue coat. And he said to me, 'Don't you know that a monkey'll kill you? It's got more strength in its fingers than you got in your whole body.' He said people had been killed in Vietnam by monkeys, bunches of them marauding while you were asleep, killing you and covering you with leaves. I didn't believe a word of it, except that when I got home and got undressed I started looking over across the room at Mary on her chair in the dark watching me. And I got the creeps. And after a while I got up and went out to the car, got a length of clothesline wire, and came back in and wired her to the doorknob through her little silver collar, then went back and tried to sleep. And I guess I must've slept the sleep of the dead—though I don't remember it—because when I got up I found Mary had tipped off her chair-back and hanged herself on the wire line. I'd made it too short."

Edna seemed badly affected by that story and slid low

in the seat so she couldn't see out over the dash. "Isn't that a shameful story, Earl, what happened to that poor little monkey?"

"I see a town! I see a town!" Cheryl started yelling from the back seat, and right up Little Duke started yapping and the whole car fell into a racket. And sure enough she had seen something I hadn't, which was Rock Springs, Wyoming, at the bottom of a long hill, a little glowing jewel in the desert with I-80 running on the north side and the black desert spread out behind.

"That's it, honey," I said. "That's where we're going. You saw it first."

"We're hungry," Cheryl said. "Little Duke wants some fish, and I want spaghetti." She put her arms around my neck and hugged me.

"Then you'll just get it," I said. "You can have anything you want. And so can Edna and so can Little Duke." I looked over at Edna, smiling, but she was staring at me with eyes that were fierce with anger. "What's wrong?" I said.

"Don't you care anything about that awful thing that happened to me?" Her mouth was drawn tight, and her eyes kept cutting back at Cheryl and Little Duke, as if they had been tormenting her.

"Of course I do," I said. "I thought that was an awful thing." I didn't want her to be unhappy. We were almost there, and pretty soon we could sit down and have a real meal without thinking somebody might be hurting us.

"You want to know what I did with that monkey?" Edna said.

"Sure I do," I said.

"I put her in a green garbage bag, put it in the trunk of my car, drove to the dump, and threw her in the trash." She was staring at me darkly, as if the story meant something to her that was real important but that only she could see and that the rest of the world was a fool for.

"Well, that's horrible," I said. "But I don't see what else you could do. You didn't mean to kill it. You'd have done it differently if you had. And then you had to get rid of it, and I don't know what else you could have done. Throwing it away might seem unsympathetic to somebody, probably, but not to me. Sometimes that's all you can do, and you can't worry about what somebody else thinks." I tried to smile at her, but the red light was staying on if I pushed the accelerator at all, and I was trying to gauge if we could coast to Rock Springs before the car gave out completely. I looked at Edna again. "What else can I say?" I said.

"Nothing," she said, and stared back at the dark highway. "I should've known that's what you'd think. You've got a character that leaves something out, Earl. I've known that a long time."

"And yet here you are," I said. "And you're not doing so bad. Things could be a lot worse. At least we're all together here."

"Things could always be worse," Edna said. "You could go to the electric chair tomorrow."

"That's right," I said. "And somewhere somebody probably will. Only it won't be you."

"I'm hungry," said Cheryl. "When're we gonna eat? Let's find a motel. I'm tired of this. Little Duke's tired of it too."

Where the car stopped rolling was some distance from the town, though you could see the clear outline of the interstate in the dark with Rock Springs lighting up the sky behind. You could hear the big tractors hitting the spacers in the overpass, revving up for the climb to the mountains.

I shut off the lights.

"What're we going to do now?" Edna said irritably, giving me a bitter look.

"I'm figuring it," I said. "It won't be hard, whatever it is. You won't have to do anything."

"I'd hope not," she said and looked the other way.

Across the road and across a dry wash a hundred yards was what looked like a huge mobile-home town, with a factory or a refinery of some kind lit up behind it and in full swing. There were lights on in a lot of the mobile homes, and there were cars moving along an access road that ended near the freeway overpass a mile the other way. The lights in the mobile homes seemed friendly to me, and I knew right then what I should do.

"Get out," I said, opening my door.

"Are we walking?" Edna said.

"We're pushing."

"I'm not pushing." Edna reached up and locked her door.

"All right," I said. "Then you just steer."

"You're pushing us to Rock Springs, are you, Earl? It doesn't look like it's more than about three miles."

"I'll push," Cheryl said from the back.

"No, hon. Daddy'll push. You just get out with Little Duke and move out of the way."

Edna gave me a threatening look, just as if I'd tried to hit her. But when I got out she slid into my seat and took the wheel, staring angrily ahead straight into the cottonwood scrub.

"Edna can't drive that car," Cheryl said from out in the dark. "She'll run it in the ditch."

"Yes, she can, hon. Edna can drive it as good as I can. Probably better."

"No she can't," Cheryl said. "No she can't either." And I thought she was about to cry, but she didn't.

I told Edna to keep the ignition on so it wouldn't lock up and to steer into the cottonwoods with the parking lights on so she could see. And when I started, she steered it straight off into the trees, and I kept pushing until we were twenty yards into the cover and the tires sank in the soft sand and nothing at all could be seen from the road.

"Now where are we?" she said, sitting at the wheel. Her voice was tired and hard, and I knew she could have put a good meal to use. She had a sweet nature, and I recognized that this wasn't her fault but mine. Only I wished she could be more hopeful.

"You stay right here, and I'll go over to that trailer park and call us a cab," I said.

"What cab?" Edna said, her mouth wrinkled as if she'd never heard anything like that in her life.

"There'll be cabs," I said, and tried to smile at her. "There's cabs everywhere."

"What're you going to tell him when he gets here? Our stolen car broke down and we need a ride to where we can steal another one? That'll be a big hit, Earl."

"I'll talk," I said. "You just listen to the radio for ten minutes and then walk on out to the shoulder like nothing was suspicious. And you and Cheryl act nice. She doesn't need to know about this car."

"Like we're not suspicious enough already, right?" Edna looked up at me out of the lighted car. "You don't think right, did you know that, Earl? You think the world's stupid and you're smart. But that's not how it is. I feel sorry for you. You might've *been* something, but things just went crazy someplace."

I had a thought about poor Danny. He was a vet and crazy as a shit-house mouse, and I was glad he wasn't in for all this. "Just get the baby in the car," I said, trying to be patient. "I'm hungry like you are."

"I'm tired of this," Edna said. "I wish I'd stayed in Montana."

"Then you can go back in the morning," I said. "I'll buy the ticket and put you on the bus. But not till then."

"Just get on with it, Earl." She slumped down in the seat, turning off the parking lights with one foot and the radio on with the other.

The mobile-home community was as big as any I'd ever seen. It was attached in some way to the plant that was lighted up behind it, because I could see a car once in a while leave one of the trailer streets, turn in the direction of the plant, then go slowly into it. Everything in the plant was white, and you could see that all the trailers were painted white and looked exactly alike. A deep hum came out of the plant, and I thought as I got closer that it wouldn't be a location I'd ever want to work in.

I went right to the first trailer where there was a light, and knocked the metal door. Kids' toys were lying in the gravel around the little wood steps, and I could hear talking on TV that suddenly went off. I heard a woman's voice talking, and then the door opened wide.

A large Negro woman with a wide, friendly face stood in the doorway. She smiled at me and moved forward as if she was going to come out, but she stopped at the top step. There was a little Negro boy behind her peeping out from behind her legs, watching me with his eyes half closed. The trailer had that feeling that no one else was inside, which was a feeling I knew something about.

"I'm sorry to intrude," I said. "But I've run up on a little bad luck tonight. My name's Earl Middleton."

The woman looked at me, then out into the night toward the freeway as if what I had said was something she was going to be able to see. "What kind of bad luck?" she said, looking down at me again.

"My car broke down out on the highway," I said. "I

can't fix it myself, and I wondered if I could use your phone to call for help."

The woman smiled down at me knowingly. "We can't live without cars, can we?"

"That's the honest truth," I said.

"They're like our hearts," she said, her face shining in the little bulb light that burned beside the door. "Where's your car situated?"

I turned and looked over into the dark, but I couldn't see anything because of where we'd put it. "It's over there," I said. "You can't see it in the dark."

"Who all's with you now?" the woman said. "Have you got your wife with you?"

"She's with my little girl and our dog in the car," I said. "My daughter's asleep or I would have brought them."

"They shouldn't be left in the dark by themselves," the woman said and frowned. "There's too much unsavoriness out there."

"The best I can do is hurry back." I tried to look sincere, since everything except Cheryl being asleep and Edna being my wife was the truth. The truth is meant to serve you if you'll let it, and I wanted it to serve me. "I'll pay for the phone call," I said. "If you'll bring the phone to the door I'll call from right here."

The woman looked at me again as if she was searching for a truth of her own, then back out into the night. She was maybe in her sixties, but I couldn't say for sure. "You're not going to rob me, are you, Mr. Middleton?" She smiled like it was a joke between us.

"Not tonight," I said, and smiled a genuine smile. "I'm not up to it tonight. Maybe another time."

"Then I guess Terrel and I can let you use our phone with Daddy not here, can't we, Terrel? This is my grandson, Terrel Junior, Mr. Middleton." She put her hand on the boy's head and looked down at him. "Terrel won't talk. Though if he did he'd tell you to use our phone. He's a sweet boy." She opened the screen for me to come in.

The trailer was a big one with a new rug and a new couch and a living room that expanded to give the space of a real house. Something good and sweet was cooking in the kitchen, and the trailer felt like it was somebody's comfortable new home instead of just temporary. I've lived in trailers, but they were just snailbacks with one room and no toilet, and they always felt cramped and unhappy—though I've thought maybe it might've been me that was unhappy in them.

There was a big Sony TV and a lot of kids' toys scattered on the floor. I recognized a Greyhound bus I'd gotten for Cheryl. The phone was beside a new leather recliner, and the Negro woman pointed for me to sit down and call and gave me the phone book. Terrel began fingering his toys and the woman sat on the couch while I called, watching me and smiling.

There were three listings for cab companies, all with one number different. I called the numbers in order and didn't get an answer until the last one, which answered with the name of the second company. I said I was on the highway beyond the interstate and that my wife and family needed to be taken to town and I would arrange for a tow later. While I was giving the location, I looked up the name of a tow service to tell the driver in case he asked.

When I hung up, the Negro woman was sitting looking at me with the same look she had been staring with into the dark, a look that seemed to want truth. She was smiling, though. Something pleased her and I reminded her of it.

"This is a very nice home," I said, resting in the recliner, which felt like the driver's seat of the Mercedes, and where I'd have been happy to stay.

"This isn't *our* house, Mr. Middleton," the Negro

woman said. "The company owns these. They give them to us for nothing. We have our own home in Rockford, Illinois."

"That's wonderful," I said.

"It's never wonderful when you have to be away from home, Mr. Middleton, though we're only here three months, and it'll be easier when Terrel Junior begins his special school. You see, our son was killed in the war, and his wife ran off without Terrel Junior. Though you shouldn't worry. He can't understand us. His little feelings can't be hurt." The woman folded her hands in her lap and smiled in a satisfied way. She was an attractive woman, and had on a blue-and-pink floral dress that made her seem bigger than she could've been, just the right woman to sit on the couch she was sitting on. She was good nature's picture, and I was glad she could be, with her little brain-damaged boy, living in a place where no one in his right mind would want to live a minute. "Where do *you* live, Mr. Middleton?" she said politely, smiling in the same sympathetic way.

"My family and I are in transit," I said. "I'm an ophthalmologist, and we're moving back to Florida, where I'm from. I'm setting up practice in some little town where it's warm year-round. I haven't decided where."

"Florida's a wonderful place," the woman said. "I think Terrel would like it there."

"Could I ask you something?" I said.

"You certainly may," the woman said. Terrel had begun pushing his Greyhound across the front of the TV screen, making a scratch that no one watching the set could miss. "Stop that, Terrel Junior," the woman said quietly. But Terrel kept pushing his bus on the glass, and she smiled at me again as if we both understood something sad. Except I knew Cheryl would never damage a television set. She had respect for nice things, and I was sorry for the lady that Terrel didn't. "What did you want to ask?" the woman said.

"What goes on in that plant or whatever it is back there beyond these trailers, where all the lights are on?"

"Gold," the woman said and smiled.

"It's what?" I said.

"Gold," the Negro woman said, smiling as she had for almost all the time I'd been there. "It's a gold mine."

"They're mining gold back there?" I said, pointing.

"Every night and every day." She smiled in a pleased way.

"Does your husband work there?" I said.

"He's the assayer," she said. "He controls the quality. He works three months a year, and we live the rest of the time at home in Rockford. We've waited a long time for this. We've been happy to have our grandson, but I won't say I'll be sorry to have him go. We're ready to start our lives over." She smiled broadly at me and then at Terrel, who was giving her a spiteful look from the floor. "You said you had a daughter," the Negro woman said. "And what's her name?"

"Irma Cheryl," I said. "She's named for my mother."

"That's nice. And she's healthy, too. I can see it in your face." She looked at Terrel Junior with pity.

"I guess I'm lucky," I said.

"So far you are. But children bring you grief, the same way they bring you joy. We were unhappy for a long time before my husband got his job in the gold mine. Now, when Terrel starts to school, we'll be kids again." She stood up. "You might miss your cab, Mr. Middleton," she said, walking toward the door, though not to be forcing me out. She was too polite. "If *we* can't see your car, the cab surely won't be able to."

"That's true." I got up off the recliner, where I'd been so comfortable. "None of us have eaten yet, and your food makes me know how hungry we probably all are."

"There are fine restaurants in town, and you'll find

them," the Negro woman said. "I'm sorry you didn't meet my husband. He's a wonderful man. He's everything to me."

"Tell him I appreciate the phone," I said. "You saved me."

"You weren't hard to save," the woman said. "Saving people is what we were all put on earth to do. I just passed you on to whatever's coming to you."

"Let's hope it's good," I said, stepping back into the dark.

"I'll be hoping, Mr. Middleton. Terrel and I will both be hoping."

I waved to her as I walked out into the darkness toward the car where it was hidden in the night.

The cab had already arrived when I got there. I could see its little red-and-green roof lights all the way across the dry wash, and it made me worry that Edna was already saying something to get us in trouble, something about the car or where we'd come from, something that would cast suspicion on us. I thought, then, how I never planned things well enough. There was always a gap between my plan and what happened, and I only responded to things as they came along and hoped I wouldn't get in trouble. I was an offender in the law's eyes. But I always *thought* differently, as if I weren't an offender and had no intention of being one, which was the truth. But as I read on a napkin once, between the idea and the act a whole kingdom lies. And I had a hard time with my acts, which were oftentimes offender's acts, and my ideas, which were as good as the gold they mined there where the bright lights were blazing.

"We're waiting for you, Daddy," Cheryl said when I crossed the road. "The taxicab's already here."

"I see, hon," I said, and gave Cheryl a big hug. The cabdriver was sitting in the driver's seat having a smoke with the lights on inside. Edna was leaning against the back of the cab between the taillights, wearing her Bailey hat. "What'd you tell him?" I said when I got close.

"Nothing," she said. "What's there to tell?"

"Did he see the car?"

She glanced over in the direction of the trees where we had hid the Mercedes. Nothing was visible in the darkness, though I could hear Little Duke combing around in the under-brush tracking something, his little collar tinkling. "Where're we going?" she said. "I'm so hungry I could pass out."

"Edna's in a terrible mood," Cheryl said. "She already snapped at me."

"We're tired, honey," I said. "So try to be nicer."

"She's never nice," Cheryl said.

"Run go get Little Duke," I said. "And hurry back."

"I guess *my* questions come last here, right?" Edna said.

I put my arm around her. "That's not true."

"Did you find somebody over there in the trailers you'd rather stay with? You were gone long enough."

"That's not a thing to say," I said. "I was just trying to make things look right, so we don't get put in jail."

"So *you* don't, you mean." Edna laughed a little laugh I didn't like hearing.

"That's right. So I don't," I said. "I'd be the one in Dutch." I stared out at the big, lighted assemblage of white buildings and white lights beyond the trailer community, plumes of white smoke escaping up into the heartless Wyo-ming sky, the whole company of buildings looking like some unbelievable castle, humming away in a distorted dream. "You know what all those buildings are there?" I said to Edna, who hadn't moved and who didn't really seem to care if she ever moved anymore ever.

"No. But I can't say it matters, because it isn't a motel and it isn't a restaurant."

"It's a gold mine," I said, staring at the gold mine, which, I knew now, was a greater distance from us than it seemed, though it seemed huge and near, up against the cold sky. I thought there should've been a wall around it with guards instead of just the lights and no fence. It seemed as if anyone could go in and take what they wanted, just the way I had gone up to that woman's trailer and used the telephone, though that obviously wasn't true.

Edna began to laugh then. Not the mean laugh I didn't like, but a laugh that had something caring behind it, a full laugh that enjoyed a joke, a laugh she was laughing the first time I laid eyes on her, in Missoula in the East Gate Bar in 1979, a laugh we used to laugh together when Cheryl was still with her mother and I was working steady at the track and not stealing cars or passing bogus checks to merchants. A better time all around. And for some reason it made me laugh just hearing her, and we both stood there behind the cab in the dark, laughing at the gold mine in the desert, me with my arm around her and Cheryl out rustling up Little Duke and the cabdriver smoking in the cab and our stolen Mercedes-Benz, which I'd had such hopes for in Florida, stuck up to its axle in sand, where I'd never get to see it again.

"I always wondered what a gold mine would look like when I saw it," Edna said, still laughing, wiping a tear from her eye.

"Me too," I said. "I was always curious about it."

"We're a couple of fools, aren't we, Earl?" she said, unable to quit laughing completely. "We're two of a kind."

"It might be a good sign, though," I said.

"How could it be? It's not our gold mine. There aren't any drive-up windows." She was still laughing.

"We've seen it," I said, pointing. "That's it right there.

It may mean we're getting closer. Some people never see it at all."

"In a pig's eye, Earl," she said. "You and me see it in a pig's eye."

And she turned and got in the cab to go.

The cabdriver didn't ask anything about our car or where it was, to mean he'd noticed something queer. All of which made me feel like we had made a clean break from the car and couldn't be connected with it until it was too late, if ever. The driver told us a lot about Rock Springs while he drove, that because of the gold mine a lot of people had moved there in just six months, people from all over, including New York, and that most of them lived out in the trailers. Prostitutes from New York City, who he called "B-girls," had come into town, he said, on the prosperity tide, and Cadillacs with New York plates cruised the little streets every night, full of Negroes with big hats who ran the women. He told us that everybody who got in his cab now wanted to know where the women were, and when he got our call he almost didn't come because some of the trailers were brothels operated by the mine for engineers and computer people away from home. He said he got tired of running back and forth out there just for vile business. He said that *60 Minutes* had even done a program about Rock Springs and that a blow-up had resulted in Cheyenne, though nothing could be done unless the boom left town. "It's prosperity's fruit," the driver said. "I'd rather be poor, which is lucky for me."

He said all the motels were sky-high, but since we were a family he could show us a nice one that was affordable. But I told him we wanted a first-rate place where they took animals, and the money didn't matter because we had had a hard day and wanted to finish on a high note. I also knew that it was in the little nowhere places that the police look for you and find you. People I'd known were always being arrested in cheap hotels and tourist courts with names you'd never heard of before. Never in Holiday Inns or TraveLodges.

I asked him to drive us to the middle of town and back out again so Cheryl could see the train station, and while we were there I saw a pink Cadillac with New York plates and a TV aerial being driven slowly by a Negro in a big hat down a narrow street where there were just bars and a Chinese restaurant. It was an odd sight, nothing you could ever expect.

"There's your pure criminal element," the cabdriver said and seemed sad. "I'm sorry for people like you to see a thing like that. We've got a nice town here, but there're some that want to ruin it for everybody. There used to be a way to deal with trash and criminals, but those days are gone forever."

"You said it," Edna said.

"You shouldn't let it get *you* down," I said to him. "There's more of you than them. And there always will be. You're the best advertisement this town has. I know Cheryl will remember you and not *that* man, won't you, honey?" But Cheryl was alseep by then, holding Little Duke in her arms on the taxi seat.

The driver took us to the Ramada Inn on the interstate, not far from where we'd broken down. I had a small pain of regret as we drove under the Ramada awning that we hadn't driven up in a cranberry-colored Mercedes but instead in a beat-up old Chrysler taxi driven by an old man full of complaints. Though I knew it was for the best. We were better off without that car; better, really, in any other car but that one, where the signs had turned bad.

I registered under another name and paid for the room in cash so there wouldn't be any questions. On the line where it said "Representing" I wrote "Ophthalmologist" and put

"M.D." after the name. It had a nice look to it, even though it wasn't my name.

When we got to the room, which was in the back where I'd asked for it, I put Cheryl on one of the beds and Little Duke beside her so they'd sleep. She'd missed dinner, but it only meant she'd be hungry in the morning, when she could have anything she wanted. A few missed meals don't make a kid bad. I'd missed a lot of them myself and haven't turned out completely bad.

"Let's have some fried chicken," I said to Edna when she came out of the bathroom. "They have good fried chicken at Ramadas, and I noticed the buffet was still up. Cheryl can stay right here, where it's safe, till we're back."

"I guess I'm not hungry anymore," Edna said. She stood at the window staring out into the dark. I could see out the window past her some yellowish foggy glow in the sky. For a moment I thought it was the gold mine out in the distance lighting the night, though it was only the interstate.

"We could order up," I said. "Whatever you want. There's a menu on the phone book. You could just have a salad."

"You go ahead," she said. "I've lost my hungry spirit." She sat on the bed beside Cheryl and Little Duke and looked at them in a sweet way and put her hand on Cheryl's cheek just as if she'd had a fever. "Sweet little girl," she said. "Everybody loves you."

"What do you want to do?" I said. "I'd like to eat. Maybe *I'll* order up some chicken."

"Why don't you do that?" she said. "It's your favorite." And she smiled at me from the bed.

I sat on the other bed and dialed room service. I asked for chicken, garden salad, potato and a roll, plus a piece of hot apple pie and iced tea. I realized I hadn't eaten all day. When I put down the phone I saw that Edna was watching me, not in a hateful way or a loving way, just in a way that seemed to say she didn't understand something and was going to ask me about it.

"When did watching me get so entertaining?" I said and smiled at her. I was trying to be friendly. I knew how tired she must be. It was after nine o'clock.

"I was just thinking how much I hated being in a motel without a car that was mine to drive. Isn't that funny? I started feeling like that last night when that purple car wasn't mine. That purple car just gave me the willies, I guess, Earl."

"One of those cars *outside* is yours," I said. "Just stand right there and pick it out."

"I know," she said. "But that's different, isn't it?" She reached and got her blue Bailey hat, put it on her head, and set it way back like Dale Evans. She looked sweet. "I used to like to go to motels, you know," she said. "There's something secret about them and free—I was never paying, of course. But you felt safe from everything and free to do what you wanted because you'd made the decision to be there and paid that price, and all the rest was the good part. Fucking and everything, you know." She smiled at me in a good-natured way.

"Isn't that the way this is?" I was sitting on the bed, watching her, not knowing what to expect her to say next.

"I don't guess it is, Earl," she said and stared out the window. "I'm thirty-two and I'm going to have to give up on motels. I can't keep that fantasy going anymore."

"Don't you like this place?" I said and looked around at the room. I appreciated the modern paintings and the lowboy bureau and the big TV. It seemed like a plenty nice enough place to me, considering where we'd been.

"No, I don't," Edna said with real conviction. "There's no use in my getting mad at you about it. It isn't your fault. You do the best you can for everybody. But every trip teaches you something. And I've learned I need to give up on motels before some bad thing happens to me. I'm sorry."

"What does that mean?" I said, because I really didn't know what she had in mind to do, though I should've guessed.

"I guess I'll take that ticket you mentioned," she said, and got up and faced the window. "Tomorrow's soon enough. We haven't got a car to take me anyhow."

"Well, that's a fine thing," I said, sitting on the bed, feeling like I was in shock. I wanted to say something to her, to argue with her, but I couldn't think what to say that seemed right. I didn't want to be mad at her, but it made me mad.

"You've got a right to be mad at me, Earl," she said, "but I don't think you can really blame me." She turned around and faced me and sat on the windowsill, her hands on her knees. Someone knocked on the door, and I just yelled for them to set the tray down and put it on the bill.

"I guess I *do* blame you," I said, and I was angry. I thought about how I could've disappeared into that trailer community and hadn't, had come back to keep things going, had tried to take control of things for everybody when they looked bad.

"Don't. I wish you wouldn't," Edna said and smiled at me like she wanted me to hug her. "Anybody ought to have their choice in things if they can. Don't you believe that, Earl? Here I am out here in the desert where I don't know anything, in a stolen car, in a motel room under an assumed name, with no money of my own, a kid that's not mine, and the law after me. And I have a choice to get out of all of it by getting on a bus. What would you do? I know exactly what you'd do."

"You think you do," I said. But I didn't want to get into an argument about it and tell her all I could've done and didn't do. Because it wouldn't have done any good. When you get to the point of arguing, you're past the point of changing anybody's mind, even though it's supposed to be the other way, and maybe for some classes of people it is, just never mine.

Edna smiled at me and came across the room and put her arms around me where I was sitting on the bed. Cheryl rolled over and looked at us and smiled, then closed her eyes, and the room was quiet. I was beginning to think of Rock Springs in a way I knew I would always think of it, a lowdown city full of crimes and whores and disappointments, a place where a woman left me, instead of a place where I got things on the straight track once and for all, a place I saw a gold mine.

"Eat your chicken, Earl," Edna said. "Then we can go to bed. I'm tired, but I'd like to make love to you anyway. None of this is a matter of not loving you, you know that."

Sometime late in the night, after Edna was asleep, I got up and walked outside into the parking lot. It could've been anytime because there was still the light from the interstate frosting the low sky and the big red Ramada sign humming motionlessly in the night and no light at all in the east to indicate it might be morning. The lot was full of cars all nosed in, a couple of them with suitcases strapped to their roofs and their trunks weighed down with belongings the people were taking someplace, to a new home or a vacation resort in the mountains. I had laid in bed a long time after Edna was asleep, watching the Atlanta Braves on television, trying to get my mind off how I'd feel when I saw that bus pull away the next day, and how I'd feel when I turned around and there stood Cheryl and Little Duke and no one to see about them but me alone, and that the first thing I had to do was get hold of some automobile and get the plates switched, then get them some breakfast and get us all on the road to Florida, all in the space of probably two hours, since that Mercedes would certainly look less hid in the daytime than the night, and word travels fast. I've always taken care of Cheryl myself as long as I've had her with me. None of the women ever did. Most of them didn't even seem to like her, though they took care of me in a way so that I could take care of her. And I knew that once Edna left, all that was going to get harder. Though what I wanted most to do was not think about it just for a little while, try to let my mind go limp so it could be strong for the rest of what there was. I thought that the difference between a successful life and an unsuccessful one, between me at that moment and all the people who owned the cars that were nosed into their proper places in the lot, maybe between me and that woman out in the trailers by the gold mine, was how well you were able to put things like this out of your mind and not be bothered by them, and maybe, too, by how many troubles like this one you had to face in a lifetime. Through luck or design they had all faced fewer troubles, and by their own characters, they forgot them faster. And that's what I wanted for me. Fewer troubles, fewer memories of trouble.

I walked over to a car, a Pontiac with Ohio tags, one of the ones with bundles and suitcases strapped to the top and a lot more in the trunk, by the way it was riding. I looked inside the driver's window. There were maps and paperback books and sunglasses and the little plastic holders for cans that hang on the window wells. And in the back there were kids' toys and some pillows and a cat box with a cat sitting in it staring up at me like I was the face of the moon. It all looked familiar to me, the very same things I would have in my car if I had a car. Nothing seemed surprising, nothing different. Though I had a funny sensation at that moment and turned and looked up at the windows along the back of the motel. All were dark except two. Mine and another one. And I wondered, because it seemed funny, what would you think a man was doing if you saw him in the middle of the night looking in the windows of cars in the parking lot of the Ramada Inn? Would you think he was trying to get his head cleared? Would you think he was trying to get ready for a day when trouble would come down on him? Would you think his girlfriend was leaving him? Would you think he had a daughter? Would you think he was anybody like you?

GREAT FALLS

This is not a happy story. I warn you.

My father was a man named Jack Russell, and when I was a young boy in my early teens, we lived with my mother in a house to the east of Great Falls, Montana, near the small town of Highwood and the Highwood Mountains and the Missouri River. It is a flat, treeless benchland there, all of it used for wheat farming, though my father was never a farmer, but was brought up near Tacoma, Washington, in a family that worked for Boeing.

He—my father—had been an Air Force sergeant and had taken his discharge in Great Falls. And instead of going home to Tacoma, where my mother wanted to go, he had taken a civilian's job with the Air Force, working on planes, which was what he liked to do. And he had rented the house out of town from a farmer who did not want it left standing empty.

The house itself is gone now—I have been to the spot. But the double row of Russian olive trees and two of the outbuildings are still standing in the milkweeds. It was a plain, two-story house with a porch on the front and no place for the cars. At the time, I rode the school bus to Great Falls every morning, and my father drove in while my mother stayed home.

My mother was a tall pretty woman, thin, with black hair and slightly sharp features that made her seem to smile when she wasn't smiling. She had grown up in Wallace, Idaho, and gone to college a year in Spokane, then moved out to the coast, which is where she met Jack Russell. She was two years older than he was, and married him, she said to me, because he was young and wonderful looking, and because she thought they could leave the sticks and see the world together—which I suppose they did for a while. That was the life she wanted, even before she knew much about wanting anything else or about the future.

When my father wasn't working on airplanes, he was going hunting or fishing, two things he could do as well as anyone. He had learned to fish, he said, in Iceland, and to hunt ducks up on the DEW line—stations he had visited in the Air Force. And during the time of this—it was 1960—he began to take me with him on what he called his "expeditions." I thought even then, with as little as I knew, that these were opportunities other boys would dream of having but probably never would. And I don't think that I was wrong in that.

It is a true thing that my father did not know limits. In the spring, when we would go east to the Judith River Basin and camp up on the banks, he would catch a hundred fish in a weekend, and sometimes more than that. It was all he did from morning until night, and it was never hard for him. He used yellow corn kernels stacked onto a #4 snelled hook, and he would rattle this rig-up along the bottom of a deep pool below a split-shot sinker, and catch fish. And most of the time, because he knew the Judith River and knew how to feel his bait down deep, he could catch fish of good size.

It was the same with ducks, the other thing he liked. When the northern birds were down, usually by mid-October, he would take me and we would build a cattail and wheat-straw blind on one of the tule ponds or sloughs he knew about down the Missouri, where the water was shallow enough to wade. We would set out his decoys to the leeward side of our blind, and he would sprinkle corn on a hunger-line from the decoys to where we were. In the evenings when he came home from the base, we would go and sit out in the blind until the roosting flights came and put down among the decoys—there was never calling involved. And after a while, sometimes it would be an hour and full dark, the ducks would find the corn, and the whole raft of them—sixty, sometimes—would swim in to us. At the moment he judged they were close enough, my father would say to me, "Shine, Jackie," and I would stand and shine a seal-beam car light out onto the pond, and he would stand up beside me and shoot all the ducks that were there, on the water if he could, but flying and getting up as well. He owned a Model 11 Remington with a long-tube magazine that would hold ten shells, and with that many, and shooting straight over the surface rather than down onto it, he could kill or wound thirty ducks in twenty seconds' time. I remember distinctly the report of that gun and the flash of it over the water into the dark air, one shot after another, not even so fast, but measured in a way to hit as many as he could.

What my father did with the ducks he killed, and the fish, too, was sell them. It was against the law then to sell wild game, and it is against the law now. And though he kept some for us, most he would take—his fish laid on ice, or his ducks still wet and bagged in the burlap corn sacks—down to the Great Northern Hotel, which was still open then on Second Street in Great Falls, and sell them to the Negro caterer who bought them for his wealthy customers and for the dining car passengers who came through. We would drive in my father's Plymouth to the back of the hotel—always this was after dark—to a concrete loading ramp and lighted door that were close enough to the yards that I could sometimes see passenger trains waiting at the station, their car lights yellow and warm inside, the passengers dressed in suits, all bound for someplace far away from Montana—Milwaukee or Chicago or New York City, unimaginable places to me, a boy fourteen years old, with my father in the cold dark selling illegal game.

The caterer was a tall, stooped-back man in a white jacket, who my father called "Professor Ducks" or "Professor Fish," and the Professor referred to my father as "Sarge." He paid a quarter per pound for trout, a dime for whitefish, a dollar for a mallard duck, two for a speckle or a blue goose, and four dollars for a Canada. I have been with my father when he took away a hundred dollars for fish he'd caught and, in the fall, more than that for ducks and geese. When he had sold game in that way, we would drive out 10th Avenue and stop at a bar called The Mermaid which was by the air base, and he would drink with some friends he knew there, and they would laugh about hunting and fishing while I played pinball and wasted money in the jukebox.

It was on such a night as this that the unhappy things came about. It was in late October. I remember the time because Halloween had not been yet, and in the windows of the houses that I passed every day on the bus to Great Falls, people had put pumpkin lanterns, and set scarecrows in their yards in chairs.

My father and I had been shooting ducks in a slough

on the Smith River, upstream from where it enters on the Missouri. He had killed thirty ducks, and we'd driven them down to the Great Northern and sold them there, though my father had kept two back in his corn sack. And when we had driven away, he suddenly said, "Jackie, let's us go back home tonight. Who cares about those hard-dicks at The Mermaid. I'll cook these ducks on the grill. We'll do something different tonight." He smiled at me in an odd way. This was not a thing he usually said, or the way he usually talked. He liked The Mermaid, and my mother—as far as I knew—didn't mind it if he went there.

"That sounds good," I said.

"We'll surprise your mother," he said. "We'll make her happy."

We drove out past the air base on Highway 87, past where there were planes taking off into the night. The darkness was dotted by the green and red beacons, and the tower light swept the sky and trapped planes as they disappeared over the flat landscape toward Canada or Alaska and the Pacific.

"Boy-oh-boy," my father said—just out of the dark. I looked at him and his eyes were narrow, and he seemed to be thinking about something. "You know, Jackie," he said, "your mother said something to me once I've never forgotten. She said, 'Nobody dies of a broken heart.' This was somewhat before you were born. We were living down in Texas and we'd had some big blow-up, and that was the idea she had. I don't know why." He shook his head.

He ran his hand under the seat, found a half-pint bottle of whiskey, and held it up to the lights of the car behind us to see what there was left of it. He unscrewed the cap and took a drink, then held the bottle out to me. "Have a drink, son," he said. "Something oughta be good in life." And I felt that something was wrong. Not because of the whiskey, which I had drunk before and he had reason to know about, but because of some sound in his voice, something I didn't recognize and did not know the importance of, though I was certain it was important.

I took a drink and gave the bottle back to him, holding the whiskey in my mouth until it stopped burning and I could swallow it a little at a time. When we turned out the road to Highwood, the lights of Great Falls sank below the horizon, and I could see the small white lights of farms, burning at wide distances in the dark.

"What do you worry about, Jackie," my father said. "Do you worry about girls? Do you worry about your future sex life? Is that some of it?" He glanced at me, then back at the road.

"I don't worry about that," I said.

"Well, what then?" my father said. "What else is there?"

"I worry if you're going to die before I do," I said, though I hated saying that, "or if Mother is. That worries me."

"It'd be a miracle if we didn't," my father said, with the half-pint held in the same hand he held the steering wheel. I had seen him drive that way before. "Things pass too fast in your life, Jackie. Don't worry about that. If I were you, I'd worry we might not." He smiled at me, and it was not the worried, nervous smile from before, but a smile that meant he was pleased. And I don't remember him ever smiling at me that way again.

We drove on out behind the town of Highwood and onto the flat field roads toward our house. I could see, out on the prairie, a moving light where the farmer who rented our house to us was disking his field for winter wheat. "He's waited too late with that business," my father said and took a drink, then threw the bottle right out the window. "He'll lose that," he said, "the cold'll kill it." I did not answer him, but what I thought was that my father knew nothing about farming, and if he was right it would be an accident. He knew about planes and hunting game, and that seemed all to me.

"I want to respect your privacy," he said then, for no reason at all that I understood. I am not even certain he said it, only that it is in my memory that way. I don't know what he was thinking of. Just words. But I said to him, I remember well, "It's all right. Thank you."

We did not go straight out the Geraldine Road to our house. Instead my father went down another mile and turned, went a mile and turned back again so that we came home from the other direction. "I want to stop and listen now," he said. "The geese should be in the stubble." We stopped and he cut the lights and engine, and we opened the car windows and listened. It was eight o'clock at night and it was getting colder, though it was dry. But I could hear nothing, just the sound of air moving lightly through the cut field, and not a goose sound. Though I could smell the whiskey on my father's breath and on mine, could hear the motor ticking, could hear him breathe, hear the sound we made sitting side by side on the car seat, our clothes, our feet, almost our hearts beating. And I could see out in the night the yellow lights of our house, shining through the olive trees south of us like a ship on the sea. "I hear them, by God," my father said, his head stuck out the window. "But they're high up. They won't stop here now, Jackie. They're high flyers, those boys. Long gone geese."

There was a car parked off the road, down the line of wind-break trees, beside a steel thresher the farmer had left there to rust. You could see moonlight off the taillight chrome. It was a Pontiac, a two-door hard-top.

My father said nothing about it and I didn't either, though I think now for different reasons.

The floodlight was on over the side door of our house and lights were on inside, upstairs and down. My mother had a pumpkin on the front porch, and the wind chime she had hung by the door was tinkling. My dog, Major, came out of the quonset shed and stood in the car lights when we drove up.

"Let's see what's happening here," my father said, opening the door and stepping out quickly. He looked at me inside the car, and his eyes were wide and his mouth drawn tight.

We walked in the side door and up the basement steps into the kitchen, and a man was standing there—a man I had never seen before, a young man with blond hair, who might've been twenty or twenty-five. He was tall and was wearing a short-sleeved shirt and beige slacks with pleats. He was on the other side of the breakfast table, his fingertips just touching the wooden tabletop. His blue eyes were on my father, who was dressed in hunting clothes.

"Hello," my father said.

"Hello," the young man said, and nothing else. And for some reason I looked at his arms, which were long and pale. They looked like a young man's arms, like my arms. His short sleeves had each been neatly rolled up, and I could see the bottom of a small green tattoo edging out from underneath. There was a glass of whiskey on the table, but no bottle.

"What's your name?" my father said, standing in the kitchen under the bright ceiling light. He sounded like he might be going to laugh.

"Woody," the young man said and cleared his throat. He looked at me, then he touched the glass of whiskey, just the rim of the glass. He wasn't nervous, I could tell that. He did not seem to be afraid of anything.

"Woody," my father said and looked at the glass of whiskey. He looked at me, then sighed and shook his head. "Where's Mrs. Russell, Woody? I guess you aren't robbing my house, are you?"

Woody smiled. "No," he said. "Upstairs. I think she went upstairs."

"Good," my father said, "that's a good place." And he walked straight out of the room, but came back and stood in the doorway. "Jackie, you and Woody step outside and wait on me. Just stay there and I'll come out." He looked at Woody then in a way I would not have liked him to look at me, a look that meant he was studying Woody. "I guess that's your car," he said.

"That Pontiac." Woody nodded.

"Okay. Right," my father said. Then he went out again and up the stairs. At that moment the phone started to ring in the living room, and I heard my mother say, "Who's that?" And my father say, "It's me. It's Jack." And I decided I wouldn't go answer the phone. Woody looked at me, and I understood he wasn't sure what to do. Run, maybe. But he didn't have run in him. Though I thought he would probably do what I said if I would say it.

"Let's just go outside," I said.

And he said, "All right."

Woody and I walked outside and stood in the light of the floodlamp above the side door. I had on my wool jacket, but Woody was cold and stood with his hands in his pockets, and his arms bare, moving from foot to foot. Inside, the phone was ringing again. Once I looked up and saw my mother come to the window and look down at Woody and me. Woody didn't look up or see her, but I did. I waved at her, and she waved back at me and smiled. She was wearing a powder-blue dress. In another minute the phone stopped ringing.

Woody took a cigarette out of his shirt pocket and lit it. Smoke shot through his nose into the cold air, and he sniffed, looked around the ground and threw his match on the gravel. His blond hair was combed backwards and neat on the sides, and I could smell his aftershave on him, a sweet, lemon smell. And for the first time I noticed his shoes. They were two-tones, black with white tops and black laces. They stuck out below his baggy pants and were long and polished and shiny, as if he had been planning on a big occasion. They looked like shoes some country singer would wear, or a salesman. He was handsome, but only like someone you would see beside you in a dime store and not notice again.

"I like it out here," Woody said, his head down, looking at his shoes. "Nothing to bother you. I bet you'd see Chicago if the world was flat. The Great Plains commence here."

"I don't know," I said.

Woody looked up at me, cupping his smoke with one hand. "Do you play football?"

"No," I said. I thought about asking him something about my mother. But I had no idea what it would be.

"I *have* been drinking," Woody said, "but I'm not drunk now."

The wind rose then, and from behind the house I could hear Major bark once from far away, and I could smell the irrigation ditch, hear it hiss in the field. It ran down from Highwood Creek to the Missouri, twenty miles away. It was nothing Woody knew about, nothing he could hear or smell. He knew nothing about anything that was here. I heard my father say the words, "That's a real joke," from inside the house, then the sound of a drawer being opened and shut, and a door closing. Then nothing else.

Woody turned and looked into the dark toward where the glow of Great Falls rose on the horizon, and we both could see the flashing lights of a plane lowering to land there.

"I once passed my brother in the Los Angeles airport and didn't even recognize him," Woody said, staring into the night. "He recognized *me,* though. He said, 'Hey, bro, are you mad at me, or what?' I wasn't mad at him. We both had to laugh."

Woody turned and looked at the house. His hands were still in his pockets, his cigarette clenched between his teeth, his arms taut. They were, I saw, bigger, stronger arms than I had thought. A vein went down the front of each of them. I wondered what Woody knew that I didn't. Not about my mother—I didn't know anything about that and didn't want to—but about a lot of things, about the life out in the dark, about coming out here, about airports, even about me. He and I were not so far apart in age, I knew that. But Woody was one thing, and I was another. And I wondered how I would ever get to be like him, since it didn't necessarily seem so bad a thing to be.

"Did you know your mother was married before?" Woody said.

"Yes," I said. "I knew that."

"It happens to all of them, now," he said. "They can't wait to get divorced."

"I guess so," I said.

Woody dropped his cigarette into the gravel and toed it out with his black-and-white shoe. He looked up at me and smiled the way he had inside the house, a smile that said he knew something he wouldn't tell, a smile to make you feel bad because you weren't Woody and never could be.

It was then that my father came out of the house. He still had on his plaid hunting coat and his wool cap, but his face was as white as snow, as white as I have ever seen a human being's face to be. It was odd. I had the feeling that he might've fallen inside, because he looked roughed up, as though he had hurt himself somehow.

My mother came out the door behind him and stood in the floodlight at the top of the steps. She was wearing the powder-blue dress I'd seen through the window, a dress I had never seen her wear before, though she was also wearing a car coat and carrying a suitcase. She looked at me and shook her head in a way that only I was supposed to notice, as if it was not a good idea to talk now.

My father had his hands in his pockets, and he walked right up to Woody. He did not even look at me. "What do you do for a living?" he said, and he was very close to Woody. His coat was close enough to touch Woody's shirt.

"I'm in the Air Force," Woody said. He looked at me and then at my father. He could tell my father was excited.

"Is this your day off, then?" my father said. He moved even closer to Woody, his hands still in his pockets. He pushed Woody with his chest, and Woody seemed willing to let my father push him.

"No," he said, shaking his head.

I looked at my mother. She was just standing, watching. It was as if someone had given her an order, and she was obeying it. She did not smile at me, though I thought she was thinking about me, which made me feel strange.

"What's the matter with you?" my father said into Woody's face, right into his face—his voice tight, as if it had gotten hard for him to talk. "Whatever in the world is the matter with you? Don't you understand something?" My father took a revolver pistol out of his coat and put it up under Woody's chin, into the soft pocket behind the bone, so that Woody's whole face rose, but his arms stayed at his sides, his hands open. "I don't know what to do with you," my father said. "I don't have any idea what to do with you. I just don't." Though I thought that what he wanted to do was hold Woody there just like that until something important took place, or until he could simply forget about all this.

My father pulled the hammer back on the pistol and raised it tighter under Woody's chin, breathing into Woody's face—my mother in the light with her suitcase, watching them, and me watching them. A half a minute must've gone by.

And then my mother said, "Jack, let's stop now. Let's just stop."

My father stared into Woody's face as if he wanted Woody to consider doing something—moving or turning around or anything on his own to stop this—that my father would then put a stop to. My father's eyes grew narrowed, and his teeth were gritted together, his lips snarling up to resemble a smile. "You're crazy, aren't you?" he said. "You're a god-damned crazy man. Are you in love with her, too? Are you, crazy man? Are you? Do you say you love her? Say you love her! Say you love her so I can blow your fucking brains in the sky."

"All right," Woody said. "No. It's all right."

"He doesn't love me, Jack. For God's sake," my mother said. She seemed so calm. She shook her head at me again. I do not think she thought my father would shoot Woody. And I don't think Woody thought so. Nobody did, I think, except my father himself. But I think he did, and was trying to find out how to.

My father turned suddenly and glared at my mother, his eyes shiny and moving, but with the gun still on Woody's skin. I think he was afraid, afraid he was doing this wrong and could mess all of it up and make matters worse without accomplishing anything.

"You're leaving," he yelled at her. "That's why you're packed. Get out. Go on."

"Jackie has to be at school in the morning," my mother said in just her normal voice. And without another word to any one of us, she walked out of the floodlamp light carrying her bag, turned the corner at the front porch steps and disappeared toward the olive trees that ran in rows back into the wheat.

My father looked back at me where I was standing in the gravel, as if he expected to see me go with my mother toward Woody's car. But I hadn't thought about that—though later I would. Later I would think I should have gone with her, and that things between them might've been different. But that isn't how it happened.

"You're sure you're going to get away now, aren't you, mister?" my father said into Woody's face. He was crazy himself, then. Anyone would've been. Everything must have seemed out of hand to him.

"I'd like to," Woody said. "I'd like to get away from here."

"And I'd like to think of some way to hurt you," my father said and blinked his eyes. "I feel helpless about it." We all heard the door to Woody's car close in the dark. "Do you think that I'm a fool?" my father said.

"No," Woody said. "I don't think that."

"Do you think you're important?"

"No," Woody said. "I'm not."

My father blinked again. He seemed to be becoming someone else at that moment, someone I didn't know. "Where are you from?"

And Woody closed his eyes. He breathed in, then out, a long sigh. It was as if this was somehow the hardest part, something he hadn't expected to be asked to say.

"Chicago," Woody said. "A suburb of there."

"Are your parents alive?" my father said, all the time with his blue magnum pistol pushed under Woody's chin.

"Yes," Woody said. "Yessir."

"That's too bad," my father said. "Too bad they have to know what you are. I'm sure you stopped meaning anything to them a long time ago. I'm sure they both wish you were dead. You didn't know that. But I know it. I can't help them out, though. Somebody else'll have to kill you. I don't want to have to think about you anymore. I guess that's it."

My father brought the gun down to his side and stood looking at Woody. He did not back away, just stood, waiting for what I don't know to happen. Woody stood a moment, then he cut his eyes at me uncomfortably. And I know that I looked down. That's all I could do. Though I remember wondering if Woody's heart was broken and what any of this meant to him. Not to me, or my mother, or my father. But to him, since he seemed to be the one left out somehow, the one who would be lonely soon, the one who had done something he would someday wish he hadn't and would have no one to tell him that it was all right, that they forgave him, that these things happen in the world.

Woody took a step back, looked at my father and at me again as if he intended to speak, then stepped aside and walked away toward the front of our house, where the wind chime made a noise in the new cold air.

My father looked at me, his big pistol in his hand. "Does this seem stupid to you?" he said. "All this? Yelling and threatening and going nuts? I wouldn't blame you if it did. You shouldn't even see this. I'm sorry. I don't know what to do now."

"It'll be all right," I said. And I walked out to the road. Woody's car started up behind the olive trees. I stood and watched it back out, its red taillights clouded by exhaust. I could see their two heads inside, with the headlights shining behind them. When they got into the road, Woody touched his brakes, and for a moment I could see that they were talking, their heads turned toward each other, nodding. Woody's head and my mother's. They sat that way for a few seconds, then drove slowly off. And I wondered what they had to say to each other, something important enough that they had to stop right at that moment and say it. Did she say, *I love you*? Did she say, *This is not what I expected to happen*? Did she say, *This is what I've wanted all along*? And did he say, *I'm sorry for all this*, or *I'm glad*, or *None of this matters to me*? These are not the kinds of things you can know if you were not there. And I was not there and did not want to be. It did not seem like I should be there. I heard the door slam when my father went inside, and I turned back from the road where I could still see their taillights disappearing, and went back into the house where I was to be alone with my father.

Things seldom end in one event. In the morning I went to school on the bus as usual, and my father drove in to the air base in his car. We had not said very much about all that had happened. Harsh words, in a sense, are all alike. You can make them up yourself and be right. I think we both believed that we were in a fog we couldn't see through yet, though in a while, maybe not even a long while, we would see lights and know something.

In my third-period class that day a messenger brought a note for me that said I was excused from school at noon, and I should meet my mother at a motel down 10th Avenue South—a place not so far from my school—and we would eat lunch together.

It was a gray day in Great Falls that day. The leaves were off the trees and the mountains to the east of town were obscured by a low sky. The night before had been cold and clear, but today it seemed as if it would rain. It was the beginning of winter in earnest. In a few days there would be snow everywhere.

The motel where my mother was staying was called the

Tropicana, and was beside the city golf course. There was a neon parrot on the sign out front, and the cabins made a U shape behind a little white office building. Only a couple of cars were parked in front of cabins, and no car was in front of my mother's cabin. I wondered if Woody would be here, or if he was at the air base. I wondered if my father would see him there, and what they would say.

I walked back to cabin 9. The door was open, though a DO NOT DISTURB sign was hung on the knob outside. I looked through the screen and saw my mother sitting on the bed alone. The television was on, but she was looking at me. She was wearing the powder-blue dress she had had on the night before. She was smiling at me, and I liked the way she looked at that moment, through the screen, in shadows. Her features did not seem as sharp as they had before. She looked comfortable where she was, and I felt like we were going to get along, no matter what had happened, and that I wasn't mad at her—that I had never been mad at her.

She sat forward and turned the television off. "Come in, Jackie," she said, and I opened the screen door and came inside. "It's the height of grandeur in here, isn't it?" My mother looked around the room. Her suitcase was open on the floor by the bathroom door, which I could see through and out the window onto the golf course, where three men were playing under the milky sky. "Privacy can be a burden, sometimes," she said, and reached down and put on her high-heeled shoes. "I didn't sleep very well last night, did you?"

"No," I said, though I had slept all right. I wanted to ask her where Woody was, but it occurred to me at that moment that he was gone now and wouldn't be back, that she wasn't thinking in terms of him and didn't care where he was or ever would be.

"I'd like a nice compliment from you," she said. "Do you have one of those to spend?"

"Yes," I said. "I'm glad to see you."

"That's a nice one," she said and nodded. She had both her shoes on now. "Would you like to go have lunch? We can walk across the street to the cafeteria. You can get hot food."

"No," I said. "I'm not really hungry now."

"That's okay," she said and smiled at me again. And, as I said before, I liked the way she looked. She looked pretty in a way I didn't remember seeing her, as if something that had had a hold on her had let her go, and she could be different about things. Even about me.

"Sometimes, you know," she said, "I'll think about something I did. Just anything. Years ago in Idaho, or last week, even. And it's as if I'd read it. Like a story. Isn't that strange?"

"Yes," I said. And it did seem strange to me because I was certain then what the difference was between what had happened and what hadn't, and knew I always would be.

"Sometimes," she said, and she folded her hands in her lap and stared out the little side window of her cabin at the parking lot and the curving row of other cabins. "Sometimes I even have a moment when I completely forget what life's like. Just altogether." She smiled. "That's not so bad, finally. Maybe it's a disease I have. Do you think I'm just sick and I'll get well?"

"No. I don't know," I said. "Maybe. I hope so." I looked out the bathroom window and saw the three men walking down the golf course fairway carrying golf clubs.

"I'm not very good at sharing things right now," my mother said. "I'm sorry." She cleared her throat, and then she didn't say anything for almost a minute while I stood there. "I *will* answer anything you'd like me to answer, though. Just ask me anything, and I'll answer it the truth, whether I want to or not. Okay? I will. You don't even have to trust me. That's not a big issue with us. We're both grown-ups now."

And I said, "Were you ever married before?"

My mother looked at me strangely. Her eyes got small, and for a moment she looked the way I was used to seeing her—sharp-faced, her mouth set and taut. "No," she said. "Who told you that? That isn't true. I never was. Did Jack say that to you? Did your father say that? That's an awful thing to say. I haven't been that bad."

"He didn't say that," I said.

"Oh, of course he did," my mother said. "He doesn't know just to let things go when they're bad enough."

"I wanted to know that," I said. "I just thought about it. It doesn't matter."

"No, it doesn't," my mother said. "I could've been married eight times. I'm just sorry he said that to you. He's not generous sometimes."

"He didn't say that," I said. But I'd said it enough, and I didn't care if she believed me or didn't. It was true that trust was not a big issue between us then. And in any event, I know now that the whole truth of anything is an idea that stops existing finally.

"Is that all you want to know, then?" my mother said. She seemed mad, but not at me, I didn't think. Just at things in general. And I sympathized with her. "Your life's your own business, Jackie," she said. "Sometimes it scares you to death it's so much your own business. You just want to run."

"I guess so," I said.

"I'd like a less domestic life, is all." She looked at me, but I didn't say anything. I didn't see what she meant by that, though I knew there was nothing I could say to change the way her life would be from then on. And I kept quiet.

In a while we walked across 10th Avenue and ate lunch in the cafeteria. When she paid for the meal I saw that she had my father's silver-dollar money clip in her purse and that there was money in it. And I understood that he had been to see her already that day, and no one cared if I knew it. We were all of us on our own in this.

When we walked out onto the street, it was colder and the wind was blowing. Car exhausts were visible and some drivers had their lights on, though it was only two o'clock in the afternoon. My mother had called a taxi, and we stood and waited for it. I didn't know where she was going, but I wasn't going with her.

"Your father won't let me come back," she said, standing on the curb. It was just a fact to her, not that she hoped I would talk to him or stand up for her or take her part. But I did wish then that I had never let her go the night before. Things can be fixed by staying; but to go out into the night and not come back hazards life, and everything can get out of hand.

My mother's taxi came. She kissed me and hugged me very hard, then got inside the cab in her powder-blue dress and high heels and her car coat. I smelled her perfume on my cheeks as I stood watching her. "I used to be afraid of more things than I am now," she said, looking up at me, and smiled. "I've got a knot in my stomach, of all things." And she closed the cab door, waved at me, and rode away.

I walked back toward my school. I thought I could take the bus home if I got there by three. I walked a long way down 10th Avenue to Second Street, beside the Missouri River, then over to town. I walked by the Great Northern Hotel, where my father had sold ducks and geese and fish of all kinds. There were no passenger trains in the yard and the loading dock looked small. Garbage cans were lined along the edge of it, and the door was closed and locked.

As I walked toward school I thought to myself that my life had turned suddenly, and that I might not know exactly how or which way for possibly a long time. Maybe, in fact, I might never know. It was a thing that happened to you—I knew that—and it had happened to me in this way now. And as I walked on up the cold street that afternoon in Great Falls, the questions I asked myself were these: why wouldn't my father let my mother come back? Why would Woody stand in the cold with me outside my house and risk being killed? Why would he say my mother had been married before, if she hadn't been? And my mother herself—why would she do what she did? In five years my father had gone off to Ely, Nevada, to ride out the oil strike there, and been killed by accident. And in the years since then I have seen my mother from time to time—in one place or another, with one man or other—and I can say, at least, that we know each other. But I have never known the answer to these questions, have never asked anyone their answers. Though possibly it—the answer—is simple: it is just low-life, some coldness in us all, some helplessness that causes us to misunderstand life when it is pure and plain, makes our existence seem like a border between two nothings, and makes us no more or less than animals who meet on the road—watchful, unforgiving, without patience or desire.

SWEETHEARTS

I was standing in the kitchen while Arlene was in the living room saying good-bye to her ex-husband, Bobby. I had already been out to the store for groceries and come back and made coffee, and was drinking it and staring out the window while the two of them said whatever they had to say. It was a quarter to six in the morning.

This was not going to be a good day in Bobby's life, that was clear, because he was headed to jail. He had written several bad checks, and before he could be sentenced for that he had robbed a convenience store with a pistol—completely gone off his mind. And everything had gone to hell, as you might expect. Arlene had put up the money for his bail, and there was some expensive talk about an appeal. But there

61

wasn't any use to that. He was guilty. It would cost money and then he would go to jail anyway.

Arlene had said she would drive him to the sheriff's department this morning, if I would fix him breakfast, so he could surrender on a full stomach. and that had seemed all right. Early in the morning Bobby had brought his motorcycle around to the backyard and tied up his dog to the handlebars. I had watched him from the window. He hugged the dog, kissed it on the head and whispered something in its ear, then came inside. The dog was a black Lab, and it sat beside the motorcycle now and stared with blank interest across the river at the buildings of town, where the sky was beginning to turn pinkish and the day was opening up. It was going to be our dog for a while now, I guessed.

Arlene and I had been together almost a year. She had divorced Bobby long before and had gone back to school and gotten real estate training and bought the house we lived in, then quit that and taught high school a year, and finally quit that and just went to work in a bar in town, which is where I came upon her. She and Bobby had been childhood sweethearts and run crazy for fifteen years. But when I came into the picture, things with Bobby were settled, more or less. No one had hard feelings left, and when he came around I didn't have any trouble with him. We had things we talked about—our pasts, our past troubles. It was not the worst you could hope for.

From the living room I heard Bobby say, "So how am I going to keep up my self-respect. Answer me that. That's my big problem."

"You have to get centered," Arlene said in an upbeat voice. "Be within yourself if you can."

"I feel like I'm catching a cold right now," Bobby said. "On the day I enter prison I catch cold."

"Take Contac," Arlene said. "I've got some somewhere." I heard a chair scrape the floor. She was going to get it for him.

"I already took that," Bobby said. "I had some at home."

"You'll feel better then," Arlene said. "They'll have Contac in prison."

"I put all my faith in women," Bobby said softly. "I see now that was wrong."

"I couldn't say," Arlene said. And then no one spoke.

I looked out the window at Bobby's dog. It was still staring across the river at town as if it knew about something there.

The door to the back bedroom opened then, and my daughter Cherry came out wearing her little white nightgown with red valentines on it. BE MINE was on all the valentines. She was still asleep, though she was up. Bobby's voice had waked her up.

"Did you feed my fish?" she said and stared at me. She was barefoot and holding a doll, and looked pretty as a doll herself.

"You were asleep already," I said.

She shook her head and looked at the open living-room door. "Who's that?" she said.

"Bobby's here," I said. "He's talking to Arlene."

Cherry came over to the window where I was and looked out at Bobby's dog. She liked Bobby, but she liked his dog better. "There's Buck," she said. Buck was the dog's name. A tube of sausage was lying on the sink top and I wanted to cook it, for Bobby to eat, and then have him get out. I wanted Cherry to go to school, and for the day to flatten out and hold fewer people in it. Just Arlene and me would be enough.

"You know, Bobby, sweetheart," Arlene said now in the other room, "in our own lifetime we'll see the last of the people who were born in the nineteenth century. They'll all be gone soon. Every one of them."

"We should've stayed together, I think," Bobby whispered. I was not supposed to hear that, I knew. "I wouldn't be going to prison if we'd loved each other."

"I wanted to get divorced, though," Arlene said.

"That was a stupid idea."

"Not for me it wasn't," Arlene said. I heard her stand up.

"It's water over the bridge now, I guess, isn't it?" I heard Bobby's hands hit his knees three times in a row.

"Let's watch TV," Cherry said to me, and went and turned on the little set on the kitchen table. There was a man talking on a news show.

"Not loud," I said. "Keep it soft."

"Let's let Buck in," she said. "Buck's lonely."

"Leave Buck outside," I said.

Cherry looked at me without any interest. She left her doll on top of the TV. "Poor Buck," she said. "Buck's crying. Do you hear him?"

"No," I said. "I can't hear him."

Bobby ate his eggs and stared out the window as if he was having a hard time concentrating on what he was doing. Bobby is a handsome small man with thick black hair and pale eyes. He is likable, and it is easy to see why women would like him. This morning he was dressed in jeans and a red T-shirt and boots. He looked like somebody on his way to jail.

He stared out the back window for a long time and then he sniffed and nodded. "You have to face that empty moment, Russ." He cut his eyes at me. "How often have you done that?"

"Russ's done that, Bob," Arlene said. "We've all done that now. We're adults."

"Well, that's where I am right now," Bobby said. "I'm at the empty moment here. I've lost everything."

"You're among friends, though, sweetheart." Arlene smiled. She was smoking a cigarette.

"I'm calling you up. Guess who I am," Cherry said to Bobby. She had her eyes squeezed tight and her nose and mouth pinched up together. She was moving her head back and forth.

"Who are you?" Bobby said and smiled.

"I'm the bumblebee."

"Can't you fly?" Arlene said.

"No. My wings are much too short and I'm too fat." Cherry opened her eyes at us suddenly.

"Well, you're in big trouble then," Arlene said.

"A turkey can go forty-five miles an hour," Cherry said and looked shocked.

"Go change your clothes," I said.

"Go ahead now, sweetheart." Arlene smiled at her. "I'll come help you."

Cherry squinted at Bobby, then went back to her room. When she opened her door I could see her aquarium in the dark against the wall, a pale green light with pink rocks and tiny dots of fish.

Bobby ran his hands back through his hair and stared up at the ceiling. "Okay," he said, "here's the awful criminal now, ready for jail." He looked at us then, and he looked wild, as wild and desperate as I have ever seen a man look. And it was not for no reason.

"That's off the wall," Arlene said. "That's just completely boring. I'd never be married to a man who was a fucking criminal." She looked at me, but Bobby looked at me too.

"Somebody ought to come take her away," Bobby said. "You know that, Russell? Just put her in a truck and take her away. She always has such a wonderful fucking outlook. You wonder how she got in this fix here." He looked around the little kitchen, which was shabby and white. At one time Arlene's house had been a jewelry store, and there was a black security camera above the kitchen door, though it wasn't connected now.

"Just try to be nice, Bobby," Arlene said.

"I just oughta slap you," Bobby said, and I could see his jaw muscles tighten, and I thought he might slap her then. In the bedroom I saw Cherry standing naked in the dark, sprinkling food in her aquarium. The light made her skin look the color of water.

"Try to calm down, Bob," I said and stayed put in my chair. "We're all your friends."

"I don't know why people came out here," Bobby said. "The West is fucked up. It's ruined. I wish somebody would take me away from here."

"Somebody's going to, I guess," Arlene said, and I knew she was mad at him and I didn't blame her, though I wished she hadn't said that.

Bobby's blue eyes got small, and he smiled at her in a hateful way. I could see Cherry looking in at us. She had not heard this kind of talk yet. Jail talk. Mean talk. The kind you don't forget. "Do you think I'm jealous of you two?" Bobby said. "Is that it?"

"I don't know what you are," Arlene said.

"Well, I'm not. I'm not jealous of you two. I don't want a kid. I don't want a house. I don't want anything you got. I'd rather go to Deer Lodge." His eyes flashed out at us.

"That's lucky, then," Arlene said. She stubbed out her cigarette on her plate, blew smoke, then stood up to go help Cherry. "Here I am now, hon," she said and closed the bedroom door.

Bobby sat at the kitchen table for a while and did not say anything. I knew he was mad but that he was not mad at me. Probably, in fact, he couldn't even think why I was the one here with him now—some man he hardly knew, who slept with a woman he had loved all his life and, at that moment, thought he still loved, but who—among his other troubles— didn't love him anymore. I knew he wanted to say that and a hundred things more then. But words can seem weak. And I felt sorry for him, and wanted to be as sympathetic as I could be.

"I don't like to tell people I'm divorced, Russell," Bobby said very clearly and blinked his eyes. "Does that make any sense to you?" He looked at me as if he thought I was going to lie to him, which I wasn't.

"That makes plenty of sense," I said.

"You've been married, haven't you? You have your daughter."

"That's right," I said.

"You're divorced, aren't you?"

"Yes."

Bobby looked up at the security camera above the kitchen door, and with his finger and thumb made a gun that he pointed at the camera, and made a soft popping with his lips, then he looked at me and smiled. It seemed to make him calmer. It was a strange thing.

"Before my mother died, okay?" Bobby said, "I used to call her on the phone. And it took her a long time to get out of bed. And I used to wait and wait and wait while it rang. And sometimes I knew she just wouldn't answer it, because she couldn't get up. Right? And it would ring forever because it was me, and I was willing to wait. Sometimes I'd just let it ring, and so would she, and I wouldn't know what the fuck was going on. Maybe she was dead, right?" He shook his head.

"I'll bet she knew it was you," I said. "I bet it made her feel better."

"You think?" Bobby said.

"It's possible. It seems possible."

"What would you do, though?" Bobby said. He bit his lower lip and thought about the subject. "When would you let it stop ringing? Would you let it go twenty-five or fifty? I wanted her to have time to decide. But I didn't want to drive her crazy. Okay?"

"Twenty-five seems right," I said.

Bobby nodded. "That's interesting. I guess we all do things different. I always did fifty."

"That's fine."

"Fifty's way too many, I think."

"It's what you think *now*," I said. "But then was different."

"There's a familiar story," Bobby said.

"It's everybody's story," I said. "The then-and-now story."

"We're just short of paradise, aren't we, Russell?"

"Yes we are," I said.

Bobby smiled at me then in a sweet way, a way to let anyone know he wasn't a bad man, no matter what he'd robbed.

"What would you do if you were me," Bobby said, "if you were on your way to Deer Lodge for a year?"

I said, "I'd think about when I was going to get out, and what kind of day that was going to be, and that it wasn't very far in the future."

"I'm just afraid it'll be too noisy to sleep in there," he said and looked concerned about that.

"It'll be all right," I said. "A year can go by quick."

"Not if you never sleep," he said. "That worries me."

"You'll sleep," I said. "You'll sleep fine."

And Bobby looked at me then, across the kitchen table, like a man who knows half of something and who is supposed to know everything, who sees exactly what trouble he's in and is scared to death by it.

"I feel like a dead man, you know?" And tears suddenly came into his pale eyes. "I'm really sorry," he said. "I know you're mad at me. I'm sorry." He put his head in his hands then and cried. And I thought: What else could he do? He couldn't avoid this now. It was all right.

"It's okay, bud," I said.

"I'm happy for you and Arlene, Russ," Bobby said, his face still in tears. "You have my word on that. I just wish she and I had stayed together, and I wasn't such an asshole. You know what I mean?"

"I know exactly," I said. I did not move to touch him, though maybe I should have. But Bobby was not my brother, and for a moment I wished I wasn't tied to all this. I was sorry I had to see any of it, sorry that each of us would have to remember it.

On the drive to town Bobby was in better spirits. He and Cherry sat in the back, and Arlene in the front. I drove. Cherry held Bobby's hand and giggled, and Bobby let her put on his black silk Cam Ranh Bay jacket he had won playing cards, and Cherry said that she had been a soldier in some war.

The morning had started out sunny, but now it had begun to be foggy, though there was sun high up, and you could see the Bitterroots to the south. The river was cool and in a mist, and from the bridge you could not see the pulp yard or the motels a half mile away.

"Let's just drive, Russ," Bobby said from the backseat. "Head to Idaho. We'll all become Mormons and act right."

"That'd be good, wouldn't it?" Arlene turned and

smiled at him. She wasn't mad now. It was her nicest trait, not to stay mad at anybody for long.

"Good day," Cherry said.

"Who's that talking," Bobby asked.

"I'm Paul Harvey," Cherry said.

"He always says that, doesn't he?" Arlene said.

"Good day," Cherry said again.

"That's all Cherry's going to say all day now, Daddy," Arlene said to me.

"You've got a honeybunch back here," Bobby said and tickled Cherry's ribs. "She's her daddy's girl all the way."

"Good day," Cherry said again and giggled.

"Children pick up your life, don't they, Russ?" Bobby said. "I can tell that."

"Yes, they do," I said. "They can."

"I'm not so sure about that one back there, though," Arlene said. She was dressed in a red cowboy shirt and jeans, and she looked tired to me. But I knew she didn't want Bobby to go to jail by himself.

"I am. I'm sure of it," Bobby said, and then didn't say anything else.

We were on a wide avenue where it was foggy, and there were shopping centers and drive-ins and car lots. A few cars had their headlights on, and Arlene stared out the window at the fog. "You know what I used to want to be?" she said.

"What?" I said when no one else said anything.

Arlene stared a moment out the window and touched the corner of her mouth with her fingernail and smoothed something away. "A Tri-Delt," she said and smiled. "I didn't really know what they were, but I wanted to be one. I was already married to him, then, of course. And they wouldn't take married girls in."

"That's a joke," Bobby said, and Cherry laughed.

"No. It's not a joke," Arlene said. "It's just something you don't understand and that I missed out on in life." She took my hand on the seat and kept looking out the window. And it was as if Bobby wasn't there then, as if he had already gone to jail.

"What I miss is seafood," Bobby said in an ironic way. "Maybe they'll have it in prison. You think they will?"

"I hope so, if you miss it," Arlene said.

"I bet they will," I said. "I bet they have fish of some kind in there."

"Fish and seafood aren't the same," Bobby said.

We turned onto the street where the jail was. It was an older part of town and there were some old white two-story residences that had been turned into lawyers' offices and bail bondsmen's rooms. Some bars were farther on, and the bus station. At the end of the street was the courthouse. I slowed so we wouldn't get there too fast.

"You're going to jail right now," Cherry said to Bobby.

"Isn't that something?" Bobby said. I watched him up in the rearview; he looked down at Cherry and shook his head as if it amazed him.

"I'm going to school soon as that's over," Cherry said.

"Why don't I just go to school with you?" Bobby said. "I think I'd rather do that."

"No sir," Cherry said.

"Oh Cherry, please don't make me go to jail. I'm innocent," Bobby said. "I don't want to go."

"Too bad," Cherry said and crossed her arms.

"Be nice," Arlene said. Though I know Cherry thought she was being nice. She liked Bobby.

"She's teasing, Mama. Aren't we, Cherry baby? We understand each other."

"I'm not her mama," Arlene said.

"That's right, I forgot," Bobby said. And he widened his eyes at her. "What's your hurry, Russ?" Bobby said, and I saw I had almost come to a stop in the street. The jail was a half block ahead of us. It was a tall modern building built on the back of the old stone courthouse. Two people were standing in the little front yard looking up at a window. A station wagon was parked on the street in front. The fog had begun to burn away now.

"I didn't want to rush you," I said.

"Cherry's already dying for me to go in there, aren't you, baby?"

"No, she's not. She doesn't know anything about that," Arlene said.

"You go to hell," Bobby said. And he grabbed Arlene's shoulder with his hand and squeezed it back hard against the seat. "This is not your business, it's not your business at all. Look, Russ," Bobby said, and he reached in the black plastic bag he was taking with him and pulled a pistol out of it and threw it over onto the front seat between Arlene and me. "I thought I might kill Arlene, but I changed my mind." He grinned at me, and I could tell he was crazy and afraid and at the end of all he could do to help himself anymore.

"Jesus Christ," Arlene said. "Jesus, Jesus Christ."

"Take it, goddamn it. It's for you," Bobby said with a crazy look. "It's what you wanted. Boom," Bobby said. "Boom-boom-boom."

"I'll take it," I said and pulled the gun under my leg. I wanted to get it out of sight.

"What is it?" Cherry said. "Lemme see." She pushed up to see.

"It's nothing, honey," I said. "Just something of Bobby's."

"Is it a gun?" Cherry said.

"No, sweetheart," I said, "it's not." I pushed the gun down on the floor under my foot. I did not know if it was loaded, and I hoped it wasn't. I wanted Bobby out of the car then. I have had my troubles, but I am not a person who likes violence or guns. I pulled over to the curb in front of the jail, behind the brown station wagon. "You better make a move now," I said to Bobby. I looked at Arlene, but she was staring straight ahead. I know she wanted Bobby gone, too.

"I didn't plan this. This just happened," Bobby said. "Okay? You understand that? Nothing's planned."

"Get out," Arlene said and did not turn to look at him.

"Give Bobby back his jacket," I said to Cherry.

"Forget it, it's yours," Bobby said. And he grabbed his plastic string bag.

"She doesn't want it," Arlene said.

"Yes I do," Cherry said. "I want it."

"Okay," I said. "That's nice, sweetheart."

Bobby sat in the seat and did not move then. None of us moved in the car. I could see out the window into the little jailyard. Two Indians were sitting in plastic chairs outside the double doors. A man in a gray uniform stepped out the door and said something to them, and one got up and went inside. There was a large, red-faced woman standing on the grass, staring at our car.

I got out and walked around the car to Bobby's door and opened it. It was cool out, and I could smell the sour pulp-mill smell being held in the fog, and I could hear a car laying rubber on another street.

"Bye-bye, Bobby," Cherry said in the car. She reached over and kissed him.

"Bye-bye," Bobby said. "Bye-bye."

The man in the gray uniform had come down off the steps and stopped halfway to the car, watching us. He was waiting for Bobby, I was sure of that.

Bobby got out and stood up on the curb. He looked around and shivered. He looked cold and I felt bad for him. But I would be glad when he was gone and I could live a normal life again.

"What do we do now?" Bobby said. He saw the man in the gray uniform, but would not look at him. Cherry was saying something to Arlene in the car, but Arlene didn't say anything. "Maybe I oughta run for it," Bobby said, and I could see his pale eyes were jumping as if he was eager for something now, eager for things to happen to him. Suddenly he grabbed both my arms and pushed me back against the door and pushed his face right up to my face. "Fight me," he whispered and smiled a wild smile. "Knock the shit out of me. See what they do." I pushed against him, and for a moment he held me there, and I held him, and it was as if we were dancing without moving. And I smelled his breath and felt his cold, thin arms and his body struggling against me, and I knew what he wanted was for me not to let him go, and for all this to be a dream he could forget about.

"What're you doing?" Arlene said, and she turned around and glared at us. She was mad, and she wanted Bobby to be in jail now. "Are you kissing each other?" she said. "Is that what you're doing? Kissing good-bye?"

"We're kissing each other, that's right," Bobby said. "That's what we're doing. I always wanted to kiss Russell. We're queers." He looked at her then, and I know he wanted to say something more to her, to tell her that he hated her or that he loved her or wanted to kill her or that he was sorry. But he couldn't come to the words for that. And I felt him go rigid and shiver, and I didn't know what he would do. Though I knew that in the end he would give in to things and go along without a struggle. He was not a man to struggle against odds. That was his character, and it is the character of many people.

"Isn't this the height of something, Russell?" Bobby

said, and I knew he was going to be calm now. He let go my arms and shook his head. "You and me out here like trash, fighting over a woman."

And there was nothing I could say then that would save him or make life better for him at that moment or change the way he saw things. And I went and got back in the car while Bobby turned himself in to the uniformed man who was waiting.

I drove Cherry to school then, and when I came back outside Arléne had risen to a better mood and suggested that we take a drive. She didn't start work until noon, and I had the whole day to wait until Cherry came home. "We should open up some emotional distance," she said. And that seemed right to me.

We drove up onto the interstate and went toward Spokane, where I had lived once and Arlene had, too, though we didn't know each other then—the old days, before marriage and children and divorce, before we met the lives we would eventually lead, and that we would be happy with or not.

We drove along the Clark Fork for a while, above the fog that stayed with the river, until the river turned north and there seemed less reason to be driving anywhere. For a time I thought we should just drive to Spokane and put up in a motel. But that, even I knew, was not a good idea. And when we had driven on far enough for each of us to think about things besides Bobby, Arlene said, "Let's throw that gun away, Russ." I had forgotten all about it, and I moved it on the floor with my foot to where I could see it—the gun Bobby had used, I guessed, to commit crimes and steal people's money for some crazy reason. "Let's throw it in the river," Arlene said. And I turned the car around.

We drove back to where the river turned down even with the highway again, and went off on a dirt-and-gravel road for a mile. I stopped under some pine trees and picked up the gun and looked at it to see if it was loaded and found it wasn't. Then Arlene took it by the barrel and flung it out the window without even leaving the car, spun it not very far from the bank, but into deep water where it hit with no splash and was gone in an instant. "Maybe that'll change his luck," I said. And I felt better about Bobby for having the gun out of the car, as if he was safer now, in less danger of ruining his life and other people's, too.

When we had sat there for a minute or two, Arlene said, "Did he ever cry? When you two were sitting in the kitchen? I wondered about that."

"No," I said. "He was scared. But I don't blame him for that."

"What did he say?" And she looked as if the subject interested her now, whereas before it hadn't.

"He didn't say too much. He said he loved you, which I knew anyway."

Arlene looked out the side window at the river. There were still traces of fog that had not burned off in the sun. Maybe it was nine o'clock in the morning. You could hear the interstate back behind us, trucks going east at high speed.

"I'm not real unhappy that Bobby's out of the picture now. I have to say that," Arlene said. "I should be more—I guess—sympathetic. It's hard to love pain if you're me, though."

"It's not really my business," I said. And I truly did not think it was or ever would be. It was not where my life was leading me, I hoped.

"Maybe if I'm drunk enough someday I'll tell you about how we got apart," Arlene said. She opened the glove box and got out a package of cigarettes and closed the latch with her foot. "Nothing should surprise anyone, though, when the sun goes down. I'll just say that. It's all just melo-drama." She thumped the pack against the heel of her hand and put her feet up on the dash. And I thought about poor Bobby, being frisked and handcuffed out in the yard of the jail and being led away to become a prisoner, like a piece of useless machinery. I didn't think anyone could blame him for any-thing he ever thought or said or became after that. He could die in jail and we would still be outside and free. "Would you tell me something if I asked you?" Arlene said, opening her package of cigarettes. "Your word's worth something, isn't it?"

"To me it is," I said.

She looked over at me and smiled because that was a question she had asked me before, and an answer I had said. She reached across the car seat and squeezed my hand, then looked down the gravel road to where the Clark Fork went north and the receding fog had changed the colors of the trees and made them greener and the moving water a darker shade of blue-black.

"What do you think when you get in bed with me every night? I don't know why I want to know that. I just do," Arlene said. "It seems important to me."

And in truth I did not have to think about that at all, because I knew the answer, and had thought about it already, had wondered, in fact, if it was in my mind because of the time in my life it was, or because a former husband was involved, or because I had a daughter to raise alone, and no one else I could be absolutely sure of.

"I just think," I said, "here's another day that's gone. A day I've had with you. And now it's over."

"There's some loss in that, isn't there?" Arlene nodded at me and smiled.

"I guess so," I said.

"It's not so all-bad though, is it? There can be a next day."

"That's true," I said.

"We don't know where any of this is going, do we?" she said, and she squeezed my hand tight.

"No," I said. And I knew that was not a bad thing at all, not for anyone, in any life.

"You're not going to leave me for some other woman, now, are you? You're still my sweetheart. I'm not crazy, am I?"

"I never thought that," I said.

"It's your hole card, you know," Arlene said. "You can't leave twice. Bobby proved that." She smiled at me again.

And I knew she was right about that, though I did not want to hear about Bobby anymore for a while. He and I were not alike. Arlene and I had nothing to do with him. Though I knew, then, how you became a criminal in the world and lost it all. Somehow, and for no apparent reason, your decisions got tipped over and you lost your hold. And one day you woke up and you found yourself in the very situation you said you would never ever be in, and you did not know what was most important to you anymore. And after *that*, it was all over. And I did not want that to happen to me—did not, in fact, think it ever would. I knew what love was about. It was about not giving trouble or inviting it. It was about not leaving a woman for the thought of another one. It was about never being in that place you said you'd never be in. And it was not about being alone. Never that. Never that.

CHILDREN

Claude Phillips was a half-Blackfeet Indian, and his father, Sherman, was a full-blood, and in 1961 our families rented out farm houses from the bank in Great Falls—the homes of wheat farmers gone bust on the prairie east of Sunburst, Montana. People were going broke even then, and leaving. Claude Phillips and I were seventeen, and in a year from the day I am going to tell about, in May, I would be long gone from there myself, and so would Claude.

Where all of this took place was in that remote part of Montana near the Canada border and west of the Sweetgrass Hills. That is called the Hi-line, there, and it is an empty, lonely place if you are not a wheat farmer. I make this a point only because I have thought possibly it was the place itself, as much as the time in our lives or our characters, that took part in the small things that happened and made them memorable.

Claude Phillips was a small boy with long arms who boxed in the same amateurs club I boxed in—up in Sweetgrass and across the border in Canada, wherever we could box. He was ten months younger than I was, but he was hard-nosed and had fight courage. His real mother was his father's first wife, and was Irish, and Claude did not look like an Indian— his cheeks wore more color in them and his eyes were gray. His father had later married another woman—an Indian, an Assiniboin, named Hazel Tevitts—whom Claude did not talk about. I didn't know much about their life then, only that it didn't seem much different from mine. You did not learn much of other people in that locality, and though Claude and I were friends, I would not say I knew him very well, because there was no chance for it.

Claude's father had stayed the night in the motel in town and called Claude in the morning and told him to come down there at noon. On the way Claude stopped at my house—just out of the blue—and said I should come along. We were due to be in school that day, but my father worked on the Great Northern as a brakeman in Shelby, and was usually gone two nights together, and my mother was gone for good by then, though we didn't know that. But I did not go to school so much, as a result, and when Claude drove up in the yard, I just got in with him and we rode to town.

"What're we going in for?" I said when we were out on the Nine Mile Road, riding across the tops of the wheat prairies.

"Sherman's brought a woman in," Claude said. He was smoking a cigarette clenched in his teeth. "That's typical. He likes to put something on display."

"What does your mother think about it?" I said. We referred to Hazel as Claude's mother even though she wasn't.

"She married a gash hound. She's a Catholic," Claude said. "Maybe she can see the future. Maybe she thinks it's superior." He shook his head and put his arms up around the steering wheel as if he was thinking about that. "There might not be actual words for what Hazel thinks, yet. This ought to be funny." He grinned.

"I'll still have a look," I said. "I'll do it."

"Sure you will. Then you'll just have to give her a pumping, right?" Claude flexed up the muscle of his right arm.

"I might have to," I said.

"That's typical, too," he said. Claude was wearing the yellow silk jacket his father had brought back from the war, one with a red dragon coiled around a map of Korea on the back, and *I died there* embroidered under it in red. He reached inside it and brought out a half-pint bottle of Canadian gin. "Rocket fuel," he said. "Sherman forgets where he hides it." He handed the bottle over to me. "Fire up your missile."

I took a big drink and swallowed it. I didn't like whiskey and had not drunk it much, and when it went down I had to look out the car window. The wheat fields running by were two inches up and green then as far as you could see. The only trees alive were the olive breaks planted in rows on the rises and out distant, alongside some house or a quonset where a farm still ran. The little town of Sunburst was ahead, lower than where we were driving. I could see the grain elevator and the narrow collection of houses down one side of the railroad spur.

Claude said suddenly, "Maybe Sherman's going to give her to us." He held the bottle up and took a drink. "He doesn't care what happens. He's been in Deer Lodge twice already. Twice *I* know of."

"For what?" I said.

"Stealing and fighting. Then fighting and stealing. He stole two cows once, and they caught him there. Then he stole two trucks and beat a guy up for fun. He went down for that."

"I don't need to beat anybody up," I said.

"There's Mr. Conscience talking now," Claude said. "Have another drink, Mr. Conscience." He had another drink of the gin, then I took another one, then he threw the bottle in the back, where the seat of his Buick had been torn out and the floor boarded in with plywood. Two fishing rods were rattling back in the dust.

"Who is this woman," I asked, feeling the gin tightening my scalp.

"He brought her over in the caboose last night from Havre. He dead-headed her in. She's Canadian. I didn't actually catch her name." Claude laughed, and we both laughed about it, and then we were down among the first poor houses of Sunburst.

Sunburst had one paved street, which was the Canada highway, and the rest dirt streets. There was the elevator, a café, an implement company, a sawdust burner, one bar and the motel. It was the show-up for the Shelby crews that worked the GN going south. A switch engine hauled in a caboose and three cars two times a day, switched out the elevator spur, and took the crews back and forth to the main line. A green bull-pen shack was across the tracks, and my father's brown truck sat parked beside it with other crew trucks.

The motel was a little cottage camp across the highway—six white cottages and a skinny gravel lot. The closest cabin had a sign on top that said ROOMS FOR TOURISTS, and there was only one car, with an Alberta plate, parked at the cabin nearest the street.

Claude drove in the lot and gunned his engine. I saw a woman look out through the blinds of the office cabin. I wondered if she would know me if she saw me. Claude and I did not go to school in this town, but at the Consolidated in Sweetgrass.

Claude honked the horn and his father stepped out of one of the cabins. "Here comes the great lady's man," he said. "The big Indian." Claude grinned. We were both a little drunk now. He revved the engine again and kicked out gravel.

Sherman Philips was a large dark man with a big belly. He walked bent forward and took very small steps. He had on a long-sleeved white shirt, and his black hair was slicked back and tied in a long ponytail. He wore glasses and a pair of bedroom slippers with no socks. I didn't see how any woman would like how he looked. He drank a lot, is what my father said, and sometimes had been seen carrying a loaded gun.

"Clear conscience is no conscience," Claude said to his father out the car window. He was still smiling.

Sherman leaned on the car door and looked in at me. His big face had pockmarks, and a scar below his left ear. I had never been this close to him. He had narrow eyes and he was clean shaven. A pack of cigarettes was in his pocket, and I could smell his aftershave.

"You two're drunk as monkeys," he said in a mean way.

"No, we're not drunk at all," Claude said.

I could hear Claude's father breathe in his chest. The lines in his face behind his glasses were deep lines. He looked back over his shoulder at the cabin. Behind the screen in the shadows, there was a blond woman in a green dress watching us, but who didn't want us to see her.

"I've got to get home right now," Claude's father said. "You understand? Hazel thinks I'm in Havre."

"Maybe you are," Claude said. "Maybe we're all in Havre. What's *her* name." He was looking at the cabin door where the blond woman was.

"Lucy," Sherman said, and breathed in deeply. "She's a nice girl."

"She likes you, though, I guess," Claude said. "Maybe she'll like us."

Sherman stood up and looked down the row of cabins to the office, where a phone booth was outside. The woman was gone from the office window, and I thought that she probably knew Claude's father because he had been here before, and that probably she knew all the railroad men—including my father.

"I'm going to bring her out here," Sherman said.

"You going to give her to us as a present?" Claude said.

And Sherman suddenly reached his big hand through the window and caught Claude's hair in the back and twisted it. Claude's hair was as short as mine, for boxing, but Sherman had enough of it to hurt. He had a big silver and turquoise ring on his index finger that pushed into Claude's scalp.

"You're not funny. You're clucks. You're stupid clucks." Sherman forced Claude's head almost out the window. He seemed dangerous to me, then—just suddenly. He was an Indian, and I wanted to get out of the car.

Sherman opened the door, pulled Claude out by his hair and away from the car, and put his big face down into Claude's face and said something I didn't hear. I looked the other way, at my father's Dodge truck parked over beside the bull-pen. I didn't think he would be back until late tonight. He stayed in Shelby in the bars sometimes, and went home with women. I wondered where my mother was right at that moment. California? Hawaii? I wondered if she was having a good time.

"Okay now, wise ass?" I heard Sherman say. "How's that, now?" He still had Claude's hair, but had raised his voice as if he wanted me to hear, too. Claude was much smaller than his father, and he had not said anything. "I'll just break your goddamn arm, now," Sherman said and grabbed Claude up closer, then pushed him away. Sherman glared over at me in

84

the car, then turned and walked back toward the cabin he'd come out of.

Claude got back in the car and turned off the engine. "So fuck him," he said. His face was red, and he put both his hands in his lap. He didn't try to touch the back of his head, he just stared out at the Polar Bar, beside the motel. A little red Polar bear sign was shining dimly in the sunlight. A man came out the side door wearing a cowboy hat. He looked at us sitting in the car, then walked around the side of the building and disappeared. No one else was in town that I could see. I didn't say anything for a few moments.

Finally I said, "What're we doing?" The car engine was ticking.

Claude stared ahead still. "We're taking her off somewhere and bringing her back tonight. He doesn't want her out in the street where people'll see her. He's an asshole."

Behind the cabin screen I could see Claude's father in his white shirt. He was kissing the woman in the green dress, his big arms wrapped around her. One leg was hooked behind her so he could get all of her against him and hold her. I could hardly see the woman at all.

"I think we should kill her," Claude said, "just to piss him off."

"What *will* happen to her?"

"I don't know. What's going to happen to you? Maybe you two'll get married. Or maybe you'll kill each other. Who cares?"

The screen opened and Sherman came out again. He looked bigger. He walked in his short steps across the lot, the sun gleaming off his glasses. He had dollar bills in his hand.

"This is shut-up money," he said when he looked in the window again. He stuffed the bills down in Claude's shirt pocket. "So shut up." He looked across at me. "Go the hell home, George. Your old man's cooking dinner. He needs you home."

I didn't smile at him, but I did not talk back either.

"I'll take him home," Claude said.

"He'll spew this."

"No, he won't," Claude said.

"I don't spew anything," I said.

Claude's father glared at me. "Don't talk toward me now, George. Just don't begin that."

I looked at him, and I wanted him to know what I was thinking: that I was sorry Claude had to be his son. I wanted the woman inside the cabin to come with us, though, and I wanted Sherman to leave. I knew Claude would not take me home.

Sherman motioned toward the cabin door, and for a few seconds nothing happened, then the screen opened and the woman came out. She closed the cabin door behind her and walked across the lot carrying a paper sack. She was wearing a man's sunglasses and was thin and flat-chested and wore green high heels. I wasn't sure how old she was. Claude and I watched her while Sherman policed up and down the street to see who was watching us. The woman in the office was not at the window. A car drove by the motel going north. A switch engine had started shunting grain cars out to the elevator, and I could smell diesel. Nobody was paying attention to any of this.

"So, all right now," Sherman said when the woman arrived. I could see through the window that she wasn't a woman but a girl. She was older than we were, but not by very much. "This is Claude," Sherman said. "He's my son. This is his close friend George, who's not going. Claude's going to take you fishing." He looked across the street at the switch engine. "This is Lucy."

The girl just stood there, holding her folded paper sack. She was tall and pretty and pale-skinned, and she didn't seem happy.

"You don't want to go fishing with us," Claude said. He had not made a move to let her in.

"Let her get in," I said. "She wants to go."

The girl bent and looked in the back where there was no seat. A crate was there with a jack, the two rods, and a jumper set.

"I'm not riding in that back," the girl said, and looked at me.

"Let her in front," I told Claude.

I don't think he wanted the girl in the car. And I didn't know why, because I wanted her in. Maybe he had thought his father had an Indian woman, and he wasn't sure what to do now.

Claude opened the door, and when he stood up I could see that the girl was taller than he was. I didn't think that kind of thing mattered though, because Claude had already whipped boys with his fists who were bigger than he was.

When the girl got in she had to pull her knees up. She was wearing stockings, and her green shoes were the kind without toes.

"Hello, George," she said, and smiled. I could smell Sherman's aftershave.

"Hello," I said.

"Don't cause me any fucking trouble, or I'll break you up," Sherman said. And before Claude could get in, Sherman was starting back to the motel in his bedroom slippers, his ponytail swinging down his back.

"You're a real odd match," Lucy said when Claude had gotten in the driver's seat. "You don't look like each other."

"Who do I look like?" Claude said. He was angry.

"Some Greek," Lucy said. She looked around Claude as Sherman disappeared into the motel room and closed the door. "Maybe your mother, though," she said as an afterthought.

"Where's she now?" Claude said. "My mother." He started the car.

The girl looked at him from behind her glasses. "At home. I guess. Wherever you live."

"No. She's dead," Claude said. "Are those my father's glasses?"

"He gave them to me. Do you want them back?"

"Are you divorced?" Claude said.

"I'm not old enough," the girl said. "I'm not even married yet."

"How old *are* you?" Claude said.

"Twenty, nineteen. How does that sound?" She looked at me and smiled. She had small teeth and her breath had beer on it. "How old do I look?"

"Eight," Claude said. "Or maybe a hundred."

"Are we going fishing, today?" she said.

"We talk about things we don't intend to do," Claude said. He hit the motor then, and snapped the clutch, and we went swerving out of the lot onto the hardtop, heading out of Sunburst and back onto the green wheat prairie.

Claude drove out the Canada highway eight miles, then off on the county road that went between the fields and past my house toward the west mountains a hundred miles away, where there was still snow and it was cold. My house flashed by in back of its belt of olive trees—just a square gray two-story house, unprotected toward the east. Claude was driving to Mormon Creek, I knew, though we were only doing what his father had told us to and not anything on our own. We were only boys, and nothing about us would interest a woman, or even a girl the age of this girl. You aren't ignorant of that fact when it is true about you, and sometimes when it isn't. And there was a strange feeling of suspense in me then—that once we were there I did not know what would happen and possibly nothing good would.

"That's a pretty green dress," Claude said as he drove. The girl had not been saying anything. None of us had, though she seemed to have her mind on something—getting back to the motel maybe, or getting back where she'd come from.

"It's not for this season," she said, staring out at the new fields where the air was tawny. "It's already too dry to farm."

"Where are you from?" I said.

"In Sceptre, Saskatchewan," she said, "where it looks just like this. A little town and a bunch of houses. The rest knifed up with these farms." She said *house* the way Canadians do, but otherwise she did not talk that way.

"What did your family do?" Claude said. "Are they a bunch of cheddar-head Swedes?" He seemed to expect everything she said to make him mad.

"He farmed," she said. "Then he worked in a tractor shop in Leader. In the fall he cleans geese. He's up to that right now."

"What do you mean, he cleans geese?" Claude said. He smiled a mean smile at her, then at me.

"Hunters bring geese they shoot. It's just out on the open prairie there. And they leave them at our garage. My father dips 'em to get the feathers out, then guts 'em and wraps 'em. It's easy. He's an American. He's from Wyoming. He was against the draft."

"He plucks 'em, you mean—right?" Claude said, driving. "Is that what you mean he does?"

"They smell better than this car does. I wouldn't have known you two were Indians if it wasn't for this car. This is a reservation beater is what we call these."

"That's what *we* call them," Claude said. "And we call those motels where you were at whorehouses."

"What do you call that guy I was with?" Lucy said.

"Do you think George looks like an Indian?" Claude said. "I think George is a Sioux, don't you?" He smiled at me. "George isn't a goddamn Indian. I am."

"An Indian's a bump in the road to me," she said.

"That's true," Claude said. And something about her had made him feel better. I didn't believe that this girl was a whore though, and I didn't believe she thought she was, or that he did. Claude's father did, but he was wrong. I just didn't know why she would come over from Havre in the middle of the night and end up out here with us. It was a mystery.

We started down the steep car path to Mormon Creek bottom, where the water was high but not too muddy to shine. Across the bridge and a hundred yards downstream was a sawmill that had made fence posts but had been wrecked. Behind it was a pitch clay bluff the creek had cut, and beyond that were shallows and a cottonwood swale. On the near side was a green willow bank and a rusted car body that had been caught in the willow roots. It was a place Claude and I had fished for whitefish.

"Not much of a lumber place," Lucy said.

"That's why the sawyers did so great," Claude said.

"Which way's west?"

"That is," I said, pointing to where the white peaks of mountains could just be seen above the coulee rim.

She looked back the other way. "And what're those mountains back there?"

"Those're hills," Claude said. "We keep them separate in this country."

"It is a nice atmosphere though," she said. "I like to be oriented to the light."

"You can't see light with those glasses," Claude said.

She turned to face me. "I see George here. I see well enough. He's nicer than you are so far. He's not an asshole."

"Why don't you take those glasses off?" Claude said. We were crossing the low bridge over Mormon Creek. The Buick clattered and shimmied on the boards. I looked down. I could see through the clear surface to gravel.

"Where does *this* water go?" Lucy was looking around me.

"Up," I said. "To the Milk River. It goes north."

"Did Sherman bust you, is that the trouble?" Claude said. He stopped us right on the bridge, and grabbed at the glasses, tried taking them off Lucy's face. "You got a big busted eye?"

"No," Lucy said. And she took off the glasses and looked at me first, then Claude. She had blue eyes and blond eyebrows the color of her hair. And what she was hiding was not a black eye, but that she had been crying. Not when she'd been with us, but when she woke up, maybe, and saw where she was, or who she was with, or what the day looked like ahead of her.

"I don't see why you have to have them on," Claude said. Then he drove off the bridge and turned onto the post mill road downstream, the Buick bucking and rocking over the bumps.

"It's too bright," she said and pulled the hem of her dress over her knees. It was a wool dress, as green as grass, and it felt hot against me. "What's the fun out here," she said. "That's a well-kept secret."

"You are," Claude said. "The blond bombshell. You're our reward for being able to put up with you."

"Good luck for that party." She clutched her paper bag. Her fingers were short and pink, and her fingernails were clean and not bitten, just a regular girl's hands. "Where's *your* mother and father?" she said to me.

"His old man runs the rails. He's a gash hound, too,"

Claude said as we drove in under the cottonwoods that grew to the creek bank. "His mother already hit the road. This is wild country up here. Nobody's safe." Claude looked at me in a disgusted way, but he knew I didn't like that talk. I didn't think that was true of my father, and he did not know my mother—though what he said about her was what I thought. It was not unusual that people left that part of Montana. She had never liked it, and neither my father nor me ever blamed her.

"Are you boys men now?" Lucy said and put her glasses back on. "Am I supposed to think that, now that we're out here?"

"It doesn't matter what you think," I said. I opened the door and got out.

"At least somebody accepts truth," Lucy said.

"George'll say anything to get on your pretty side," Claude said. "Him and me are different. Aren't we, George?"

But I had already started toward the creek and couldn't hear what the girl said back, though she and Claude were in the car together for a little while. I heard him say, "Hope means wait to me," and laugh, and I heard his door slam, with her left inside.

Claude took his casting rod to the creek bank with his jelly jar of white maggots, and tied up a cork-and-hook rig, then went to the shallows where sawdust from the mill had laid a warm-water bottom and a sluice down the center of the creek. Sometimes we had caught fifteen whitefish in a school there, when they'd fed. One after another. You could put your bait where they were and bring one back. They were big fish and steady fighters, and Claude liked them because they were easy to catch.

It was three o'clock then, and warm, but I did not want to fish. I did not like the waiting of fishing. I'd hunted for birds with my father, walked them up out of the rosebush thickets. But I did not care so much for fishing, and not for whitefish at all.

Claude had taken off his yellow jacket, and the girl had brought it back up—walking on the toes of her shoes—and spread it in the sun, then sat facing the creek. She raised her dress to her knees and took off her shoes and stockings and pushed up her sleeves. She'd unbuttoned her front enough to let sun on her neck and leaned on one elbow, smoking a cigarette, blowing the smoke in the warm air.

"I wish I could play the piano," she said when I walked up from the bank. "Do you play one?"

"No," I said. My mother had played a piano when we'd lived in Great Falls. She played Dixieland in the house we'd rented there.

"Out here makes me think about that," she said. "I'd like to go in somebody's house and sit down and play some song." She blew smoke out the side of her mouth. She still had on Sherman's sunglasses. Her long legs were so white they looked gray, and thin enough that her calf bones stood out. She had shaved them above her knees, and I could see where the blond hair began. She looked at me as if she wanted me to say something else, but I had nothing else to say. "Do you ever have the dream that somebody you know is leading you into a river and just when you're knee-deep, you step in a hole and you fall under. Then you jump in your sleep, it scares you so much?"

"I have that," I said. "Sometimes."

"Everybody probably does," she said.

I sat beside her on the grass, and we watched Claude. He was casting out toward the car body and walking his bobber down through the sluice. Now and then he'd look back at us and make a phony gesture of having a fish on his line, and then he would ignore us. I could smell the cotton-woods and the sawdust air from the mill.

"Do you have a suitcase full of your clothes?" I said.

"Where?" she said. She was smoking another cigarette.

"I don't know. Someplace else."

"I just left," the girl said. "I wanted to take a trip suddenly—to someplace warmer. I'm not sure I had this in mind, though." She looked at Claude, who had looked up at us again then turned around. Whitefish made little dimples on the flat water, seizing insects I could not even see. It was not a good sign for the rig Claude was using; though at any time fish can do another thing and you will begin to catch them. "His father's not so terrible," she said and touched her nylon stockings, which were in a pile on the grass. She lifted one up with her little finger. "You certainly wouldn't think he'd sit in the dark in the middle of the night and pray in a motel. But he does. He's nice, really. He's pretty big, too. His son's scrawny."

I tried to think about Sherman praying but couldn't think of what he'd want to pray for or hope to have come to him. "Where'd you meet him?"

"At the Trails End Bar in Havre, where I was too young to get in, or should've been. You get in odd situations sometimes."

"How old *are* you?"

She widened her eyes at me. "You're now a criminal. I'm just sixteen, though I look older than that, I know it. Some day I'll regret it." She reached for her paper sack and brought out a can of beer, a cold hot dog, and a red transistor radio. "I've accumulated this much so far."

"When did you leave home?"

"Exactly one night before last," she said. "I didn't think I could trust anybody up there—maybe I was wrong. Who knows?" When she opened the beer it spewed up her arm. She took a drink and handed it to me, and I drank some. "Drinking distances you," she said. "I *would* like to see the Space Needle, still." She picked up the little radio, leaning on her elbow, and stared at it. "Batteries are my next assignment. For this thing." She thumped it with her finger as if she wanted that to turn it on. "I'm not going to eat *this* either." She picked up the hot dog and tossed it in the grass.

"You didn't want to come out here, did you?" I said.

"I didn't want to stay back in that room. Sunburst? Is that what that place is called? You accept help where you get it, I guess."

"Uh-oh, now. Uh-oh," Claude shouted. His rod was curved over, and his line was cutting around the water this way and that. "Here, now. Here he is," Claude said, and looked over his shoulder and wound in on the reel. "This is the big whitefish," he yelled.

Lucy sat up and watched. Claude had walked into the shallows in his shoes, holding his rod up as the fish toured around him. "Look how excited he gets," she said and took a drink of her warm beer. "A monkey could catch a whitefish. They're trash fish. He's stupid."

I saw the fish shine through the surface, then turn down in the cold water. It was a big fish, you could tell by how deep it took the line. I knew Claude wanted to get it in to show.

"He's going to break that one off," Lucy said, "and I bet he doesn't have another hook." And I thought he would break it off myself. I'd seen him break off big fish before.

Claude brought his rod butt down then, and struck it with the edge of his hand, struck it hard enough that the rod tip snapped. "They hate this," he shouted, and he smacked his rod butt again. "A fish feels pain."

The rod dipped, then rose. The line ran out toward the willow bank twenty yards away, then the fish turned on the surface, its white belly visible as Claude began backing it out, and I saw that the fish was falling in the current, losing distance.

"That trick works," Claude shouted at us. "Pain works. Come see this thing."

I walked down to where he'd waded back onto the mud bank. The fish was already on its side, finning sideways in the shallows. "It's huge," Claude said, hoisting the fish up with his rod. And it was a huge fish, long and deep-chested and silvery as it touched up out of the silt. "You can't catch this fish every day, can you?" He was sweating and jittery. He wanted Lucy to see the fish. He looked around, but she'd stayed sitting, smoking her cigarette.

"Great," she said and waved a hand at him. "Catch two more and we can all throw one away."

Claude smiled a mean smile. "Get it off," he said, and dragged the big fish back onto the grass where it lay with its gills cupping air. It was not a pretty fish. It was two feet long, and scaly and silver-white. "Use this," Claude said. He pulled his black spring-knife out of his pocket and clicked down the blade. "Just cut the hook out."

And I got on my knees in the grass, held the fish across its cold body, and cut up right through the bottom of its gill, using the point of the blade. I opened the cut out, pushed under the hook and dug it loose. The fish made a strangled sound when I put my weight on it, but it didn't move.

"Hooked in the gills," Claude said, watching the fish begin to bleed where I'd cut it. "It'll eat good."

I stood up and gave Claude his knife. The fish still breathed, but it was too badly cut to live in the water again. It was too worn out and too big. It wouldn't have lived, I didn't think, even if I hadn't cut it.

Claude pinched the hook between his fingers and the knife blade, straightening the point. "I'm going to catch a bigger one," he said. "They're out there in rows. I'll catch every one of them." Claude looked over his shoulder at Lucy, who was still watching us. He bit his bottom lip. "You're into something, aren't you?" He said this in a whisper.

"I hope so," I said.

"She's a sweetheart." He closed the knife on his pants leg. "Things can happen when you're by yourself, can't they?" He smiled.

"Tell secrets, now," Lucy said and looked up at the sky and shook her head.

"It's not a secret," Claude yelled. "We don't have any secrets. We're friends."

"Great," she said. "Then you and Sherman are all alike. You got nothing worth hiding."

I went back up and sat beside Lucy. Swallows were appearing now, hitting the creek surface and catching the insects that had hatched in the afternoon air.

Lucy was at her red radio, thumbing its little plastic dial back and forth. "I wish this worked," she said. "We could get some entertainment in the wilderness. We could dance. Do you like dancing?"

"Yes," I said.

"Do you have a girlfriend, too?"

"No," I said, though I did have a girlfriend—in Sweet-grass—a half-Blackfeet girl I had not known very long.

Lucy lay in the grass and stared at where a jet was leaving a trail of white cloud, like a silvery speck inching westward. She had her green dress a little farther up her legs so the sun could be on them. "Do you understand radar, yet?"

"I've read about it."

"Don't you see things that aren't there? Is that right?"

"They're still there," I said, "but they're out of sight."

"That's the thing I liked about fishing when my father used to go with me," she said, gazing up. "You only saw half what was there. It was a mystery. I liked that." She pursed up her lips and watched the jet going east. To Germany, I decided. "I don't mind feeling lonely out here." She put her hands behind her head and looked at me through Sherman's dark glasses. "Tell me something shameful you've done. That's an act of faith. You already know something about me, right? Though that wasn't so bad. I've probably done worse."

Claude yelled from down in the creek. His rod was bent and he had it raised high in both hands, the line shooting upstream. Then suddenly the rod snapped straight and the line fell back on the surface. "There's his long-line release," Claude said, then laughed. He was in better spirits just from fishing. "If I didn't horse 'em, I'd catch 'em," he said and did not look where we were.

"He's a fool," Lucy said. "Indians are fools. I'd hate to have their kids."

"He's not," I said. "He's not a fool."

"Okay. I guess I'm too hard on him."

"He doesn't care."

She looked at Claude, who was beginning to rebait his hook, standing to his knees in the creek. "Well," she said, "you'll never see me after today, either. What have you done that's shameful?"

"Nothing," I said. "I haven't done anything shameful."

"Lying is it, then," she said. "That's shameful. You lied because you're ashamed. There isn't any out to this. It's a game, and you lost it."

"You're not ashamed of anything, are you?"

"Yes I am," she said. "I'm ashamed of leaving home without saying anything to anybody. And of spending the night with Sherman at that motel. That's just two days of things. I'll give you a second chance. Are you ashamed of being out here with me—whatever kind of person I am? That's easy, isn't it?"

"I haven't done anything to you I'm ashamed of," I said, though I wanted to think of something I might be ashamed of—that I'd hurt someone or hated them or been glad a terrible thing had happened. It seemed wrong to know nothing about that. I looked at Claude, who was throwing his line onto the current, his bobber catching the sluice and riding it. In forty-five minutes we would lose daylight, and it would be colder. After that we'd take Lucy back to the motel for Claude's father, if he remembered. My own father would never even know I had been here, wouldn't know about this day. I felt on my own, which was not so unusual. "I was glad when my mother left," I said.

"Why?" Lucy said.

"We didn't need her. She didn't need us, either." Neither of those things was true, but I could say them, and it didn't bother me to hear them.

"Where is she now?" Lucy said.

"I don't know," I said. "I don't care."

Though just from her voice then I could tell this didn't matter to her. Shame didn't mean any more to her than some other way you could feel on a day—like feeling tired or cold or crying. It went away, finally. And I thought that I would like to feel that way about shame if I could.

Lucy took her sunglasses off. She reached over and put her hands on my arm and kissed my arm above the wrist. It was a strange thing for her to do. "What he said about your parents was a lie," she said. "It was too harsh. If they're happy, you'll be the same way. I bet my parents are happy I'm gone. I don't even blame them." I didn't say anything, because I didn't know what kind of people they could've been—some man who'd gone across the border to stay out of the war. "Why don't you kiss me?" Lucy said. "Just for a minute?"

I looked at Claude. I saw he had another fish on but wasn't yelling about it. He was just pulling it in.

"He can see us," she said. "I don't care. Let him." She pushed her face up into my face and kissed me. She kissed me hard and opened her mouth too wide and put her tongue in mine, then pushed me on the grass and onto her stockings and her shoes. "Just do this," she said. "Kiss me back. Kiss me all you want to. I like that."

And I kissed her, put both my arms around her and felt her skinny back and her sides and up to her breasts and her face and her hair, and held her on top of me, pushing against me until my heart beat hard, and I thought my breath would stop. "You boys," she whispered to me, "I love you boys. I wish I was staying with you tonight. You're so wonderful."

But I knew that wasn't what she meant. It was just a thing to say, and nothing was wrong with it at all. "You're wonderful," I said. "I love you."

"You're drunk," I heard Claude call out. "You're both fuck drunk."

I was on my back and my mouth was dry. Lucy pulled away from me and looked at him. "Don't act jealously," she said, then reached for her can of beer and took a drink.

"I'm down here fishing," Claude said. "Come look at this. It's a great fish."

"Let's let him have something," Lucy said and stood up, though I didn't want her to leave but to kiss me again, to stay. But she got up and started down barefoot to where Claude was kneeling in the grass. "Let's see your poor fish," she said.

Claude had another whitefish in the grass. The one I'd killed was dry and lying beside it, and the second one was smaller, but it was bright and bending in the grass. Claude had his hand on it and his spring-knife ready to pry out the hook himself.

"It's smaller," he said, "but it's prettier. It's livelier."

Lucy looked down at the fish. She said, "That's a picture of helplessness, I guess, isn't it?"

"It's a whitefish," Claude said as the fish tried to twist free under his hand. "They're the best. And it's helpless. Right. You bet it is."

"What a surprise that must be," Lucy said, watching the fish struggle. "For the fish. Everything just goes crazy at once. I wonder what it thinks."

"They don't. Fish don't think," Claude said.

"Don't they have little perfect spirits?" Lucy looked at me and smiled. She didn't care about any of this. I could tell.

"Not this one," Claude said.

He moved his hand around to the top of the fish to make a better grip so he could use his knife, but the fish twisted again, and with its top fin it jabbed Claude's hand into the meat below his thumb.

"Look at that!" Lucy said.

And Claude let the fish go and wrung his hand and flung blood on the fish and on his face and on Lucy. He dropped his knife and squeezed his hand where the fish had cut him, his jaws set tight. "Son of a bitch thing, he said. He put his hand in his mouth and sucked it, then looked at it. The wound was small and narrow, and it had begun to seep blood on his wet skin. "Fucking thing," Claude said. "Fucking fish is dangerous." He put his hand back in his mouth and sucked the cut again. He looked at Lucy, who was watching him. And for an instant I thought Claude would do something terrible—say something to her or do something to the fish that would make her turn her head away, something he would later be sorry for. I had seen that in him. He was able to do bad things easily.

But what he did was take his hand out of his mouth and stick it in the grass and lean hard on it to stop the blood. It might've been an Indian way. "Who cares," he said, and he seemed calm. He pushed his hand harder in the grass. The blood had dried already on his face. The fish was still twisting in the grass, its stiff gills trapping air, its scales growing dry and dull. "This is your fish," Claude said to Lucy. "Do something with it. I don't want it." I knew his hand hurt him by the way he talked so quietly.

Lucy looked at the fish, and I thought her body, which I was close to, became relaxed somehow, as if something that had been bothering her or that was hard for her suddenly wasn't.

"Okay," Lucy said. "My fish. Let me have that knife."

Claude picked the knife up and handed it to her, the blade forward in the dangerous way. "This is sharp," he said, and as she reached for it, he jabbed it at her, though she only moved her hand out of the way and did not take a step back. "You think we're handsome?" Claude said. "Us two?"

"You're the most handsome boys I ever saw," Lucy said, "in this particular light." She put her hand back out for Claude's knife. "Let me have that."

"We could kill you, right now," Claude said. "Who'd know about it?"

Lucy looked at me and back at Claude. "That woman in the motel would probably be the first one. I had a talk with her this morning before what's-his-name came back to life. Not that it matters."

Claude smiled at her. "You plan to kill me when I give you this knife?"

I could see Lucy's toes twitching in the grass. "No. I'm going to kill my fish," she said.

"Okay," Claude said, and handed her the knife by the blade. Lucy stepped by him and, without getting down on her knees, leaned over and pushed the knife down straight into the fish Claude had caught—pushed it through in the middle behind the gills that were still working, and on into the ground. Then she pulled the knife back far enough to get it out of the ground, picked the fish up by the handle, and flung it off the blade into Mormon Creek. She looked at Claude in a casual way, then threw his knife out into the deep water, where it hit with hardly a splash and disappeared down among the fish.

She looked around at me. "There you go," she said.

And Claude was smiling at her because I think he didn't know what else to do. He was sitting on the ground in his wet shoes, and he wasn't squeezing his hand anymore. "You'll do anything, won't you?" he said.

"I always commit the wrong sins," she said. "I thought we'd have fun out here. That must prove something."

"I bet you'd fuck a pig in knickers," Claude said, "you Canada girls."

"You want me to take my dress off?" she said. "Is that what you mean? I'll do that. Who cares. That's what *you* said."

"Do that, then. I'll watch it," Claude said. "George can watch. That'll be okay." I thought about kissing her then, sitting on Claude's jacket in the grass, and I was ready to watch her take her dress off.

And that's what she did, with Claude on the ground and me standing close to the side of Mormon Creek. She unbuttoned her green dress front, reached down, crossed her arms, and pulled her dress over her head so that she was only in her loose petticoat. And you could tell from her face that she was occupied by something—I don't know what. She pulled down the loose straps off her shoulders and let her petticoat drop off of her so that she had on only a pink brassiere and pants that looked like the cotton pants I wore. Her legs and stomach were white and soft and a little fat, and I didn't think she looked as good as when she'd had her dress on. Not as good as I thought would be the case. There were red marks and scratches on her back and down the backs of her legs, which I thought were the marks Sherman had made on her. I thought of them in the motel in Sunburst, under some blanket together, making noise and rolling and grabbing at each other in the dark.

And then she took off the rest. The brassiere first and then the cotton pants. Her breasts were small and up-pointed, and her ass was hardly even there. I didn't look much at the rest of her. Though I could see then—or so I thought at the time—how *young* she was by how she stood on her pale thin legs, with her thin arms, and how she turned only at the waist and looked at me, so she could be sure I saw her, too. Like a girl. Younger, maybe even than I was, younger than Claude.

But it did not matter because she was already someone who could be by herself in the world. And neither Claude nor I were anything like that, and we never would be, never if we lived to be old men. Maybe she was born that way, or raised to it or had simply become that in the last two days. But it embarrassed me at that moment—for myself—and I know I looked away from her.

"What's next?" she said.

"What do you think you're good for now," Claude said, sitting in the grass, looking up to her. "Everybody thinks they're good for something. You must think you are. Or are you just good for nothing?" And he surprised me, because I didn't think he was taunting her. I think he wanted to know the answer—that something about her seemed odd to him, maybe in the way it seemed to me.

"A lot of this seems a lot alike to me," she said and sighed. "You can take me back to the motel. I ve had all the fun I'm going to." She looked around at her clothes on the ground, as if she was trying to decide what to pick up first.

"You don't have to act that way," Claude said. "I'm not mad at you." And his voice seemed strange to me, some soft voice I hadn't heard him speak in—almost as if he was worried. "No, no," he said. "You don't." I watched him extend his hand and touch her bare ankle, saw her look at him on the ground. I knew what was going to happen after that, and it did not involve me, and I didn't feel the need to be there for it. Claude had a serious look on his face, a look that said this was for him now. And I just turned and walked back toward the Buick at the edge of the cottonwoods.

I heard Lucy say, "You can't ever read other people's minds, can you? That's the trouble." Then I quit listening to them altogether.

I will say how all of this turned out because in a way it is surprising, and because it did not turn out badly.

In the car I didn't wait a long while for them. They were not there long. I thought I wouldn't watch them, but I did, from the distance of the car. I happen to think it is what she wanted, though it might seem she wouldn't have. In any case I don't think she knew what she wanted from me. What we did, I thought, didn't matter so much. Not to us, or to anyone. She might've been with me instead of Claude, or with Claude's father, or another man none of us knew. She was pushing everything out. She was just an average girl.

I turned on the car radio and listened to the news from the Canadian station. Snow and bad weather were on their way again, it said, and I could feel the evening grow colder as it went to dark and the air turned blue. Trout moved against the far willow bank—swirling, deep rises that weren't like other fish, and created in me a feeling of anticipation high up in my chest. It was that way I had felt early in the day, when we'd driven down to this very place to fish. Though the place now seemed different—the creek, the tree line, the millshed— all in new arrangements, in different light.

But I did not, as I waited, want to think about only myself. I realized that was all I had ever really done, and that possibly it was all you could ever do, and that it would make you bitter and lonesome and useless. So I tried to think instead about Lucy. But I had no idea where to begin. I thought about my mother, someplace far off—on a *flyer,* is how my father had described it. He thought she would walk back into our house one day, and that life would start all over. But I was accustomed to the idea that things ended and didn't start up again—it is not a hard lesson to learn when that is all around you. And I only, at that moment, wondered if she'd ever lied to me, and if so, what about, wondered if she was someplace with a boy like me or Claude Philips. I put a picture in my mind that she was, though I thought it was wrong.

After a while the two of them walked back up to the car. It was dark and Lucy had her shoes and her stockings and her sack, and Claude had his fishing rod and his one fish he put behind the seat. They were drinking another beer, and for a minute or so they were quiet. But then Lucy said, just in a passing way, straightening her green dress, "I hope you aren't what you wear."

"You *are* judged by it, though," I said. Then that tension was over, and we all seemed to know what was happening to us.

We got in the car and drove around over the wheat prairie roads at night, drove by my house, where it was still dark, then by Claude's, where there were yellow lights and smoke out the chimney, and we could see figures through the windows. His father's truck was parked against the house side. Claude honked as we passed, but didn't stop.

We drove down into Sunburst, stopped at the Polar Bar, and bought a package of beer. When Claude was inside, Lucy said to me that she hoped to rise in the world someday. She asked me in what situations I would tell her a lie, and I said not any, then she kissed me again while we sat waiting in sight of the dark train yard and the grain elevator, ribboned in its lights, and the empty motel where I had seen her first that day. The sky was growing marbly against the moon, and she said she hated a marble sky. The air in the truck was cold, and I wondered if Sherman was already on his way to town.

When Claude came back with the beers, we all sat and drank one, and then he said we should drive Lucy to Great Falls, a hundred miles away, and forget all about Sherman. And that is what we did. We drove her there that night, took her to the bus station in the middle of town, where Claude and I gave her all the money we had and what Sherman had given him as the shut-up money. And we left her there, just at midnight, going toward what and where neither of us knew or even talked about.

On the drive back up along the Great Northern tracks we passed a long train coming north, sparks popping off its brakeshoes and out its journal boxes, the lighted caboose seeming to move alone and unaided through the dark. Snow was beginning to mist in the black air.

"Sherman wouldn't have come back." Claude was watching the train as it raced along beside us. "She wanted to stay with me. She admitted that. I wish I could marry her. I wish I was old."

"You could be old," I said, "and it could still be the same way."

"Don't belittle me now," Claude said. "Don't do that."

"No," I said. "I'm not."

"And don't belittle her." And I thought Claude was a fool then, and this was how you knew what a fool was— someone who didn't know what mattered to him in the long run. "I wonder what she's thinking about," Claude said, driving.

"She's thinking about you," I said. "Or about your old man."

"He could never love a woman like I can," Claude said and smiled at me. "Never in his life. It's a shame."

"That's right. He couldn't," I said, even though I thought that shame was something else. And I felt my own life, exactly at that instant, begin to go by me—fast and plummeting—almost without my notice.

Claude raised his fist and held it out like a boxer in the dark of the car. "I'm strong and I'm invincible," he said. "Nothing's on my conscience." I don't know why he said that. He was just lost in his thinking. He held his fist up in the dark for a long time as we drove on toward north. And I wondered then: what was I good for? What was terrible about me? What was best? Claude and I couldn't see the world and what would happen to us in it—what we would do, where we would go. How could we? Outside was a place that seemed not even to exist, an empty place you could stay in for a long time and never find a thing you admired or loved or hoped to keep. And we were unnoticeable in it—both of us. Though I did not want to say that to him. We were friends. But when you are older, nothing you did when you were young matters at all. I know that now, though I didn't know it then. We were simply young.

GOING TO THE DOGS

My wife had just gone out West with a groom from the local dog track, and I was waiting around the house for things to clear up, thinking about catching the train to Florida to change my luck. I already had my ticket in my wallet.

It was the day before Thanksgiving, and all week long there had been hunters parked down at the gate: pickups and a couple of old Chevys sitting empty all day—mostly with out-of-state tags—occasionally, two men standing beside their car doors drinking coffee and talking. I hadn't given them any thought. Gainsborough—who I was thinking at that time of stiffing for the rent—had said not to antagonize them, and let them hunt unless they shot near the house, and then to call the state police and let them handle it. No one had shot near the house, though I had heard shooting back in the woods and had seen one of the Chevys drive off fast with a deer on top, but I didn't think there would be any trouble.

I wanted to get out before it began to snow and before the electricity bills started coming. Since my wife had sold our car before she left, getting my business settled wasn't easy, and I hadn't had time to pay much attention.

Just after ten o'clock in the morning there was a knock on the front door. Standing out in the frozen grass were two fat women with a dead deer.

"Where's Gainsborough?" the one fat woman said. They were both dressed like hunters. One had on a red plaid lumberjack's jacket and the other a green camouflage suit. Both of them had the little orange cushions that hang from your back belt loops and get hot when you sit on them. Both of them had guns.

"He's not here," I said. "He's gone back to England. Some trouble with the government. I don't know about it."

Both women were staring at me as if they were trying to get me in better focus. They had green-and-black camouflage paste on their faces and looked like they had something on their minds. I still had on my bathrobe.

"We wanted to give Gainsborough a deer steak," said the one who was wearing the red lumberjack's jacket and who had spoken first. She turned and looked at the dead deer, whose tongue was out the side of his mouth and whose eyes looked like a stuffed deer's eyes. "He lets us hunt, and we wanted to thank him in that way," she said.

"You could give *me* a deer steak," I said. "I could keep it for him."

"I suppose we could do that," the one who was doing the talking said. But the other one, who was wearing the camouflage suit, gave her a look that said she knew Gainsborough would never see the steak if it got in my hands.

"Why don't you come in," I said. "I'll make some coffee and you can warm up."

"We *are* pretty cold," the one in the plaid jacket said and patted her hands together. "If Phyllis wouldn't mind."

Phyllis said she didn't mind at all, though it was clear that accepting an invitation to have coffee had nothing to do with giving away a deer steak.

"Phyllis is the one who actually brought him down," the pleasant fat woman said when they had their coffee and were holding their mugs cupped between their fat hands, sitting on the davenport. She said her name was Bonnie and that they were from across the state line. They were big women, in their forties with fat faces, and their clothes made them look like all their parts were sized too big. Both of them were jolly, though—even Phyllis, when she forgot about the deer steaks and got some color back in her cheeks. They seemed to fill up the house and make *it* feel jolly. "He ran sixty yards after she hit him, and went down when he jumped the fence," Bonnie said authoritatively. "It was a heart shot, and sometimes those take time to take effect."

"He ran like a scalded dog," Phyllis said, "and dropped like a load of shit." Phyllis had short blond hair and a hard mouth that seemed to want to say hard things.

"We saw a wounded doe, too," Bonnie said and looked aggravated about it. "That really makes you mad."

"The man may have tracked it, though," I said. "It may have been a mistake. You can't tell about those things."

"That's true enough," Bonnie said and looked at Phyllis hopefully, but Phyllis didn't look up. I tried to imagine the two of them dragging a dead deer out of the woods, and it was easy.

I went out to the kitchen to get a coffee cake I had put in the oven, and they were whispering to each other when I came back in. The whispering, though, seemed good-natured, and I gave them the coffee cake without mentioning it. I was happy they were here. My wife is a slender, petite woman who bought all her clothes in the children's sections of department stores and said they were the best clothes you could buy because they were made for hard wearing. But she didn't have much presence in the house; there just wasn't enough of her to occupy the space—not that the house was so big. In fact it was very small—a prefab Gainsborough had had pulled in on a trailer. But these women seemed to fill everything and to make it seem like Thanksgiving was already here. Being that big never seemed to have a good side before, but now it did.

"Do you ever go to the dogs?" Phyllis asked with part of her coffee cake in her mouth and part floating in her mug.

"I do," I said. "How did you know that?"

"Phyllis says she thinks she's seen you at the dogs a few times," Bonnie said and smiled.

"I just bet the quinellas," Phyllis said. "But Bon will bet anything, won't you, Bon? Trifectas, daily doubles, anything at all. She doesn't care."

"I sure will." Bon smiled again and moved her orange hot-seat cushion from under her seat so that it was on top of the davenport arm. "Phyllis said she thought she saw you with a woman there once, a little, tiny woman who was pretty."

"Could be," I said.

"Who was *she?*" Phyllis said gruffly.

"My wife," I said.

"Is she here now?" Bon asked, looking pleasantly around the room as if someone was hiding behind a chair.

"No," I said. "She's on a trip. She's gone out West."

"What happened?" said Phyllis in an unfriendly way. "Did you blow all your money on the dogs and have her bolt?"

"No." I didn't like Phyllis nearly as well as Bon, though in a way Phyllis seemed more reliable if it ever came to that, and I didn't think it ever could. But I didn't like it that Phyllis knew so much, even if the particulars were not right on the money. We had, my wife and I, moved up from the city. I had some ideas about selling advertising for the dog track in the local restaurants and gas stations, and arranging coupon discounts for evenings out at the dogs that would make everybody some money. I had spent a lot of time, used up my capital. And now I had a basement full of coupon boxes that nobody wanted, and they weren't paid for. My wife came in laughing one day and said my ideas wouldn't make a Coke fizz in Denver, and the next day she left in the car and didn't come back. Later, a fellow had called to ask if I had the service records on the car—which I didn't—and that's how I knew it was sold, and who she'd left with.

Phyllis took a little plastic flask out from under her camouflage coat, unscrewed the top, and handed it across the coffee table to me. It was early in the day but, I thought, what the hell. Thanksgiving was tomorrow. I was alone and about to jump the lease on Gainsborough. It wouldn't make any difference.

"This place is a mess." Phyllis took back the flask and looked at how much I'd had of it. "It looks like an animal starved in here."

"It needs a woman's touch," Bon said and winked at me. She was not really bad looking, even though she was a little heavy. The camouflage paste on her face made her look a little like a clown, but you could tell she had a nice face.

"I'm just about to leave," I said and reached for the flask, but Phyllis put it back in her hunting jacket. "I'm just getting things organized back in the back."

"Do you have a car?" Phyllis said.

"I'm getting antifreeze put in it," I said. "It's down at the BP. It's a blue Camaro. You probably passed it. Are you girls married?" I was happy to steer away from my own troubles.

Bon and Phyllis exchanged a look of annoyance, and it disappointed me. I was disappointed to see any kind of displeasure cloud up on Bon's nice round features.

"We're married to a couple of rubber-band salesmen down in Petersburg. That's across the state line," Phyllis said. "A real pair of monkeys, if you know what I mean."

I tried to imagine Bonnie's and Phyllis's husbands. I pictured two skinny men wearing nylon jackets, shaking hands in the dark parking lot of a shopping mall in front of a bowling alley bar. I couldn't imagine anything else. "What do you think about Gainsborough?" Phyllis said. Bon was just smiling at me now.

"I don't know him very well," I said. "He told me he was a direct descendant of the English painter. But I don't believe it."

"Neither do I," said Bonnie and gave me another wink.

"He's farting through silk," Phyllis said.

"He has two children who come snooping around here sometimes," I said. "One's a dancer in the city. And one's a computer repairman. I think they want to get in the house and live in it. But I've got the lease."

"Are you going to stiff him?" Phyllis said.

"No. I wouldn't do that. He's been fair to me, even if he lies sometimes."

"He's farting through silk," Phyllis said.

Phyllis and Bonnie looked at each other knowingly. Out the little picture window I saw it had begun to snow, just a mist, but unmistakable.

"You act to me like you could use a good snuggle," Bon said, and she broke a big smile at me so I could see her teeth. They were all there and white and small. Phyllis looked at Bonnie without any expression, as if she'd heard the words before. "What do you think about that?" Bonnie said and sat forward over her big knees.

At first I didn't know what to think about it. And then I thought it sounded pretty good, even if Bonnie was a little heavy. I told her it sounded all right with me.

"I don't even know your name," Bonnie said, and stood up and looked around the sad little room for the door to the back.

"Henderson," I lied. "Lloyd Henderson is my name. I've lived here six months." I stood up.

"I don't like *Lloyd*," Bonnie said and looked at me up and down now that I was up, in my bathrobe. "I think I'll call you Curly, because you've got curly hair. As curly as a Negro's," she said and laughed so that she shook under her clothes.

"You can call me anything you want," I said and felt good.

"If you two're going into the other room, I think I'm going to clean some things up around here," Phyllis said. She let her big hand fall on the davenport arm as if she thought dust would puff out. "You don't care if I do that, do you, Lloyd?"

"Curly," said Bonnie, "say Curly."

"No, I certainly don't," I said, and looked out the window at the snow as it began to sift over the field down the hill. It looked like a Christmas card.

"Then don't mind a little noise," she said and began collecting the cups and plates on the coffee table.

Without her clothes on Bonnie wasn't all that bad looking. It was just as though there were a lot of heavy layers of her, but at the middle of all those layers you knew she was generous and loving and as nice as anybody you'd ever meet. She was just fat, though probably not as fat as Phyllis if you'd put them side by side.

A lot of clothes were heaped on my bed and I put them all on the floor. But when Bon sat on the cover she sat on a metal tie tack and some pieces of loose change and she yelled and laughed, and we both laughed. I felt good.

"This is what we always hope we'll find in the woods," Bonnie said and giggled. "Somebody like you."

"Same here," I said. It wasn't at all bad to touch her, just soft everywhere. I've often thought that fat women might be better because they don't get to do it so much and have more time to sit around and think about it and get ready to do it right.

"Do you know a lot of funny stories about fatties," Bonnie asked.

"A few," I said. "I used to know a lot more, though." I could hear Phyllis out in the kitchen, running water and shuffling dishes around in the sink.

"My favorite is the one about driving the truck," Bonnie said.

I didn't know that one. "I don't know that one," I said.

"You don't know the one about driving the truck?" she said, surprised and astonished.

"I'm sorry," I said.

"Maybe I'll tell you sometime, Curly," she said. "You'd get a big kick out of it."

I thought about the two men in the nylon jackets shaking hands in the dark parking lot, and I decided they wouldn't care if I was doing it to Bonnie or to Phyllis, or if they did they wouldn't find out until I was in Florida and had a car. And then Gainsborough could explain it to them, along with why he hadn't gotten his rent or his utilities. And maybe they'd rough him up before they went home.

"You're a nice-looking man," Bonnie said. "A lot of

men are fat, but you're not. You've got arms like a wheelchair athlete."

I liked that. It made me feel good. It made me feel reckless, as if I had killed a deer myself and had a lot of ideas to show to the world.

"I broke one dish," Phyllis said when Bonnie and I were back in the living room. "You probably heard me break it. I found some Magic Glue in the drawer, though, and it's better now than ever. Gainsborough'll never know."

While we were gone, Phyllis had cleaned up almost everything and put away all the dishes. But now she had on her camouflage coat and looked like she was ready to leave. We were all standing in the little living room, filling it, it seemed to me, right up to the walls. I had on my bathrobe and felt like asking them to stay over. I felt like I could grow to like Phyllis better in a matter of time, and maybe we would eat some of the deer for Thanksgiving. Outside, snow was all over everything. It was too early for snow. It felt like the beginning of a bad winter.

"Can't I get you girls to stay over tonight?" I said and smiled hopefully.

"No can do, Curly," Phyllis said. They were at the door. Through the three glass portals I could see the buck lying outside in the grass with snow melting in its insides. Bonnie and Phyllis had their guns back over their shoulders. Bonnie seemed genuinely sorry to be leaving.

"You should see his arms," she was saying and winked at me a last time. She had on her lumberjack's jacket and her orange cushion fastened to her belt loops. "He doesn't look strong. But he is strong. Oh my God! You should see his arms," she said.

I stood in the door and watched them. They had the deer by the horns and were pulling him off down the road toward their car.

"You be careful, Lloyd," Phyllis said. Bonnie smiled over her shoulder.

"I certainly will," I said. "You can count on me."

I closed the door, then went and stood in the little picture window watching them walk down the road to the fence, sledding the deer through the snow, making a swath behind them. I watched them drag the deer under Gains-borough's fence, and laugh when they stood by the car, then haul it up into the trunk and tie down the lid with string. The deer's head stuck out the crack to pass inspection. They stood up then and looked at me in the window and waved, each of them , big wide waves. Phyllis in her camouflage and Bonnie in her lumber-jack's jacket. And I waved back from inside. Then they got in their car, a new red Pontiac, and drove away.

I stayed around in the living room most of the after-noon, wishing I had a television, watching it snow, and being glad that Phyllis had cleaned up everything so that when I cleared out I wouldn't have to do that myself. I thought about how much I would've liked one of those deer steaks.

It began to seem after a while like a wonderful idea to leave, just call a town cab, take it all the way in to the train station, get on for Florida and forget about everything, about Tina on her way to Phoenix with a guy who only knew about greyhounds and nothing else.

But when I went to the dinette to have a look at my ticket in my wallet, there was nothing but some change and some matchbooks, and I realized it was only the beginning of bad luck.

EMPIRE

Sims and his wife Marge were on the train to Minot from their home in Spokane. They had left Spokane at five, when Marge got off her shift, and it was after nine now and black outside. Sims had paid for a roomette which Marge said she intended to be asleep in by nine, but she wasn't in it yet. She had talked Sims into having a drink.

"How would you hate to die most?" Marge said, waggling a ballpoint in her fingers. She was working a crossword puzzle book that had been left on the seat. She had finished the hardest puzzle and gone on to the quiz in the back. The quiz predicted how long people would live by how they answered certain questions, and Marge was comparing her chances to Sims's. "This will be revealing," Marge said.

"I'm sure you've thought about it, knowing you." She smiled at Sims.

"I'd hate to be bored to death," Sims said. He stared out at the glassy darkness of Montana where you could see nothing. No lights. No motion. He'd never been here before.

"Okay. That's *E*," Marge said. "That's good. It's ten. I'm ten because I said none of the above." She wrote a number down. "You can see the psychology in this thing. If *E* is your answer for all of these, you live forever."

"I wouldn't like that," Sims answered.

At the front of the parlor car a group of uniformed Army people were making a lot of noise, shuffling cards, opening beer cans and leaning over seats to talk loud and laugh. Every now and then a big laugh would go up and one of the Army people would look back down the car with a grin on his face. Two of the soldiers were women, Sims noticed, and most of the goings-on seemed intended to make them laugh and to present the men a chance to give one of them a squeeze.

"Okay, hon." Marge took a drink of her drink and repositioned the booklet under the shiny light. "Would you rather live in a country of high suicide or a high crime rate? This thing's nutty, isn't it?" Marge smiled. "Sweden's high suicide, I know that. Everywhere else is high crime, I suppose. I'll answer *E* for you on this one. *E* for me, too." She marked the boxes and scored the points.

"Neither one sounds all that great," Sims said. The train flashed through a small Montana town without stopping—two crossing gates with bells and red lanterns, a row of darkened stores, an empty rodeo corral with two cows standing alone under a bright floodlight. A single car was waiting to cross, its parking lights shining. It all disappeared. Sims could hear a train whistle far off.

"Here's the last one," Marge said. She took another sip

and cleared her throat as if she was taking this seriously. "The rest are . . . I don't know what. Weird. But just answer this one. Do you feel protective often, or do you often feel in need of protection?"

At the front of the car the Army people all roared with laughter at something one of them had said in a loud whisper. A couple more beer cans popped and somebody shuffled cards, cracking them together hard. "Put your money where *your* mouth is, sucker. Not where *mine* is," one of the women said, and everybody roared again. Marge smiled at one of the Army men who turned to see who else was enjoying all the fun they were having. He winked at Marge and made circles around his ear with his finger. He was a big sergeant with an enormous head. He had his tie loosened. "Answer," Marge said to Sims.

"Both," Sims said.

"Both," Marge said and shook her head. "Boy, you've got this test figured out. That's an extra five points. *Neither* would've taken points off, incidentally. Ten for me. Fifteen for you." She entered the numbers. "If there weren't twenty taken off yours right from the start, you'd live longer by a long shot." She folded the book and stuck it down between the seat cushions, and squeezed Sims's arm to her. "Unfortunately, I still live five years longer. Sorry."

"That's all right with me," Sims said and sniffed.

One of the Army women got up and walked back down the aisle. She was a sergeant, too. They were all sergeants. She was wearing a green shirt and a regulation skirt and a little black tie. She was a big, shapely woman in her thirties, an ash blond with reddish cheeks and dark eyes that sparkled. She was not wearing a wedding ring, Sims also noticed. When she passed their seat she gave Marge a nice smile and gave Sims a smaller one. Sims wondered if she was the jokester. BENTON was the name on her brass name tag.

SGT. BENTON. Her epaulettes had little black-and-white sergeant's stripes snapped on them. The woman went back and entered the rest room.

"I wonder if they're on duty," Marge said.

"I can't even remember the Army, now," Sims said. "Isn't that funny? I can't remember anybody I was even in it with." The toilet door clicked locked.

"You weren't overseas. You'd remember things, then," Marge said. "Carl had a horror movie in his head. I'll never forget it." Carl, Marge's first husband, lived in Florida. Sims had met him, and they'd been friendly. Carl was a stumpy, hairy man with a huge chest, whereas Sims was taller. "Carl was in the Navy," Marge said.

"That's right," Sims said. Sims himself had been stationed in Oklahoma, a hot, snaky, hellish place in the middle of a bigger hellish place he'd been glad to stay in instead of shipping out to where everybody else was going. How long ago was that, Sims thought? 1969. Long before he'd met Marge. A different life altogether.

"I'm taking a snooze pill now," Marge said. "I worked today, unlike some people. I need a snooze." She began fishing around inside her purse for some pills. Marge waitressed in a bar out by the airport, from nine in the morning until five. Airline people and manufacturers' reps were her customers, and she liked that crowd. When Sims had worked, they had had the same hours, and Sims had sometimes come in the bar for lunch. But he had quit his job selling insurance, and hadn't thought about working since then. Sims thought he'd work again, but he wasn't a glutton for it.

"I'll come join you in a little while," Sims said. "I'm not sleepy yet. I'll have another one of these, though." He drank the last of his gin from his plastic cup and jiggled the ice cubes.

"Who's counting?" Marge smiled. She had a pill in her hand, but she took a leather-bound glass flask out of her purse and poured Sims some gin while he jiggled the ice.

"Perfect. It'll make me sleepy," Sims said.

Marge put her pill in her mouth. "Snoozeroosky," she said, and washed it down with the rest of her drink. "Don't be Mr. Night Owl." She reached and kissed Sims on the cheek. "There's a pretty girl in the sleeping car who loves you. She's waiting for you."

"I'll keep that in mind," Sims said and smiled. He reached across and kissed Marge and patted her shoulder.

"Tomorrow'll be fine. Don't brood," Marge said.

"I wasn't even thinking about it."

"Nothing's normal, right? That's just a concept."

"Nothing I've seen yet," Sims said.

"Just a figure of the mind, right?" Marge smiled, then went off down the aisle toward the sleeper.

The Army people at the front of the car all laughed again, this time not so loud, and two of them—there were eight or so—turned and watched Marge go back down the aisle toward the sleeping car. One of these two was the big guy. The big guy looked at Marge, then at Sims, then turned back around. Sims thought they were talking about the woman in the rest room, telling something on her she wouldn't like to hear. "Oh, you guys. Jesus," the remaining woman said. "You guys are just awful. I mean, really. You're *awful.*"

All the worry was about Marge's sister, Pauline, who was currently in a mental health unit somewhere in Minot—probably, Sims thought, in a straitjacket, tied to a wall, tranquilized out of her brain. Pauline was younger than Marge, two years younger, and she was a hippie. Once, years ago, she had taught school in Seattle. That had been three husbands back. Now she lived with a Sioux Indian who made metal sculptures from car parts on a reservation outside of Minot. Dan was his name. Pauline had changed her own name to an Indian word that sounded like Monica. Pauline was also a Scientologist and talked all the time about "getting clear." She talked all the time, anyway.

At four o'clock yesterday morning Pauline had called up in a wild state of mind. They had both been asleep. The police had come and gotten Dan, she said, and arrested him for embezzling money using stolen cars. The F.B.I., too, she said. Dan was in jail down in Bismarck now. She said she knew nothing about any of it. She was there in the house with Dan's dog, Eduardo, and the doors broken in from when the F.B.I. had showed up with axes.

"Do you want this dog, Victor?" Pauline had said to Sims on the phone.

"No. Not now," Sims had said from his bed. "Try to calm down, Pauline."

"Will you want it later, then?" Pauline said. He could tell she was spinning.

"I don't think so. I doubt it."

"It'll sit with its paw up. Dan taught it that. Otherwise it's useless. It has nightmares."

"Are you all right, honey?" Marge said from the kitchen phone.

"Sure, I'm fine. Yeah." Sims could hear an ice cube tinkle. A breath of cigarette smoke blown into the receiver. "I'll miss him, but he's a loser. A self-made man. I'm just sorry I gave up my teaching job. I'm going back to Seattle in two hours."

"What's there," Marge asked.

"Plenty," Pauline said. "I'm dropping Eduardo off at the pound first, though, if you don't want him."

"No thanks," Sims said. Pauline had not taught school in ten years.

"He's sitting here with his idiot paw raised. I won't miss that part."

"Maybe now's not the best time to leave Dan," Sims said. "He's had some bad luck." Sims had had his eyes closed. He opened them. The clock said 4:12 A.M. He could see the yellow light down the hall in the kitchen.

"He broke my dreams," Pauline said. "The Indian chief."

"Don't be a martyr, hon," Marge said. "Tell her that, Vic."

"You're not going to make it, acting this way," Sims said. He wished he could go back to sleep.

"I remember you," Pauline said.

"It's Victor," Marge said.

"I know who it is," Pauline said. "I want out of this. I'm getting the fuck out of this. Do you know how it feels to have F.B.I. agents wearing fucking flak jackets, chopping in your bedroom with fire axes?"

"How?" Sims said.

"Weird, that's how. Lights. Machine guns. Loud-speakers. It was like a movie set. I'm just sorry." Pauline dropped the receiver and picked it up again. "Oh shit," Sims heard her say. "There it goes." She was starting to cry. Pauline gave out a long, wailing moan that sounded like a dog howling.

"Monica?" Marge said. Marge was calling Pauline by her Indian name now. "Get hold of yourself, sweetheart. Talk to her again, Vic."

"There's no reason to think Dan's a criminal," Sims said. "No reason at all. The government harasses Indians all the time." Pauline was wailing.

"I'm going to kill myself," Pauline said. "Right now, too."

"Talk to her, Victor," Marge said from the kitchen. "I'm calling 911."

"Try to calm down, Monica," Sims had said from his bed. He heard Marge running out the back door, headed for the Krukows next door. Death was not an idle notion to Pauline, he knew that. Pauline had taken an overdose once, back in the old wild days, just to make good on a threat. "Monica," Sims had said. "This'll be all right. Pet the dog. Try to calm down." Pauline was still wailing. Then suddenly the connection was broken, and Sims was left alone in bed with the phone on his chest, staring down the empty hall where the light was on but no one was there.

When the police got to Pauline and Dan's house it was an hour later. Pauline was sitting by the phone. She had cut her wrists with a knife and bled all over the dog. The policeman who called said she had not hit a vein and couldn't have bled to death in a week. But she needed to calm down. Pauline was under arrest, he said, but she'd be turned loose in two days. He suggested Marge come out and visit her.

Sims had always been attracted to Pauline. She and Marge had been wild girls together. Drugs. Overland drives at all hours. New men. They had had imagination for wildness. They were both divorced; both small, delicate women with dark, quick eyes. They were not twins, but they looked alike, though Marge was prettier.

The first time he had seen Pauline was at a party in Spokane. Everyone was drunk or drugged. He was sitting on a couch talking to some people. Through a door to the kitchen he could see a man pressed against a woman, feeling her breast. The man pulled down the front of the woman's sundress, exposed both breasts and kissed them; the woman was holding on to the man's crotch and massaging it. Sims understood they thought no one could see them. But when the woman suddenly opened her eyes, she looked straight at Sims and smiled. She was still holding the man's dick. Sims thought it was the most inflamed look he had ever seen. His heart had raced, and a feeling had come over him like being in a car going down a hill out of control in the dark. It was Pauline.

Later that winter he walked into a bedroom at another party to get his coat, and found Pauline naked on a bed fucking a man who was naked himself. It had not been the same man he'd seen the first time. Later still, at another party, he had asked Pauline to go out to dinner with him. They had gone, first, out on a twilight rowboat ride on a lake in town, but Pauline had gotten cold and refused to talk to him anymore, and he had taken her home early. When he met Marge, sometime later, he had at first thought Marge was Pauline. And when Marge later introduced Pauline to Sims, Pauline didn't seem to remember him at all, something he was relieved about.

Sims heard the rest-room door click behind him, and suddenly he smelled marijuana. The Army crew was still yakking up front, but somebody not far away was smoking reefer. It was a smell he didn't smell often, and hadn't for a long time. A hot, sweet, thick smell. Who was having a joint right on the train? Train travel had changed since the last time he'd done it, he guessed. He turned around to see if he could find the doper, and saw the woman sergeant coming back up the aisle. She was straightening her blouse as if she'd taken it off in the rest room, and was brushing down the front of her skirt.

The woman looked at Sims looking at her and smiled a big smile. She was the one smoking dope, Sims thought. She'd slipped off from her friends and gotten loaded. He had smoked plenty of it in the Army. In Oklahoma. Everybody had stayed loaded all the time then. It was no different now, and no reason it should be.

"Where's your pretty wife?" the sergeant said casually when she got to Sims. She arched her brows and put her knee up on the armrest of Marge's seat. She was loaded, Sims thought. Her smile spoke volumes. She didn't know Sims from Adam.

"She's gone off to bed."

"Why aren't you with her," the woman asked, still smiling down over him.

"I'm not sleepy. She wanted to go to sleep," Sims said. The woman smelled like marijuana. It was a smell he liked, but it made him nervous. He wondered what the Army people would think. Being in the Army was a business now. Businessmen didn't smoke dope.

"You two have kids?"

"No," Sims said. "I don't like kids." She looked down at her friends who were playing cards in two groups. "Do you?" Sims said.

"None that I know about," the woman said. She wasn't looking at him.

"Are you a farmer?"

"No," Sims said. "Why?"

"What else is there to do out here?" The woman's look unexpectedly turned sour. "Do you say nice things to your wife?"

"Every day," Sims said.

"You must really be in love," she said. "That's the coward's way out." The woman quickly smiled. "Just kidding." She ran her fingers back through her hair and gave her head a shake as if she was clearing her thoughts. She looked down the aisle again and seemed, Sims thought, not to want to go back down there. He looked at the name BENTON on her brass tag. It also had tiny sergeant's stripes stamped on it. Sims looked at the woman's breast underneath the tag. It was in a big brassiere and couldn't be defined well. Sims thought about his own age. Forty-two.

"Your friends are having a good time, it sounds like."

"They're not my friends," she said.

This time the other Army woman in the group got up and looked back where Sergeant Benton was standing beside Sims's seat. She put her hands on her hips and shook her head

in a mock disapproving way, then waved an arm in a wide wagon-train wave at Sergeant Benton. "Get back down here, Benton," the woman shouted. "There's money to be made off these drunks."

The other sergeants said, "Whoa!" then laughed. Another beer can popped. Cards were shuffled. The other woman was fat and short with black hair.

"They think they're your friends," Sims said.

"Let 'em think it. I just met them tonight," the woman said. "It's the easygoing camaraderie of the armed forces. They're all nice people, I guess. Who knows? Where're you going if you're not a farmer?"

"Minot," Sims said.

"Which rhymes with why-not. I remember that from school. Pierre rhymes with queer." She shook her head again and touched her palm to her forehead. She had big hands, red and tough looking. Hands that had worked. Bigger than his own hands, Sims suspected. "I feel a little light-headed," the woman said.

"Must be the dope you smoked," Sims said.

She grinned at Sims. "Well, do tell." She look scandalized but wasn't scandalized at all. "You're just full of ideas, aren't you?"

"I'm a veteran myself," Sims said.

"What of? Modern life?"

"I was in Vietnam," Sims said. The words just popped out of his mouth. They shocked him. He didn't want them back, but they shocked him. How many people had been there, after all? He tried to guess how old Sergeant Benton was, if she might've been there herself. Thirty. Thirty-five. It was a long time ago.

"When was that?" the woman said.

"When was what?" Sims said.

"Vietnam? Was that a war or what?" She looked

disgustedly at Sims. "I don't believe you were in Vietnam. Do you know how many of you guys I've met?"

"How many?"

"Two million," the woman said, "possibly three."

"I was in the Navy," Sims said.

"And you were probably on a boat that patrolled the rivers shooting blindly in the jungle day and night, and you don't want to discuss it now because of your nightmares, right?"

"I worked on an air base," Sims said. This seemed safe to say.

"That's a new one," Sergeant Benton said. "The non-violent tactic."

"What's your job in the Army?" Sims felt a big smile involuntarily crossing his face. He wished he'd never mentioned Vietnam. He wished he had that part of his life story to tell over again. He was relieved Marge wasn't here.

"I'm in intelligence," Sergeant Benton said brazenly. "Don't I look smart?"

The fat woman stood up and faced Sergeant Benton again. "Stop harassing the civilians, Benton," she shouted. A laugh went up.

"You look plenty smart," Sims said. "You look great, if you ask me." Sims realized he was still grinning and wished he weren't. He wished he'd told her to go to hell in a rickshaw.

"Well, aren't you nice?" the woman said in a voice Sims thought was vulgar. The sergeant kissed her fingertips and blew him a kiss. "Sweet dreams," she said and walked off down the aisle to where the other soldiers were laughing and drinking.

Sims took a walk back to the sleeping car to check on Marge. Two of the sergeants turned and watched him leave. He heard someone chuckle and somebody say, "Gimme a break."

When he stepped out onto the vestibule he noticed it was colder, a lot colder than Spokane. It was September the eighteenth. It could freeze tonight, he thought. Canada wasn't far north of where they were. That was not an appealing world, Sims thought. Cold and boring.

The train was coming into a station when he looked in on Marge. There was one main street that came straight up to the main tracks. The sky was cloudy in front of a big harvest moon. Down the street were red bar signs and Christmas lights strung across one intersection. Here was a place, Sims thought, you'd want to stay drunk in if you could.

Marge was asleep on top of the covers, still in her clothes. The reading light was on. She had a mystery novel open on her chest. She was dead to the world.

Sims took down the extra blanket and covered Marge up to her neck. He put the book on the window ledge and turned off the light. It was cold in the roomette. There was hardly room for him in the bed.

Out the window on the station platform he saw the big sergeant walk past, then the other Army people. He could see a green Army van waiting in a parking lot, its motor running in the chilled air. A few Indian men were standing along the wall of the station in their shirt sleeves. Two dogs sat in front of them. One of the Indians saw Sims looking out and pointed to him. Sims, leaning over Marge, waved and gave him the thumbs-up. All the Indians laughed.

The Army sergeants, seven in all, carrying their bags, walked down to the parking lot and climbed in the van. The one fat woman was with them, and the big man was giving the orders. They looked cold. Where could they be going, Sims wondered. What was out here?

A bell sounded. The train moved away before the

Army van left. Sims kept watching. The Indians all gave him the thumbs-up and laughed again. They had bottles in Sneaky-Pete sacks.

"What's happening?" Marge said. She was still asleep, but she was talking. "Where are we now?"

"Nowhere. I don't know," Sims said softly, still leaning over her, watching the town slide by. "Everything's fine."

"Okay," Marge said. "That's good news."

She went back to sleep. Sims slipped out and headed back to his seat.

It was quieter in the car now. A couple of new people had gotten on, but it seemed less smoky, the lights not as bright. Sims bought a ham sandwich and a soft drink at the snack bar and sat back in his seat and ate, watching the night go by. He thought he should've taken Marge's mystery novel. That would put him to sleep fast. He wasn't going to be able to sleep in the roomette anyway.

Out the window, a highway went along the train tracks. Trucks were running in the night. A big white Winnebago seemed to be trying to keep up with the train. Lights were on in the living quarters and children's faces at the windows. The kids were pointing toy guns at the train and bouncing up and down. Their parents were up front, invisible in the dark. Sims made a pistol with his fingers and pointed it at the Winnebago. All the children—three of them—abruptly ducked out of sight. Suddenly the train was onto a long trestle, over a bottomless ravine, and the Winnebago was lost from view in the dark.

Sergeant Benton rose out of a seat at the far end of the car and looked back toward the rest room. She looked like she'd been asleep. She grabbed her shoulder purse and walked back toward Sims, pushing the sides of her hair up.

"What happened to your friends?" Sims said, though he knew perfectly well what had happened to them.

Sergeant Benton looked down at Sims as if she'd never seen him before. Her blouse was wrinkled. She looked dazed. It was the dope, Sims thought. He'd felt the same himself. Like a criminal.

"Nothing but bars in these towns," the woman said vaguely. "All social life's in the bars. Where do you eat?" She shook her head and put her fingers over one eye, leaving the other looking at Sims. "What's your name?"

"Vic," Sims said and smiled.

"Vic." The woman stared at him. "How's your wife?"

"She's fine," Sims said. "She's locked away in dreamland."

"That's good. My friends left in a hurry. They were loudmouths. Especially that Ethel. She was too loud."

"What's your name," Sims asked. He was staring at the woman's breasts again.

Sergeant Benton looked at her name tag and back at Sims. "Can I trust you?" she said. She covered her other eye and looked at Sims with the one that had been covered.

"Depends," Sims said.

"Doris," she said. "Wait a minute. Stay right here."

"I'm up all night," Sims said.

The woman went on down to the toilet and locked herself in again. Sims wondered if she'd smoke another joint. Maybe he'd smoke one himself this time. He hadn't been loaded in ten years. He could stand it. If Marge were here, she'd want to get loaded herself. He wondered what Pauline had on her mind tonight. He wondered if she'd stopped howling yet. Maybe things would get better for Pauline. Maybe she'd go back and teach school someplace, some small town in Maine, possibly, where no one knew her. Maybe Pauline was a manic depressive and needed to be on drugs.

He thought about Sergeant Benton, in the head now, washing up. His attitude toward "lifers," which is what he assumed she was, had always been that something was wrong with them. The women, especially. Something made them unsuited for the rest of life, made them need to be in a special category. The women were always almost pretty, yet not quite pretty. They had a loud laugh, or a moustache or enlarged pores, or some mannishness that went back to a farm experience with roughneck brothers and a cruel, strict father—something to run away from. Bad luck, really. Something somebody with a clearer outlook might just get over and turn into a strong point. Maybe he could find out what it was in Doris and treat her like a normal person, and that would make a difference.

Out the window, running along with the train, was the big white Winnebago again. The kids were in the windows, but they weren't shooting guns at him this time. They were just staring. Sims thought maybe they weren't staring at him, but at something else entirely.

Sergeant Benton came out of the toilet and this time no dope smell came out with her. She had puffed up her hair, straightened her green blouse and her tie, and put on some lipstick. She looked better, Sims thought, and he was happy for her to come back. But Sergeant Benton looked straight down the aisle past him, patted her hair again, raised her chin slightly and made no gesture to suggest she had ever known Sims was alive or on the earth at that moment. She turned and walked straight out through the door and into the next car.

Sims watched through the window glass as her blond head crossed the vestibule and disappeared through the second door into the lounge car. He felt surprised and vaguely disappointed, but it was actually better, he thought, if she didn't come back. He'd wanted her to sit down and talk—all a matter of being friendly and passing the time—but it wasn't going anyplace. Killing time led to trouble, he'd found. It even was possible Sergeant Benton was traveling with someone else, somebody asleep somewhere. Another sergeant.

A year ago, Marge had gotten sick and had had to go in the hospital for an operation. Marge had seemed fine, then suddenly she'd lost twenty pounds and gotten pale and weak, so weak she couldn't go to work—all in the space of what seemed like ten days. The doctor who examined Marge told her and Sims together that Marge had a tumor the size of an Easter egg deep under her arm, and in all likelihood it was cancerous. After a dangerous operation, she would have to undergo prolonged treatments at the end of which she would probably die anyway, though nothing was certain. Sims took a leave from his insurance job and spent every day and every night until nine in the hospital with Marge, who needed to be there two weeks just to get strong enough for the surgery.

Every night Sims kissed Marge good-bye in her bed, then drove off into the night streets alone. Sometimes he'd stop in a waffle house, eat a sandwich, read the paper and talk to the waitresses. But most of the time he would go home, fix his own sandwich, eat it standing at the sink and watch TV until he went off to sleep, usually by eleven. Sometimes he'd wake up in his chair at three A.M.

When he'd been alone at home for three weeks, he began to notice as he stood at the sink eating his sandwich and staring into the dark, that the woman in the house next door was always at her kitchen table at that time. A radio and an ashtray were on the tabletop, and as he stood and watched, she would start crying, put her head down on her bare arms and wag it back and forth as if there was something in her life, an important fact of some kind, she couldn't understand.

Sims knew the woman was the younger sister of Mrs. Krukow, who owned the house with her husband, Stan. The Krukows were away on a driving trip to Florida, and the sister was watching the house for them. The sister's name was Cleo. She had dyed red hair and green eyes, and Mrs. Krukow had told Sims that she was "betwixt and between" and had no place to go at the moment. Sims had seen her in the backyard hanging out clothes and, often late in the day, walking the Krukows' dachshund on the sidewalk. He had waved several times, and once or twice they'd exchanged a pleasant word.

When Sims had stood in the kitchen drinking milk and eating a sandwich three days running, and watching Cleo alone and crying, he decided he should call over to the Krukows' and ask if there was something he could do. Maybe she was worried about the house. Or maybe something had happened to the Krukows and she was in shock about it and hadn't come out of the house for days. He didn't know what she did all day. It would be an act of kindness. Marge would go herself if she weren't in the hospital.

At ten-thirty on the fourth night, just as he saw Cleo's head go down on her folded arms on the kitchen table, he called the Krukows' number from the kitchen phone. He saw Cleo wagging her head in unhappiness, then saw her look at the phone ringing on the wall, then look at the kitchen window and out into the night, as if whoever was calling was watching her, which of course was the case, though Sims had turned off his own light and stood far back in the room where he couldn't be seen. Somehow he knew Cleo was going to look his way the moment the phone rang.

"Hi, it's Vic Sims from next door," Sims said from the darkness. "Are you okay over there?"

"It's what?" Cleo said harshly. Again she turned and furrowed her brow at the window above the sink. She frowned into the night, then her eyes seemed to widen as if she could see something specific.

"It's Vic Sims," Sims said cheerfully. "Marge and I were just concerned that you were all right over there. Stan and Betty asked us to check on you and see if you needed anything. I was up late over here anyway." This was a lie, but Sims knew it could've been the truth. Stan and Betty were not good friends of theirs and had never asked them to do anything for Cleo at all.

"Where are you?" Cleo said.

"I'm at home. In my living room," Sims lied, staring at Cleo, who, he could see, had on shorts and a long T-shirt. She sniffed into the receiver.

"Are you watching me?" Cleo said, looking at the window, then up at the ceiling. She sniffed again, then Sims thought he heard her sob softly and swallow. He couldn't tell from looking through the two windows and the dark. She was turned toward the wall phone now.

"Am I watching you?" Sims laughed. "No, I'm not watching you. I'm watching the news. If you're fine, then that's all I'm calling to find out. Just checking. What are you crying about, anyway?"

"Nothing. Oh, Jesus," Cleo said. Then she was overcome by tears and sobbing. "I'm sorry," she said after what seemed to Sims like a long time. "I'm just at my wit's end over here. I have to hang up now. Good-bye."

Sims watched her hang up the phone, then turn and lean against the wall and cry again. She wagged her head just as she had when she was seated at the table. Finally, Sims saw her slide down and out of sight to the floor. It was a dramatic thing to see.

Sims stood in the dark against the kitchen wall of his own house. She could hurt herself, he thought. She could be in some real trouble and have no one to help her, whereas if someone would just talk to her she might work out whatever it was and be fine. Sims thought about calling back, but suspected she wouldn't answer now. He decided he would go over, knock on the door and offer help. He took a bottle of brandy out of the cabinet, walked across the dark grassy yard and up the back steps, and knocked.

Cleo came to the back door with tears still fresh on her cheeks. Her red hair was frizzy and damp, and she was barefooted. She looked grief-stricken, Sims thought. She also looked vulnerable and beautiful. Coming over and having a drink with redheaded Cleo seemed like a good idea for both of them.

"Who are you?" Cleo said suspiciously through the screen. She glanced down at Sims's brandy bottle and hardened her mouth.

"Vic," Sims said. "From next door. Remember me? I thought you might like a drink. It sounded like you were crying. I can leave the bottle here." He hoped leaving the bottle wouldn't be necessary, but he didn't want to seem to hope that. He hoped she'd ask him to come in.

"Come on in, I guess," Cleo said and turned around and walked away, leaving Sims on the doorstep, watching her through the screen as she disappeared back into the kitchen.

Cleo, whose last name was Middleton, told Sims her entire story. How she and Betty, who was five years older, had grown up on a farm in Iowa; that Betty had gone off to college and married Stan and Stan had enjoyed a nice, unexamined life of advancement and few financial worries working as an executive for a chain of hardware stores. She herself, Cleo, had gone to a cosmetology school and had somehow ended up in California hanging out with a motorcycle gang who robbed and beat people up for fun and sold drugs and generally rained terror on anybody they wanted to. She didn't say how this involvement had started. She showed Sims a tattoo of a Satan's head she had on her ass. She pulled up her shorts and turned her back to him from across the table, and smiled when she did it. This tattoo was involuntary, she told him, and later she showed him some cigarette burns on the soles of her feet. Cleo said she'd had two children in her life— she was twenty-nine, she said, but Sims didn't believe her. She looked much older in the dim kitchen light. Forty, Sims guessed, though possibly younger. One child had died soon after birth. But the other, a little boy named Archie, was still living with his father down in Rio Vista, but Cleo couldn't see him because his father, who was a biker, had threatened to cut her head off if he ever so much as saw her again. "The courts are helpless against that kind of attitude," Cleo said and looked stern. She told Sims about waking up one night and finding herself being dragged out of her bed by a bunch of her husband's biker friends—Satan's Diplomats. They put her in the back of a car and drove off to the mountains. She could hear them talking about Satan, she said, and his evil empire, and she heard one man, a biker named Loser, say they were going to sacrifice her to Satan and then laugh about it. She said she'd screamed and yelled but no one paid attention. Eventually, she said, the car ran out of gas, and all the bikers had gotten out and abandoned it with her left in it. The next morning a policeman came along and that was how she got out. She said she hadn't gone back home after that, but that her husband, whose name was Savage, sent her a letter care of Betty telling her all he would do to her if he ever laid eyes on her.

Cleo shivered when she told this story, then she took out a cigarette and smoked it, holding it between her teeth. There was a sense about Cleo, Sims thought, that all she said might not be true. Yet she'd obviously had a kind of life that made inventing such a story an attractive possibility, and that was enough.

Cleo told Sims she knew his wife was in the hospital, and she encouraged him to talk about that. Sims had no idea how she'd found out about Marge, but he didn't really want to talk about it. Marge's illness was his terrible worry, he thought, and he didn't know what to say. Marge was sick and might die. And he hated the whole thought of it. He loved Marge, and if she died his life would be over. No ifs or ands. It would just be over. He'd already decided he'd go out in the woods and hang himself so no one but animals would ever find him. That didn't make good conversation in the middle of the night, though. Nothing he or Cleo could say would help any of that. He was happy to sit across from Cleo, who was very pretty, and get peacefully drunk and forget about illness and hospitals and people's puny insurance claims he wasn't processing.

Cleo drank brandy and said that since she'd left California, five years before, she'd had several jobs but couldn't seem to find herself, "couldn't get focused." She'd lived in Boise, she said, doing hair. She'd lived in Salt Lake. She'd gone back to California and gotten married again, but that hadn't lasted. She'd gone to Seattle, then, and come as close as she ever would to a steady job in her field, in a shopping center up in Bellingham. After that she'd gone on unemployment for a year. And then she'd accidentally run into Stan one day on the Winslow ferry. And that had panned out in her staying in Stan and Betty's house for a month. "A real cross-patch life pattern." Cleo shook her head, smiling. "A long way from Iowa, though not in actual miles."

"Things seem better now, though. Here, at least," Sims said.

"Not really," Cleo said. "What's next? It's anybody's guess."

"Maybe there'll be work here."

"I don't ever want to touch another head professionally," Cleo said. She looked down then, and Sims thought she might be ready to cry again. He didn't want that, though he didn't think he could blame her. She'd told him her whole life in ten minutes, and once the telling was finished the life itself seemed over, too. His was not that way. Not yet, anyway. Marge could get well. He could go back to work. Different and good things could happen to them. They were young. But that wasn't Cleo's lot in life. She had plenty to regret and cry about, and it wasn't over yet, not by any means.

Cleo started wagging her head again slowly, and he knew she was about to start sobbing, maybe even cracking up completely, and he would be there alone with her for that. He thought of himself waiting outside a dingy emergency room inside which Cleo, someone he didn't even know, lay strapped to a gurney, heavily sedated, while Marge, his own wife whom he loved, was asleep and dying and alone three floors up.

He could see Cleo's red head begin to lower toward the tabletop. Suddenly Sims stood up, leaned across the table over the brandy bottle, took Cleo's damp soft face in his hands. "Don't cry now, Cleo," he said. "Things'll be all right. Things're going to be a lot better. You'll see. I'll see to it myself.

"You will?" Cleo said and blinked at him. "How exactly will you do that?"

That night he slept with Cleo in Stan and Betty Krukow's big king-sized bed upstairs. Cleo insisted on leaving the television tuned to a rock music channel, but without the sound. This made the room flash with light all night long and made Sims regret he was there. Once or twice he saw Cleo peeping over his shoulder at something going on in the fantasy world where the silent music came from, a world of smoky, dark streets and Halloween masks and doors opening onto violent surprises. This was an act of kindness, Sims thought, and there was no use letting anything bother him. This was not his life and wouldn't ever be. None of it made any sense, but it didn't make any difference, either. Months from then, if Marge lived, he'd tell her about it and they'd have a big laugh together. Cleo would be long gone. Maybe he and Marge would've moved, too, to another house or to another state.

Sometime before dawn, when the light was gray and the room was still except for Cleo's breathing, Sims woke up startled out of a terrible dream. On the TV screen children were dancing and smiling around a man wearing a goat's head and playing an electric guitar. But in his dream Sims had hanged himself from a tall pine-tree limb in a forest somewhere. He'd written letters explaining everything—he'd already seen them being opened by his friends. "When you read this," the letter said, "I, Vic Sims, will already be dead." Yet, even though he was dead and hanging from a new rope with birds perched on top of his head, Marge was somehow still alive and in her hospital room, smiling out of a sunny window, looking better than she had in weeks. She would survive. But it was too late for him. All was lost and ruined forever.

When he woke up later in the morning, the TV was off and Cleo was gone. The dog was not downstairs, and Stan and Betty's other car was missing from the garage. Cleo had left the coffee pot on, but there was no note.

Sims couldn't get out fast enough. He slipped out the back door and ran across the backyard—relieved not to see Cleo drive up in the Krukows' van. Inside, he took a long shower, shaved and put on a clean suit. Then he drove straight out to the hospital, arriving an hour late with a bunch of flowers. Marge said she'd assumed he'd slept in and just unplugged the phone. She said he looked exhausted and that her illness was having bad effects on him, too. Marge cried then, and afterward said she felt better.

Marge stayed in the hospital another three weeks. At home, Sims stayed inside and saw Cleo mostly out the window—the way he'd seen her before the night he'd slept with her in the Krukows' bed—walking the dog, hanging out laundry, driving into and out of the driveway with sacks of groceries. But Cleo had begun to seem different. She never called him, and on the times he couldn't avoid seeing her outside she never acted as if he was anything more than her sister's neighbor, which was a big relief. But she referred to Sims by his first name whenever she saw him. "Hello, *Vic*," she would say, across the fence, where she was walking the dog. She would smile a kind of mean, derisive smile Sims didn't like, as if there was a joke attached to his name that he didn't know about. "How's Marge, *Vic*?" she'd say other times, though he was certain Cleo had never seen Marge. Before, Cleo had seemed out-of-luck, vulnerable, vaguely alluring and desirable. A waif. Now she seem experienced and cynical, a woman who had ridden with Satan's Diplomats and told about it. A hard woman, a woman who could cause you big trouble.

In two weeks, Sims noticed a big black Harley-David-son motorcycle in the Krukows' driveway. It was a low, sleek thing with chrome parts and high handlebars, and after a few minutes Cleo and a big, nasty-looking biker came out, got on, and rode away with a terrible roar. The biker had on black leathers, earrings, and a bandanna over his head like a pirate. Cleo had on exactly the same clothes.

For a week, the biker hung out in the Krukows' house. The bike had California plates that said LOSER, and once or twice Sims saw Cleo and the biker hanging clothes on the line in the back, smoking cigarettes and talking softly. The biker wore no shirt most of the time and drank beer, and kept on his pirate's bandanna. His chest and arms were stringy and pale and hard-looking, with tattoos. Sims understood this was the friend of Cleo's former husband, the one who'd tried to sacrifice her to Satan. He wondered what the two of them could have in common.

The Krukows came back two days before Marge was released from the hospital. The biker disappeared the same day, and the next morning Sims saw Stan carry Cleo's bags and some boxes out to the car, drive away with Cleo, then in a little while come back alone. Sims never saw Cleo again, though he did see the biker in a gas station while he was on his way to the hospital to bring Marge home.

Marge stayed home in bed another three weeks, but as it turned out she didn't have to take the horrible and pro-longed treatments the doctor had predicted. She started get-ting better almost immediately and in a month was ready to go back to her job at the bar. The doctor said that sometimes people with strong dispositions just couldn't be held down, and that Marge was lucky and would probably be fine and live a long life.

On the morning Marge was getting ready for her first day back at the bar, the phone rang in the kitchen and Sims answered it. It was almost nine and he was reading the paper while Marge was getting dressed.

"Vic," a voice said, a man's voice, a voice he didn't know. There was a long pause then, during which it sounded like the receiver was being muffled and talking was going on.

"Yes," Sims said. "Who is it?" It occurred to him that it was probably Marge's boss calling from the bar, needling Sims about being a housewife or something like that. Marge's boss, George, was a fat, good-natured Greek guy everybody liked. "Is this Big George?" Sims said. "I know what you're going to tell me, George. You better watch your step out there."

"Vic," the voice said again. Sims somehow sensed it wasn't George—though it could've been—and in the same instant he realized he had no earthly idea who it was or could be, but that it wasn't good. And in the silence that followed his own name, the feeling of a vast outside world opened up in him, and scared him so that he stood up beside the wall phone and stared at his own phone number. 876-8076. This was somebody calling from far away.

"This is Vic," Sims said stiffly. "What do you want? What's this about?" He heard Marge's footsteps in another room, heard her closet door close, smelled her perfume in the air.

"We're going to kill Marge, Vic," the man said. "If you let her out of your sight, anywhere, we'll be waiting for her. The devil needs Marge, Vic. You've given up your right to her by being an asshole and a slime, by fucking somebody else. And now you have to pay for it."

"Who is this?" Sims said.

"This is the devil calling," the voice said. "Everybody's a loser today."

Someone, a woman in the background, laughed a long, witchy, raspy laugh until she started to cough, then laughed through the cough and laughed until she couldn't stop coughing. Then a door slammed in a room at the end of the line, very far away. Sims knew who it was now. He turned and looked out the window and across the yard between his house and the Krukows'. Betty Krukow was standing at the sink, her hands down and out of sight. She looked up after an instant and saw Sims looking at her. She smiled at him through the two panes of glass and across the sunny yard with the fence in between. When Sims stared at her a moment longer, she held up a plate out of the sink, dripping with suds and dishwater, and waved it in front of her face as if it were a fan. Then her face broke into a wide laugh and she walked away from the window.

"Cleo," Sims said. "Let me speak to Cleo. Let me speak to her right now. Right this instant." Things didn't have to be this way, he thought.

"He wants to speak to Cleo," the man said to someone there where he was.

"Tell him she died," Sims heard a woman's voice say casually. "Like Marge."

"She died," the man said. "Like Marge. Who's Marge?" he heard the man say.

"His wife, you numb-nuts," the woman said, then laughed raucously.

"Let me speak to her," Sims said. "If that's Cleo, I want to talk to her. Please."

"Don't forget us," the man's voice said, suddenly very

close to the receiver. Then almost immediately the connection was broken.

Sims stood holding the buzzing phone to his ear. And after a moment of looking out the window into the daylight brightening the blue shingles of the Krukows' house and reflecting his own brown house in their kitchen window, reflecting, in fact, the very window he could see out of but not himself, Sims thought: this is not a thing that happened, not a thing I'll hear about again. Things you do pass away and are gone, and you need only to outlive them for your life to be better, steadily better. This is what you can count on.

In the chill night, the train passed slowly through another small Montana town. The business section ran along both sides of the track. Yellow crime lights were shining. Sims saw a bar with a sign that said LIVE ENTERTAINMENT and two car lots with strings of white bulbs stretched above the rows of older cars. A convenience store with customers parked into the curb was open at the end of the street. Several boys wearing football uniforms stood in front drinking beers, holding up the bottles in salute. In the rear windows of their cars, girls' faces were looking out at the train.

Down the highway, out of town, was a motel with a white neon sign that said SKYLARK. A soaring bird was outlined in delicate blue lights. He saw a woman and a man, the woman very fat and dressed in a white shift dress, walking down the row of motel rooms to where a door was ajar with light escaping. The woman was wearing high heels. Sims thought she was probably cold.

"Can you imagine a drink, Vic?" Sims looked up and Sergeant Benton was back and wearing a big grin. She was also wearing perfume and she looked fresher, Sims thought, as though she'd had a shower since he saw her.

"I thought you'd gone to sleep," he said. She had her big hands on her hips, and she wasn't wearing shoes. Just stockings. Sims noticed her feet weren't particularly big.

"Are we going to argue about this all night, or what?" Sergeant Benton said.

"I'm fresh out here," Sims said. He held up his plastic cup. "I guess the bar's closed now." He thought unhappily about the flask in Marge's purse.

"The Doris bar's still open," Sergeant Benton said. "No cover."

"Where's the Doris bar?" Sims said.

"In Doris's suite." Sergeant Benton raised her plucked eyebrows in an exaggerated way to let Sims know she was having some fun. "Vic's wife wouldn't care if he had a drink, would she?"

Marge would care, Sims thought. She'd care a lot, though Marge would certainly be happy to go herself with him and Doris if somebody were to ask her. But she was asleep and needed to get her rest for Pauline's next crisis. Meanwhile, he was here by himself, wide awake with no chance of sleep and nothing to do but stare at a dark, cheerless landscape. Anything he decided to do he would do, no questions asked.

"She wouldn't mind," Sims said. "She'd come herself if she wasn't asleep."

"We'll drink a toast to her." Doris held up an imaginary glass.

"Great," Sims said, and held up a glass himself and smiled. "Here's to Marge."

He followed Sergeant Benton into the lounge car, which was smoky. The snack bar was closed. Padlocks were on each of the steel cabinets. Two older men in cowboy hats and boots were arguing across a table full of beer cans. They were arguing about somebody named Heléna, a name they pronounced with a Spanish accent. "It'd be a mistake to underestimate Heléna," one of them said. "I'll warn you of that."

"Oh, fuck Heléna," the other cowboy said. "That fat, ugly bitch. I'm not afraid of her *or* her family."

Across from them a young Asian woman in a sari sat holding an Asian baby. They stared up at Sergeant Benton and at Sims. The woman's round belly was exposed and a tiny red jewel pierced her nose. She seemed frightened, Sims thought, frightened of whatever was going to happen next. He didn't feel that way at all, and was sorry she did.

Sergeant Benton led him out into the second, rumbling vestibule, tiptoeing across in her stocking feet and into the sleeping car where the lights were turned low. As the vestibule door closed, the sound of the moving train wheels was taken far away. Sergeant Benton turned and smiled and put her finger to her lips. "People are sleeping," she whispered.

Marge was sleeping, Sims thought, right across the hall. It made his fingers tingle and feel cold. He walked right past the little silver door and didn't look at it. She'll go right on sleeping, he thought, and wake up happy tomorow.

At the far end of the corridor a black man stuck his bald head out between the curtains of a private seat and looked at Sims and Doris. Doris was fitting a key into the lock of her compartment door. The black man was the porter who'd helped Marge and him with their suitcases and offered to bring them coffee in the morning. Sergeant Benton waved at him and went "shhhh." Sims waved at him, too, though only halfheartedly. The porter, whose name was Lewis, said nothing, and drew his head back inside the curtains.

"Give me your tired, right?" Doris said, and laughed softly as she opened the door. A bed light was on inside, and the bed had been opened and made up—probably, Sims thought, by Lewis. Out the window he could see the empty, murky night and the moon chased by clouds, and the ground shooting by below the grass. It was dizzying. He could see his own face reflected, and was surprised to see that he was smiling. "*Entrez vous*," Doris said behind him, "or we'll have tomorrow on our hands."

Sims climbed in, then slid to the foot of the bed while Doris crawled around on her hands and knees reaching for things and digging in her purse behind the pillow. She pulled out an alarm clock. "It's twelve o'clock. Do you know where your kids are?" She flashed Sims a grin. "Mine are still out there in space waiting to come in. Good luck to them, is what I say." She went back to digging in her bag.

"Mine, too," Sims said. He was cold in Doris's roomette, but he felt like he should take his shoes off. Keeping them on made him uncomfortable, but it made him uncomfortable to be in bed with Doris in the first place.

"I just couldn't stand it," Doris said. "They're just other little adults. Who needs that? One's enough."

"That's right," Sims said. Marge felt the same way he did. Children made life a misery and, once they'd finished, they did it again. That had been the first thing he and Marge had seen eye to eye on. Sims put his shoes down beside the mattress and hoped they wouldn't start to smell.

"Miracles," Doris said and held up a pint bottle of vodka. "Never fear, Doris is here," she said. "Never a dull moment. Plus there's glasses, too." She rumbled around in her bag. "Right now in a jiffy there'll be glasses," she said. "Never fear. Are you just horribly bored already, Vic? Have I completely blown this? Are you antsy? Are you mad? Don't be mad."

"I couldn't be happier," Sims said. Doris, on her hands and knees in the half-light, turned and smiled at him. Sims smiled back at her.

"Good man. Excellent." Doris held up a glass. "One glass," she said, "the fruit of patience. Did you know I look as good as I did when I was in high school. I've been told that—recently, in fact."

Sims looked at Doris's legs and her rear end. They were both good looking, he thought. Both slim and firm. "That's easy to believe," he said. "How old *are* you?"

Sergeant Benton narrowed one eye at him. "How old do you think? Or, how old do I look? I'll ask that."

She was taking all night to fix two drinks, Sims thought. "Thirty. Or near thirty, anyway," he said.

"Cute," Sergeant Benton said. "That's extremely cute." She smirked at him. "Thirty-eight is my age."

"I'm forty-two," Sims said.

Doris didn't seem to hear him. "Glass," she said, holding up another one for him to see. "Two glasses. Let's just go on and have a drink, what do you say?"

"Great," Sims said. He could smell Doris's perfume, a sweet flowery smell he liked and that came from her suitcase. He was glad to be here.

Doris turned and crossed her legs in a way that stretched her skirt across her knees. She set both glasses on her skirt and poured two drinks. Sims realized he could see up her skirt if the light in the compartment was any better.

She smiled and handed Sims a glass. "Here's to your wife," Doris said. "May sweet dreams descend."

"Here's to that," Sims said and drank a gulp of warm vodka. He hadn't known how much he'd wanted a drink until this one was down his throat.

"How fast do you think we're going now?" Doris said, peering toward the dark window where nothing was visible.

"I don't know," Sims said. "Eighty, maybe. I'd guess eighty."

"Hurtling through the dark night," Doris said and smiled. She took another drink. "What scares you ought to be interesting, right?"

"Where've you been on this trip?" Sims said.

Sergeant Benton pushed her fingers through her blond hair and gave her head another shake, then sniffed. "Visiting a relative," she said. She stared at Sims and her eyes seemed to blaze at him suddenly and for no reason Sims could see. Possibly this was a sensitive subject. He would be happy to avoid those.

"And where're you going? You told me but I forgot. It seems like a long time ago."

"Would you like to hear a little story?" Sergeant Benton said. "A recent and true-to-life story?"

"Sure." Sims raised his vodka glass to toast a story. Doris extended the bottle and poured in some more, then more for herself.

"Well," she said. She smelled the vodka in her glass, then pulled her skirt up slightly to be comfortable. "I go to visit my father, you see, out on San Juan Island. I haven't seen him in maybe eight years, since before I went in the Army—since I was married, in fact. And he's married now himself to a very nice lady. Miss Vera. They run a boarding kennels out on the island. He's sixty something and takes care of all these noisy dogs. She's fifty something. I don't know how they do it." Doris took a drink. "Or why. She's a Mormon, believes in all the angels, so he's more or less become one, too, though he drinks and smokes. He's not at all spiritual. He was in the Air Force. Also a sergeant. Anyway, the first night I get there we all eat dinner together. A big steak. And right away my father says he has to drive down to the store to get something, and he'll be back. So off he goes. And Miss Vera and I are washing dishes and watching television and chattering. And before I know it, two hours have gone by. And I say to Miss Vera, 'Where's Eddie? Hasn't he been gone a long time?' And she just says, 'Oh, he'll be back pretty soon.' So we pottered around a little more. Each of us smoked a cigarette. Then she got ready to go to bed. By herself. It was ten o'clock, and I said, 'Where's Dad?' And she said, 'Sometimes he stops and has a drink down in town.' So when she's in bed I get in the other car and drive down the hill to the bar. And there's his station wagon in front. Only when I go in and ask, he isn't there, and nobody says they know where he is. I go back outside, but then this guy steps to the door behind me and says, 'Try the trailer, hon. That's it. Try the trailer.' Nothing else. And across the road is a little house trailer with its lights on and a car sitting out front. And I just walked across the road—I still had on my uniform—walked up the steps and knocked on the door. There're some voices inside and a TV. I hear people moving around and a door close. The front door opens then and here's a woman who apparently lives there. She's completely dressed. I'd guess her age to be fifty. She's younger than Vera anyway, with a younger face. She says, 'Yes. What is it?' and I said I was sorry, but I was looking for my father, and I guessed I'd gotten the wrong place. But she says, 'Just a second,' and turns around and says, 'Eddie, your daughter's here.'

"And my father came out of a door to the next room. Maybe it was a closet, I didn't know. I didn't care. He had his pants on and an undershirt. And he said, 'Oh hi, Doris. How're you? Come on in. This is Sherry.' And the only thing I could think of was how thin his shoulders looked. He looked like he was going to die. I didn't even speak to Sherry. I just said, No, I couldn't stay. And I drove on back to the house."

"Did you leave then?" Sims said.

"No, I stayed around a couple more days. *Then* left. It didn't matter to me. It made me think, though."

"What did you think," Sims asked.

Doris put her head back against the metal wall and stared up. "Oh, I just thought about being the other woman, which I've been that enough. Everybody's done everything twice, right? At my age. You cross a line. But you can do a thing and have it mean nothing but what you feel that minute. You don't have to give yourself away. Isn't that true?"

"That's exactly true," Sims said and thought it was right. He'd done it himself plenty of times.

"Where's the real life, right? I don't think I've had mine, yet, have you?" Doris held her glass up to her lips with both hands and smiled at him.

"Not yet, I haven't," Sims said. "Not entirely."

"When I was a little girl in California and my father was teaching me to drive, I used to think, 'I'm driving now. I have to pay strict attention to everything; I have to notice everything; I have to think about my hands being on the wheel; it's possible I'll only think about this very second forever, and it'll drive me crazy.' But I'd already thought of something else." Doris wrinkled her nose at Sims. "That's my movie, right?"

"It sounds familiar," Sims said. He took a long drink of his vodka and emptied the glass. The vodka tasted metallic, as if it had been kept stored in a can. It had a good effect, though. He felt like he could stay up all night. He was seeing things from the outside, and nothing bad could happen to anyone. Everyone was protected. "Most people want to be good, though," Sims said for no reason. Just words under their own command, headed who-knows-where. Everything seemed arbitrary.

"Would you like me to take my clothes off?" Sergeant Benton said and smiled at him.

"I'd like that," Sims said. "Sure." He thought that he

would also like a small amount more of the vodka. He reached over, took the bottle off the blanket and poured himself some more.

Sergeant Benton began unbuttoning her uniform blouse. She knelt forward on her knees, pulled her shirttail out, and began with the bottom button first. She watched Sims, still half-smiling. "Do you remember the first woman you ever saw naked?" she said, opening her blouse so Sims could see her white brassiere and a line of smooth belly over her skirt.

"Yes," Sims said.

"And where was that?" Sergeant Benton said. "What state was that in?" She took her blouse off, then pulled her strap down off her shoulder and uncovered one breast, then the other one. They were breasts that went to the side and pushed outward. They were nice breasts.

"That was California, too," Sims said. "Near Sacramento, I think."

"What happened?" Sergeant Benton began unzipping her skirt.

"We were on a golf course. My friend and I and this girl. Patsy was her name. We were all twelve. We both asked her to take off her clothes, in an old caddy house by the Air Force base. And she did it. We did too. She said we'd have to." Sims wondered if Patsy's name was still Patsy.

Sergeant Benton slid her skirt down, then sat back and handed it around her ankles. She had on only panty hose now and nothing beyond that. You could see through them even in the dim light. She leaned against the metal wall and looked at Sims. He could touch her now, he thought. That was what she would like to happen. "Did you like it," Sergeant Benton asked.

"Yes. I liked it," Sims said.

"It wasn't disappointing to you?"

"It was," Sims said. "But I liked it. I knew I was going

to." Sims moved close to her, lightly touched her ankle, then her knee, then the soft skin of her belly and came down with the waist of her hosiery. Her hands touched his neck but didn't feel rough. He heard her breathe and smelled the perfume she was wearing. Nothing seemed arbitrary now.

"Sweet, that's sweet," she said, and breathed deeply once. "Sometimes I think about making love. Like now. And everything tightens up inside me, and I just squeeze and say *ahhhh* without even meaning to. It just escapes me. It's just that pleasure. Someday it'll stop, won't it?"

"No," Sims said. "That won't. That goes on forever." He was near her now, his ear to her chest. He heard a noise, a noise of releasing. Outside, in the corridor, someone began talking in a hushed voice. Someone said, "No, no. Don't say that." And then a door clicked.

"Life's on so thin a string anymore," she whispered, and turned off the tiny light. "Not that much makes it good."

"That's right, isn't it?" Sims said, close to her. "I know that."

"This isn't passion," she said. "This is something different now. I can't lose sleep over this."

"That's fine," Sims said.

"You knew this would happen, didn't you?" she said. "It wasn't a secret." He didn't know it. He didn't try to answer it. "Oh you," she whispered, "Oh you."

Sometime in the night Sims felt the train slow and then stop, then sit still in the dark. He had no idea where he was. He still had his clothes on. Outside there was sound like wind, and for a moment he thought possibly he was dead, that this is how it would feel.

Sergeant Benton lay beside him, asleep. Her clothes were around her. She was covered with a blanket. The vodka bottle was empty on the bed. What had he done here? Sims thought. How had things exactly happened? What time was it? Out the window he could see no one and nothing. The moon was gone, though the sky was red and wavering with a reflected light, as though the wind was moving it.

Sims picked up his shoes and opened the door into the corridor. The porter didn't appear this time, and Sims closed the door softly and carried his shoes down to the washroom by the vestibule. Inside, he locked the door, ran water on his hands, then rubbed soap on his face and his ears and his neck and into his hairline, then rinsed them with water out of the silver bowl until his face was clean and dripping, and he could stand to see it in the dull little mirror: a haggard face, his eyes red, his skin pale, his teeth gray and lifeless. A deceiver's face, he thought. An adulterer's face, a face to turn away from. He smiled at himself and then couldn't look. He was glad to be alone. He wouldn't see this woman again. He and Marge would get off in a few hours, and Doris would sleep around the clock.

Sims let himself back into the corridor. He thought he heard noise outside the train, and through the window to the vestibule he saw the Asian woman, standing and staring out, holding her little boy in her arms. She was talking to the conductor. He hoped there was no trouble. He wanted to get to Minot on time and get off the train.

When he let himself into Marge's roomette, Marge was awake. And out the window he saw the center of everyone's attention. A wide fire was burning on the open prairie. Out in the dark, men were moving at the edges of the fire. Trucks were in the fields and high tractors with their lights on, and dogs chasing and tumbling in the dark. Far away he could see the white stanchions of high-voltage lines traveling off into the distance.

"It's thrilling," Marge said and turned and smiled at him. "The tracks are on fire ahead of us. I heard someone outside say that. People are running all over. I watched a house disappear. It'll drive you to your remotest thoughts."

"What about *us*?" Sims said, looking out the window into the fire.

"I didn't think of that. Isn't that strange?" Marge said. "It didn't even seem to matter. It should, I guess."

The fire had turned the sky red and the wind blew flames upwards, and Sims imagined he felt heat, and his heart beat faster with the sight—a fire that could turn and sweep over them in a moment, and they would all be caught, asleep and awake. He thought of Sergeant Benton alone in her bed, dreaming dreams of safety and confidence. Nothing was wrong with her, he thought. She should be saved. A sense of powerlessness and despair rose in him, as if there was help but he couldn't offer it.

"The world's on fire, Vic," Marge said. "But it doesn't hurt anything. It just burns until it stops." She raised the covers. "Get in bed with me, sweetheart," she said, "you poor thing. You've been up all night, haven't you?" She was naked under the sheet. He could see her breasts and her stomach and the beginnings of her white legs.

He sat on the bed and put his shoes down. His heart beat faster. He could feel heat now from outside. But, he thought, there was no threat to them, to anyone on the train. "I slept a little," he said.

Marge took his hand and kissed it and held it between her hands. "When I was in my remote thoughts, you know, just watching it burn, I thought about how I get in bed sometimes and I think how happy I am, and then it makes me sad. It's crazy, isn't it? I'd like life to stop, and it won't. It just keeps running by me. It makes me jealous of Pauline. She makes life stop when she wants it to. She doesn't care what happens. That's just a way of looking at things. I guess I wouldn't want to be like her."

"You're not like her," Sims said. "You're sympathetic."

"She probably thinks no one takes her seriously."

"It's all right," Sims said.

"What's going to happen to Pauline now?" Marge moved closer to him. "Will she be all right? Do you think she will?"

"I think she will," Sims said.

"We're out on a frontier here, aren't we, sweetheart? It feels like that." Sims didn't answer. "Are you sleepy, hon," Marge asked. "You can sleep. I'm awake now. I'll watch over you." She reached and pulled down the shade, and everything, all the movement and heat outside, was gone.

He touched Marge with his fingers—the bones in her face and her shoulders, her breasts, her ribs. He touched the scar, smooth and rigid and neat under her arm, like a welt from a mean blow. This can do it, he thought, this can finish you, this small thing. He held her to him, her face against his as his heart beat. And he felt dizzy, and at that moment insufficient, but without a memory of life's having changed in that particular way.

Outside on the cold air, flames moved and divided and swarmed the sky. And Sims felt alone in a wide empire, removed and afloat, calmed, as if life was far away now, as if blackness was all around, as if stars held the only light.

WINTERKILL

I had not been back in town long. Maybe a month was all. The work had finally given out for me down at Silver Bow, and I had quit staying down there when the weather turned cold, and come back to my mother's, on the Bitterroot, to lay up and set my benefits aside for when things got worse.

My mother had her boyfriend then, an old wildcatter named Harley Reeves. And Harley and I did not get along, though I don't blame him for that. He had been laid off himself down near Gillette, Wyoming, where the boom was finished. And he was just doing what I was doing and had arrived there first. Everyone was laid off then. It was not a good time in that part of Montana, nor was it going to be. The two of them were just giving it a final try, both of them in their sixties, strangers together in the little house my father had left her.

So in a week I moved up to town, into a little misery flat across from the Burlington Northern yards, and began to wait. There was nothing to do. Watch TV. Stop in a bar. Walk down to the Clark Fork and fish where they had built a little park. Just find a way to spend the time. You think you'd like to have all the time be your own, but that is a fantasy. I was feeling my back to the wall then, and didn't know what would happen to me in a week's time, which is a feeling to stay with you and make being cheerful hard. And no one can like that.

I was at the Top Hat having a drink with Little Troy Burnham, talking about the deer season, when a woman who had been sitting at the front of the bar got up and came over to us. I had seen this woman other times in other bars in town. She would be there in the afternoons around three, and then sometimes late at night when I would be cruising back. She danced with some men from the air base, then sat drinking and talking late. I suppose she left with someone finally. She wasn't a bad-looking woman at all—blond, with wide, dark eyes set out, wide hips and dark eyebrows. She could've been thirty-four years old, although she could've been forty-four or twenty-four, because she was drinking steady, and steady drink can do both to you, especially to women. But I had thought the first time I saw her: Here's one on the way down. A miner's wife drifted up from Butte, or a rancher's daughter just suddenly run off, which can happen. Or worse. And I hadn't been tempted. Trouble comes cheap and leaves expensive, is a way of thinking about that.

"Do you suppose you could give me a light?" the woman said to us. She was standing at our table. Nola was her name. Nola Foster. I'd heard that around. She wasn't drunk. It was four o'clock in the afternoon, and no one was there but Troy Burnham and me.

"If you'll tell me a love story, I'd do anything in the world for you," Troy said. It was what he always said to women. He'd do anything in the world for something. Troy sits in a wheelchair due to a smoke jumper's injury, and can't do very much. We had been friends since high school and before. He was always short, and I was tall. But Troy had been an excellent wrestler and won awards in Montana, and I had done little of that—some boxing once was all. We had been living, recently, in the same apartments on Ryman Street, though Troy lived there permanently and drove a Checker cab to earn a living, and I was hoping to pass on to something better. "I *would* like a little love story," Troy said, and called out for whatever Nola Foster was drinking.

"Nola, Troy. Troy, Nola," I said and lit her cigarette.

"Have we met?" Nola said, taking a seat and glancing at me.

"At the East Gate. Some time ago," I said.

"That's a very nice bar," she said in a cool way. "But I hear it's changed hands."

"I'm glad to make an acquaintance," Troy said, grinning and adjusting his glasses. "Now let's hear that love story." He pulled up close to the table so that his head and his big shoulders were above the tabletop. Troy's injury had caused him not to have any hips left. There is something there, but not hips. He needs bars and a special seat in his cab. He is both frail and strong at once, though in most ways he gets on like everybody else.

"I *was* in love," Nola said quietly as the bartender set her drink down and she took a sip. "And now I'm not."

"That's a short love story," I said.

"There's more to it," Troy said, grinning. "Am I right about that? Here's cheers to you," he said, and raised his glass.

Nola glanced at me again. "All right. Cheers," she said and took another drink.

Two men had started playing a pool game at the far end of the room. They had turned on the table light, and I could hear the balls click and someone say, "Bust 'em up, Craft." And then the smack.

"You don't want to hear about that," Nola said. "You're drunk men, that's all."

"We do too," Troy said. Troy always has enthusiasm. He could very easily complain, but I have never heard it come up. And I believe he has a good heart.

"What about you? What's your name?" Nola said to me.

"Les," I said.

"Les, then," she said. "You don't want to hear this, Les."

"Yes he does," Troy said, putting his elbows on the table and raising himself. Troy was a little drunk. Maybe we all were a little.

"Why not?" I said.

"See? Sure. Les wants more. He's like me."

Nola was actually a pretty woman, with a kind of dignity to her that wasn't at once so noticeable, and Troy was thrilled by her.

"All right," Nola said, taking another sip.

"What'd I tell you?" Troy said.

"I had really thought he was dying," Nola said.

"Who?" I said.

"My husband. Harry Lyons. I don't use that name now. Someone's told you this story before, haven't they?"

"Not me. Goddamn!" Troy said. "I *want* to hear this story."

I said I hadn't heard it either, though I had heard there was a story.

She had a puff on her cigarette and gave us both a look that said she didn't believe us. But she went on. Maybe she'd thought about another drink by then.

"He had this death look. Ca-shit-ic, they call it. He was pale, and his mouth turned down like he could see death. His heart had already gone out once in June, and I had the feeling I'd come in the kitchen some morning and he'd be slumped on his toast."

"How old was this Harry?" Troy said.

"Fifty-three years old. Older than me by a lot."

"That's cardiac alley there," Troy said and nodded at me. Troy has trouble with his own organs now and then. I think they all moved lower when he hit the ground.

"A man gets strange when he's going to die," Nola said in a quiet voice. "Like he's watching it come. Though Harry was still going to work out at Champion's every day. He was an estimator. Plus he watched *me* all the time. Watched to see if I was getting ready, I guess. Checking the insurance, balancing the checkbook, locating the safe-deposit key. All that. Though I would, too. Who wouldn't?"

"Bet your ass," Troy said and nodded again. Troy was taking this all in, I could see that.

"And I admit it, I *was*," Nola said. "I loved Harry. But if he died, where was I going? Was I supposed to die, too? I had to make some plans for myself. I had to think Harry was expendable at some point. To *my* life, anyway."

"Probably that's why he was watching you," I said. "He might not have felt expendable in *his* life."

"I know." Nola looked at me seriously and smoked her cigarette. "But I had a friend whose husband killed himself. Went into the garage and left the motor running. And his wife was *not* ready. Not in her mind. She thought he was out putting on brakeshoes. And there he was dead when she went out there. She ended up having to move to Washington, D.C. Lost her balance completely over it. Lost her house, too."

"All bad things," Troy agreed.

"And that just wasn't going to be me, I thought. And if Harry had to get wind of it, well, so be it. Some days I'd wake up and look at him in bed and I'd think, Die, Harry, quit worrying about it."

"I thought this was a love story," I said. I looked down at where the two men were playing an eight-ball rack. One man was chalking a cue while the other man was leaning over to shoot.

"It's coming," Troy said. "Just be patient, Les."

Nola drained her drink. "I'll guarantee it is."

"Then let's hear it," I said. "Get on to the love part."

Nola looked at me strangely then, as if I really did know what she was going to tell, and thought maybe I might tell it first myself. She raised her chin at me. "Harry came home one evening from work, right?" she said. "Just death as usual. Only he said to me, 'Nola, I've invited some friends over, sweetheart. Why don't you go out and get a flank steak at Albertson's.' I asked when were they coming? He said, in an hour. And I thought, An hour! Because he never brought people home. We went to bars, you know. We didn't entertain. But I said, 'All right. I'll go get a flank steak.' And I got in the car and went out and bought a flank steak. I thought Harry ought to have what he wants. If he wants to have friends and steak he ought to be able to. Men, before they die, will want strange things."

"That's a fact, too," Troy said seriously. "I was full dead all of four minutes when I hit. And I dreamed about nothing but lobster the whole time. And I'd never even seen a lobster, though I have now. Maybe that's what they serve in heaven." Troy grinned at both of us.

"Well, this wasn't heaven," Nola said and signaled for another drink. "So when I got back, there was Harry with three Crow Indians, in my house, sitting in the living room drinking mai tais. A man and two women. His *friends*, he said. From the mill. He wanted to have his friends over, he said. And Harry was raised a strict Mormon. Not that it matters."

"I guess he had a change of heart," I said.

"That'll happen, too," Troy said gravely. "LDS's aren't like they used to be. They used to be bad, but that's all changed. Though I guess coloreds still can't get inside the temple all the way."

"These three were inside my house, though. I'll just say that. And I'm not prejudiced about it. Leopards with spots, leopards without. All the same to me. But I was nice. I went right in the kitchen and put the flank steak in the oven, put some potatoes in water, got out some frozen peas. And went back in to have a drink. And we sat around and talked for half an hour. Talked about the mill. Talked about Marlon Brando. The man and one of the women were married. He worked with Harry. And the other woman was her sister, Winona. There's a town in Mississippi with the same name. I looked it up. So after a while—all nice and friends—I went in to peel my potatoes. And this other woman, Bernie, came in with me to help, I guess. And I was standing there cooking over a little range, and this Bernie said to me, 'I don't know how you do it, Nola.' 'Do what, Bernie?' I said. 'Let Harry go with my sister like he does and you stay so happy about it. I couldn't ever stand that with Claude.' And I just turned around and looked at her. *Winona is what?* I thought. That name seemed so unusual for an Indian. And I just started yelling it. 'Winona, Winona,' at the top of my lungs right at the stove. I just went crazy a minute, I guess. Screaming, holding a potato in my hand, hot. The man came running into the kitchen. Claude Smart Enemy. Claude was awfully nice. He kept me from harming myself. But when I started yelling, Harry, I guess, figured everything was all up. And he and his Winona woman went right out the door. And he didn't get even to the car when his heart went. He had a myocardial infarction right out on the sidewalk at this Winona's feet. I guess he thought everything was going to be just great. We'd all have dinner together. And I'd never know what was what. Except he didn't count on Bernie saying something."

"Maybe he was trying to make you appreciate him more," I said. "Maybe he didn't like being expendable and was sending you a message."

Nola looked at me seriously again. "I thought of that," she said. "I thought about that more than once. But that would've been hurtful. And Harry Lyons wasn't a man to hurt you. He was more of a sneak. I just think he wanted us all to be friends."

"That makes sense." Troy nodded and looked at me.

"What happened to Winona," I asked.

"What happened to Winona?" Nola took a drink and gave me a hard look. "Winona moved herself to Spokane. What happened to me is a better question."

"Why? You're here with us," Troy said enthusiastically. "You're doing great. Les and me ought to do as well as you're doing. Les is out of work. And I'm out of luck. You're doing the best of the three of us, I'd say."

"I wouldn't," Nola said frankly, then turned and stared down at the men playing pool.

"What'd he leave you?" I said. "Harry."

"Two thousand," Nola said coldly.

"That's a small amount," I said.

"And it's a sad love story, too," Troy said, shaking his head. "You loved him and it ended rotten. That's like Shakespeare."

"I loved him enough," Nola said.

"How about sports. Do you like sports?" Troy said.

Nola looked at Troy oddly then. In his chair Troy doesn't look exactly like a whole man, and sometimes simple things he'll say will seem surprising. And what he'd said then surprised Nola. I've gotten used to it, myself, after all these years.

"Did you want to try skiing?" Nola said and glanced at me.

"Fishing," Troy said, up on his elbows again. "Let's all of us go fishing. Put an end to old gloomy." Troy seemed like he wanted to pound the table. And I wondered when was the last time he had slept with a woman. Fifteen years ago, maybe. And now that was all over for him. But he was excited just to be here and get to talk to Nola Foster, and I wasn't going to be in his way. "No one'll be there now," he said. "We'll catch a fish and cheer ourselves up. Ask Les. He caught a fish."

I had been going mornings in those days, when the *Today* show got over. Just to kill an hour. The river runs through the middle of town, and I could walk over in five minutes and fish downstream below the motels that are there, and could look up at the blue and white mountains up the Bitterroot, toward my mother's house, and sometimes see the geese coming back up their flyway. It was a strange winter. January was like a spring day, and the Chinook blew down over us a warm wind from the eastern slopes. Some days were cool or cold, but many days were warm, and the only ice you'd see was in the lows where the sun didn't reach. You could walk right out to the river and make a long cast to where the fish were deep down in the cold pools. And you could even think things might turn out better.

Nola turned and looked at me. The thought of fishing was seeming like a joke to her, I know. Though maybe she didn't have money for a meal and thought we might buy her one. Or maybe she'd never even been fishing. Or maybe she knew that she was on her way to the bottom, where everything is the same, and here was this something different being offered, and it was worth a try.

"Did you catch a big fish, Les," she asked.

"Yes," I said.

"See?" Troy said. "Am I a liar? Or am I not?"

"You might be." Nola looked at me oddly then, but I thought sweetly, too. "What kind of fish was it?"

"A brown trout. Caught deep, on a hare's ear," I said.

"I don't know what that is," Nola said and smiled. I could see that she wasn't minding any of this because her face was flushed, and she looked pretty.

"Which," I asked. "A brown trout? Or a hare's ear?"

"That's it," she said.

"A hare's ear is a kind of fly," I said.

"I see," Nola said.

"Let's get out of the bar for once," Troy said loudly, running his chair backwards and forwards. "We'll go fish, then we'll have chicken-in-the-ruff. Troy's paying."

"What'll I lose?" Nola said and shook her head. She looked at both of us, smiling as though she could think of something that might be lost.

"You got it all to win," Troy said. "Let's go."

"Whatever," Nola said. "Sure."

And we went out of the Top Hat, with Nola pushing Troy in his chair and me coming on behind.

On Front Street the evening was as warm as May, though the sun had gone behind the peaks already, and it was nearly dark. The sky was deep blue in the east behind the Sapphires, where the darkness was, but salmon pink above the sun. And we were in the middle of it. Half-drunk, trying to be imaginative in how we killed our time.

Troy's Checker was parked in front, and Troy rolled over to it and spun around.

"Let me show you this great trick," he said and grinned. "Get in and drive, Les. Stay there, sweetheart, and watch me."

Nola had kept her drink in her hand, and she stood by the door of the Top Hat. Troy lifted himself off his chair onto the concrete. I got in beside Troy's bars and his raised seat, and started the cab with my left hand.

"Ready," Troy shouted. "Ease forward. Ease up."

And I eased the car up.

"Oh my God," I heard Nola say and saw her put her palm to her forehead and look away.

"*Yaah. Ya-hah*," Troy yelled.

"Your poor foot," Nola said.

"It doesn't hurt me," Troy yelled. "It's just like a pressure." I couldn't see him from where I was.

"Now I know I've seen it all," Nola said. She was smiling.

"Back up, Les. Just ease it back again," Troy called out.

"Don't do it again," Nola said.

"One time's enough, Troy," I said. No one else was in the street. I thought how odd it would be for anyone to see that, without knowing something in advance. A man running over another man's foot for fun. Just drunks, you'd think, and be right.

"Sure. Okay," Troy said. I still couldn't see him. But I put the cab back in park and waited. "Help me, sweetheart, now," I heard Troy say to Nola. "It's easy getting down, but old Troy can't get up again by himself. You have to help him."

And Nola looked at me in the cab, the glass still in her hand. It was a peculiar look she gave me, a look that seemed to ask something of me, but I did not know what it was and couldn't answer. And then she put her glass on the pavement and went to put Troy back in his chair.

When we got to the river it was as good as dark, and the river was only a big space you could hear, with the south-of-town lights up behind it and the three bridges and Champion's Paper downstream a mile. And it was cold with the sun gone, and I thought there would be fog in before morning.

Troy had insisted on driving with us in the back, as if we'd hired a cab to take us fishing. On the way down he sang a smoke jumper's song, and Nola sat close to me and let her leg be beside mine. And by the time we stopped by the river, below the Lion's Head motel, I had kissed her twice, and knew all that I could do.

"I think I'll go fishing," Troy said from his little raised-up seat in front. "I'm going night fishing. And I'm going to get my own chair out and my rod and all I need. I'll have a time."

"How do you ever change a tire?" Nola said. She was not moving. It was just a question she had. People say all kinds of things to cripples.

Troy whipped around suddenly, though, and looked back at us where we sat on the cab seat. I had put my arm around Nola, and we sat there looking at his big head and big shoulders, below which there was only half a body any good to anyone. "Trust Mr. Wheels," Troy said. "Mr. Wheels can do anything a whole man can." And he smiled at us a crazy man's smile.

"I think I'll just stay in the car," Nola said. "I'll wait for chicken-in-the-ruff. That'll be my fishing."

"It's too cold for ladies now anyway," Troy said gruffly. "Only men. Only men in wheelchairs is the new rule."

I got out of the cab with Troy then and set up his chair and put him in it. I got his fishing gear out of the trunk and strung it up. Troy was not a man to fish flies, and I put a silver dace on his spin line and told him to hurl it far out and let it flow for a time into the deep current and then to work it, and work it all the way in. I said he would catch a fish with that strategy in five minutes, or ten.

"Les," Troy said to me in the cold dark behind the cab.

"What?" I said.

"Do you ever just think of just doing a criminal thing sometime? Just do something terrible. Change everything."

"Yes," I said. "I think about that."

Troy had his fishing rod across his chair now, and he was gripping it and looking down the sandy bank toward the dark and sparkling water.

"Why don't you do it?" he said.

"I don't know what I'd choose to do," I said.

"Mayhem," Troy said. "Commit mayhem."

"And go to Deer Lodge forever," I said. "Or maybe they'd hang me and let me dangle. That would be worse than this."

"Okay, that's right," Troy said, still staring. "But *I* should do it, shouldn't I? I should do the worst thing there is."

"No, you shouldn't," I said.

And then he laughed. "Hah. Right. Never do that," he said. And he wheeled himself down toward the river into the darkness, laughing all the way.

In the cold cab, after that, I held Nola Foster for a long time. Just held her with my arms around her, breathing and waiting. From the back window I could see the Lion's Head motel, see the restaurant there that faces the river and that is lighted with candles, and where people were eating. I could see the WELCOME out front, though not who was welcomed. I could see cars on the bridge going home for the night. And it made me think of Harley Reeves in my father's little house on the Bitterroot. I thought about him in bed with my mother. Warm. I thought about the faded old tattoo on Harley's shoulder. VICTORY, that said. And I could not connect it easily with what I knew about Harley Reeves, though I thought possibly that he had won a victory of kinds over me just by being where he was.

171

"A man who isn't trusted is the worst thing," Nola Foster said. "You know that, don't you?" I suppose her mind was wandering. She was cold, I could tell by the way she held me. Troy was gone out in the dark now. We were alone, and her skirt had come up a good ways.

"Yes, that's bad," I said, though I couldn't think at that moment of what trust could mean to me. It was not an issue in my life, and I hoped it never would be. "You're right," I said to make her happy.

"What was your name again?"

"Les," I said. "Lester Snow. Call me Les."

"Les Snow," Nola said. "Do you like less snow?"

"Usually I do." And I put my hand then where I wanted it most.

"How old are you, Les?" she said.

"Thirty-seven."

"You're an old man."

"How old are you?" I said.

"It's my business, isn't it?"

"I guess it is," I said.

"I'll do this, you know," Nola said, "and not even care about it. Just do a thing. It means nothing more than how I feel at this time. You know? Do you know what I mean, Les?"

"I know it," I said.

"But *you* need to be trusted. Or you aren't anything. Do you know that too?"

We were close to each other. I couldn't see the lights of town or the motel or anything more. Nothing moved.

"I know that, I guess," I said. It was whiskey talking.

"Warm me up then, Les," Nola said. "Warm. Warm."

"You'll get warm," I said.

"I'll think about Florida."

"I'll make you warm," I said.

What I thought I heard at first was a train. So many things can sound like a train when you live near trains. This was a *woo* sound, you would say. Like a train. And I lay and listened for a long time, thinking about a train and its light shining through the darkness along the side of some mountain pass north of there and about something else I don't even remember now. And then Troy came around to my thinking, and I knew then that the *woo* sound had been him.

Nola Foster said, "It's Mr. Wheels. He's caught a fish, maybe. Or else drowned."

"Yes," I said. I sat up and looked out the window but could see nothing. It had become foggy in just that little time, and tomorrow, I thought, would be warm again, though it was cold now. Nola and I had not even taken off our clothes to do what we'd done.

"Let me see," I said.

I got out and walked into the fog to where I could only see fog and hear the river running. Troy had not made a *woo*-ing sound again, and I thought to myself, There is no trouble here. Nothing's wrong.

Though when I walked a ways up the sandy bank, I saw Troy's chair come visible in the fog. And he was not in it, and I couldn't see him. And my heart went then. I heard it go click in my chest. And I thought: This is the worst. What's happened here will be the worst. And I called out, "Troy. Where are you? Call out now."

And Troy called out, "Here I am, here."

I went for the sound, ahead of me, which was not out in the river but on the bank. And when I had gone farther, I saw him, out of his chair, of course, on his belly, holding on to his fishing rod with both hands, the line out into the river as though it meant to drag him to the water.

"Help me!" he yelled. "I've got a huge fish. Do something to help me."

"I will," I said. Though I didn't see what I could do. I would not dare to take the rod, and it would only have been a mistake to take the line. Never give a straight pull to the fish, is an old rule. So that my only choice was to grab Troy and hold him until the fish was either in or lost, just as if Troy was a part of a rod *I* was fishing with.

I squatted in the cold sand behind him, put my heels down and took up his legs, which felt like matchsticks, and began to hold him there away from the water.

But Troy suddenly twisted toward me. "Turn me loose, Les. Don't be here. Go out. It's snagged. You've got to go out."

"That's crazy," I said. "It's too deep there."

"It's not deep," Troy yelled. "I've got it in close now."

"You're crazy," I said.

"Oh, Christ, Les, go get it. I don't want to lose it."

I looked a moment at Troy's face then, in the dark. His glasses were gone off of him. His face was wet. And he had the look of a desperate man, a man who has nothing to hope for but, in some strange way, everything in the world to lose.

"Stupid. This is stupid," I said, because it seemed to me to be. But I got up, walked to the edge and stepped out into the cold water.

Then, it was at least a month before the runoff would begin in the mountains, and the water I stepped in was cold and painful as broken glass, though the wet parts of me numbed at once, and my feet felt like bricks bumping the bottom.

Troy had been wrong all the way about the depth. Because when I stepped out ten yards, keeping touch of his line with the back of my hand, I had already gone above my knees, and on the bottom I felt large rocks, and there was a loud rushing around me that suddenly made me afraid.

But when I had gone five more yards, and the water was on my thighs and hurting, I hit the snag Troy's fish was hooked to, and I realized then I had no way at all to hold a fish or catch it with my numbed hands. And that all I could really hope for was to break the snag and let the fish slip down into the current and hope Troy could bring it in, or that I could go back and beach it.

"Can you see it, Les?" Troy yelled out of the dark. "Goddamn it."

"It isn't easy," I said, and I had to hold the snag then to keep my balance. My legs were numb. And I thought: This might be the time and the place I die. What an odd place it is. And what an odd reason for it to happen.

"Hurry up," Troy yelled.

And I wanted to hurry. Except when I ran the line as far as where the snag was, I felt something there that was not a fish and not the snag but something else entirely, some thing I thought I recognized, though I am not sure why. A man, I thought. This is a man.

Though when I reached farther into the snag branches and woods scruff, deeper into the water, what I felt was an animal. With my fingers I touched its hard rib-side, its legs, its short slick coat. I felt to its neck and head and touched its nose and teeth, and it was a deer, though not a big deer, not even a yearling. And I knew when I found where Troy's dace had gone up in the neck flesh, that he had hooked a deer already snagged here, and that he had pulled himself out of his chair trying to work it free.

"What is it? I know it's a big *Brown*. Don't tell me, Les, don't even tell me."

"I've got it," I said. "I'll bring it in."

"Sure, hell yes," Troy said out of the fog.

It was not so hard to work the deer off the snag brush and float it up free. Though once I did, it was dangerous to get turned in the current on numb legs, and hard to keep from going down, and I had to hold on to the deer to keep balance enough to heave myself into the slower water. And as I did that, I thought: In the Clark Fork many people drown doing less dangerous things than I am doing.

"Throw it way far up," Troy shouted when he could see me. He had righted himself on the sand and was sitting up like a little doll. "Get it way up safe."

"It's safe," I said. I had the deer beside me, floating, but I knew Troy couldn't see it.

"What did I catch?" Troy yelled.

"Something unusual," I said, and with effort I hauled the little deer a foot up onto the sand, dropped it, and put my cold hands under my arms. I heard a car door close back where I had come from, up the riverbank.

"What *is* that?" Troy said and put his hand out to touch the deer's side. He looked up at me. "I can't see without my glasses."

"It's a deer," I said.

Troy moved his hand around on the deer, then looked at me again in a painful way.

"What is it?" he said.

"A deer," I said. "You caught a dead deer."

Troy looked back at the little deer for a moment, and stared as if he did not know what to say about it. And sitting on the wet sand, in the foggy night, he all at once looked scary to me, as though it was him who had washed up there and was finished. "I don't see it," he said and sat there.

"It's what you caught," I said. "I thought you'd want to see it."

"It's crazy, Les," he said. "Isn't it?" And he smiled at me in a wild, blind-eyed way.

"It's unusual," I said.

"I never shot a deer before."

"I don't believe you shot this one," I said.

He smiled at me again, but then suddenly he gasped back a sob, something I had never seen before. "Goddamn it," he said. "Just goddamn it."

"It's an odd thing to catch," I said, standing above him in the grimy fog.

"I can't change a fucking tire," he said and sobbed. "But I'll catch a fucking deer with my fucking fishing rod."

"Not everyone can say that," I said.

"Why would they want to?" He looked up at me crazy again, and broke his spinning rod into two pieces with only his hands. And I knew he must've been drunk still, because I was still drunk a little, and that by itself made me want to cry. And we were there for a time just silent.

"Who killed a deer?" Nola said. She had come behind me in the cold and was looking. I had not known, when I heard the car door, if she wasn't starting back up to town. But it was too cold for that, and I put my arm around her because she was shivering. "Did Mr. Wheels kill it?"

"It drowned," Troy said.

"And why is that?" Nola said and pushed closer to me to be warm, though that was all.

"They get weak and they fall over," I said. "It happens in the mountains. This one fell in the water and couldn't get up."

"So a gimp man can catch it on a fishing rod in a shitty town," Troy said and gasped with bitterness. Real bitterness. The worst I have ever heard from any man, and I have heard bitterness voiced, though it was a union matter then.

"Maybe it isn't so bad," Nola said.

"Hah!" Troy said from the wet ground. "Hah, hah, hah." And I wished that I had never shown him the deer, wished I had spared him that, though the river's rushing came up then and snuffed his sound right out of hearing, and drew it away from us into the foggy night beyond all accounting.

Nola and I pushed the deer back into the river while Troy watched, and then we all three drove up into town and ate chicken-in-the-ruff at the Two Fronts, where the lights were bright and they cooked the chicken fresh for you. I bought a jug of wine and we drank that while we ate, though no one talked. Each of us had done something that night. Something different. That was plain enough. And there was nothing more to talk about.

When we were finished we walked outside, and I asked Nola where she'd like to go. It was only eight o'clock, and there was no place to go but to my little room. She said she wanted to go back to the Top Hat, that she had someone to meet there later, and there was something about the band that night that she liked. She said she wanted to dance.

I told her I was not much for dancing, and she said fine. And when Troy came out from paying, we said good-bye, and she shook my hand and said that she would see me again. Then she and Troy got in the Checker and drove away together down the foggy street, leaving me alone, where I didn't mind being at all.

For a long time I just walked then. My clothes were wet, but it wasn't so cold if you kept moving, though it stayed foggy. I walked to the river again and across on the bridge and a long way down into the south part of town on a wide avenue where there were houses with little porches and little yards, all the way, until it became commercial, and bright lights lit the drive-ins and car lots. I could've walked then, I thought, clear to my mother's house twenty miles away. But I turned back, and walked the same way, only on the other side of the street. Though when I got near the bridge, I came past the Senior Citizen Recreation, where there were soft lights on inside a big room, and I could see through a window in the pinkish glow, old people dancing across the floor to a record player that played in the corner. It was a rumba or something like a rumba that was being played, and the old people were dancing the box step, smooth and graceful and courteous, moving across the linoleum like real dancers, their arms on each other's shoulders like husbands and wives. And it pleased me to see that. And I thought that it was too bad my mother and father could not be here now, too bad they couldn't come up and dance and go home happy, and have me to watch them. Or even for my mother and Harley Reeves to do that. It didn't seem like too much to wish for. Just a normal life other people had.

I stood and watched them a while, then I walked back home across the river. Though for some reason I could not sleep that night, and simply lay in bed with the radio turned on to Denver, and smoked cigarettes until it was light. Of course I thought about Nola Foster, that I didn't know where she lived, though for some reason I thought she might live in Frenchtown, near the pulp plant. Not far. Never-never land, they called that. And I thought about my father, who had once gone to Deer Lodge prison for stealing hay from a friend, and had never recovered from it, though that meant little to me now.

And I thought about the matter of trust. That I would always lie if it would save someone an unhappiness. That was easy. And that I would rather a person mistrust me than dislike me. Though I thought you could always trust me to act a certain way, to be a place, or to say a thing if it ever were to matter. You could predict within human reason what I'd do— that I would not, for example, commit a vicious crime—trust that I would risk my own life for you if I knew it meant enough. And as I lay in the gray light, smoking, while the refrigerator clicked and the switcher in the Burlington Northern yard shunted cars and made their couplings, I thought that though my life at that moment seemed to have taken a bad turn and paused, it still meant something to me as a life, and that before long it would start again in some promising way.

I know I must've dozed a little, because I woke suddenly and there was the light. Earl Nightingale was on the radio, and I heard a door close. It was that that woke me.

I knew it would be Troy, and I thought I would step out and meet him, fix coffee for us before he went to bed and slept all day, the way he always did. But when I stood up I heard Nola Foster's voice. I could not mistake that. She was drunk, and laughing about something. "Mr. Wheels," she said. Mr. Wheels this, Mr. Wheels that. Troy was laughing. And I heard them come in the little entry, heard Troy's chair bump the sill. And I waited to see if they would knock on my door. And when they didn't, and I heard Troy's door shut and the chain go up, I thought that we had all had a good night finally. Nothing had happened that hadn't turned out all right. None of us had been harmed. And I put on my pants, then my shirt and shoes, turned off my radio, went into the kitchen where I kept my fishing rod, and with it went out into the warm, foggy morning, using just this once the back door, the quiet way, so as not to see or be seen by anyone.

OPTIMISTS

All of this that I am about to tell happened when I was only fifteen years old, in 1959, the year my parents were divorced, the year when my father killed a man and went to prison for it, the year I left home and school, told a lie about my age to fool the Army, and then did not come back. The year, in other words, when life changed for all of us and forever—ended, really, in a way none of us could ever have imagined in our most brilliant dreams of life.

My father was named Roy Brinson, and he worked on the Great Northern Railway, in Great Falls, Montana. He was a switch-engine fireman, and when he could not hold that job on the seniority list, he worked the extra-board as a hostler, or as a hostler's helper, shunting engines through the yard, onto and off the freight trains that went south and east. He was thirty-seven or thirty-eight years old in 1959, a small, young-appearing man, with dark blue eyes. The railroad was a job he liked, because it paid high wages and the work was not hard, and because you could take off days when you wanted to, or even months, and have no one to ask you questions. It was a union shop, and there were people who looked out for you when your back was turned. "It's a workingman's paradise," my father would say, and then laugh.

My mother did not work then, though she *had* worked—at waitressing and in the bars in town—and she had liked working. My father thought, though, that Great Falls was coming to be a rougher town than it had been when he grew up there, a town going downhill, like its name, and that my mother should be at home more, because I was at an age when trouble came easily. We lived in a rented two-story house on Edith Street, close to the freight yards and the Missouri River, a house where from my window at night I could hear the engines as they sat throbbing, could see their lights move along the dark rails. My mother was at home most of her time, reading or watching television or cooking meals, though sometimes she would go out to movies in the afternoon, or would go to the YWCA and swim in the indoor pool. Where she was from—in Havre, Montana, much farther north—there was never such a thing as a pool indoors, and she thought that to swim in the winter, with snow on the ground and the wind howling, was the greatest luxury. And she would come home late in the afternoon, with her brown hair wet and her face flushed, and in high spirits, saying she felt freer.

The night that I want to tell about happened in November. It was not then a good time for railroads—not in Montana especially—and for firemen not at all, anywhere. It was the featherbed time, and everyone knew, including my father, that they would—all of them—eventually lose their jobs, though no one knew exactly when, or who would go first, or, clearly, what the future would be. My father had been hired out ten years, and had worked on coal-burners and oil-burners out of Forsythe, Montana, on the Sheridan spur. But he was still young in the job and low on the list, and he felt that when the cut came young heads would go first. "They'll do something for us, but it might not be enough," he said, and I had heard him say that other times—in the kitchen, with my mother, or out in front, working on his motorcycle, or with me, fishing the whitefish flats up the Missouri. But I do not know if he truly thought that or in fact had any reason to think it. He was an optimist. Both of them were optimists, I think.

I know that by the end of summer in that year he had stopped taking days off to fish, had stopped going out along the coulee rims to spot deer. He worked more then and was gone more, and he talked more about work when he was home: about what the union said on this subject and that, about court cases in Washington, D.C., a place I knew nothing of, and about injuries and illnesses to men he knew, that threatened their livelihoods, and by association with them, threatened his own—threatened, he must've felt, our whole life.

Because my mother swam at the YWCA she had met people there and made friends. One was a large woman named Esther, who came home with her once and drank coffee in the kitchen and talked about her boyfriend and laughed out loud for a long time, but who I never saw again. And another was a woman named Penny Mitchell whose husband, Boyd, worked for the Red Cross in Great Falls and had an office upstairs in the building with the YWCA, and who my mother would sometime play canasta with on the nights my father worked late. They would set up a card table in the living room, the three of them, and drink and eat sandwiches until midnight. And I would lie in bed with my radio tuned low to the Calgary station, listening to a hockey match beamed out over the great empty prairie, and could hear the cards snap and laughter downstairs, and later I would hear footsteps leaving, hear the door shut, the dishes rattle in the sink, cabinets close. And in a while the door to my room would open and the light would fall inside, and my mother would set a chair back in. I could see her silhouette. She would always say, "Go back to sleep, Frank." And then the door would shut again, and I would almost always go to sleep in a minute.

It was on a night that Penny and Boyd Mitchell were in our house that trouble came about. My father had been working his regular bid-in job on the switch engine, plus a helper's job off the extra-board—a practice that was illegal by the railroad's rules, but ignored by the union, who could see bad times coming and knew there would be nothing to help it when they came, and so would let men work if they wanted to. I was in the kitchen, eating a sandwich alone at the table, and my mother was in the living room playing cards with Penny and Boyd Mitchell. They were drinking vodka and eating the other sandwiches my mother had made, when I heard my father's motorcycle outside in the dark. It was eight o'clock at night, and I knew he was not expected home until midnight.

"Roy's home," I heard my mother say. "I hear Roy. That's wonderful." I heard chairs scrape and glasses tap.

"Maybe he'll want to play," Penny Mitchell said. "We can play four-hands."

I went to the kitchen door and stood looking through the dining room at the front. I don't think I knew something was wrong, but I think I knew something was unusual, something I would want to know about firsthand.

My mother was standing beside the card table when my father came inside. She was smiling. But I have never seen a look on a man's face that was like the look on my father's face at that moment. He looked wild. His eyes were wild. His whole face was. It was cold outside, and the wind was coming up, and he had ridden home from the train yard in only his flannel shirt. His face was red, and his hair was strewn around his bare head, and I remember his fists were clenched white, as if there was no blood in them at all.

"My God," my mother said. "What is it, Roy? You look crazy." She turned and looked for me, and I knew she was thinking that this was something I might not need to see. But she didn't say anything. She just looked back at my father, stepped toward him and touched his hand, where he must've been coldest. Penny and Boyd Mitchell sat at the card table, looking up. Boyd Mitchell was smiling for some reason.

"Something awful happened," my father said. He reached and took a corduroy jacket off the coat nail and put it on, right in the living room, then sat down on the couch and hugged his arms. His face seemed to get redder then. He was wearing black steel-toe boots, the boots he wore every day, and I stared at them and felt how cold he must be, even in his own house. I did not come any closer.

"Roy, what is it?" my mother said, and she sat down beside him on the couch and held his hand in both of hers.

My father looked at Boyd Mitchell and at his wife, as if he hadn't known they were in the room until then. He did not know them very well, and I thought he might tell them to get out, but he didn't.

"I saw a man be killed tonight," he said to my mother, then shook his head and looked down. He said, "We were pushing into that old hump yard on Ninth Avenue. A cut of coal cars. It wasn't even an hour ago. I was looking out my side, the way you do when you push out a curve. And I could see this one open boxcar in the cut, which isn't unusual. Only this guy was in it and was trying to get off, sitting in the door, scooting. I guess he was a hobo. Those cars had come in from Glasgow tonight. And just the second he started to go off, the whole cut buckled up. It's a thing that'll happen. But he lost his balance just when he hit the gravel, and he fell backwards underneath. I looked right at him. And one set of trucks rolled right over his foot." My father looked at my mother then. "It hit his foot," he said.

"My God," my mother said and looked down at her lap.

My father squinted. "But then he moved, he sort of bucked himself like he was trying to get away. He didn't yell, and I could see his face. I'll never forget that. He didn't look scared, he just looked like a man doing something that was hard for him to do. He looked like he was concentrating on something. But when he bucked he pushed back, and the other trucks caught his hand." My father looked at his own hands then, and made fists out of them and squeezed them.

"What did you do?" my mother said. She looked terrified.

"I yelled out. And Sherman stopped pushing. But it wasn't that fast."

"Did you do anything then," Boyd Mitchell said.

"I got down," my father said, "and I went up there. But here's a man cut in three pieces in front of me. What can you do? You can't do very much. I squatted down and touched his good hand. And it was like ice. His eyes were open and roaming all up in the sky."

"Did he say anything?" my mother said.

"He said, 'Where am I today?' And I said to him, 'It's all right, bud, you're in Montana. You'll be all right.' Though, my God, he wasn't. I took my jacket off and put it over him. I didn't want him to see what had happened."

"You should've put tourniquets on," Boyd Mitchell said gruffly. "That could've helped. That could've saved his life."

My father looked at Boyd Mitchell then as if he had forgotten he was there and was surprised that he spoke. "I don't know about that," my father said. "I don't know anything about those things. He was already dead. A boxcar had run over him. He was breathing, but he was already dead to me."

"That's only for a licensed doctor to decide," Boyd Mitchell said. "You're morally obligated to do all you can." And I could tell from his tone of voice that he did not like my father. He hardly knew him, but he did not like him. I had no idea why. Boyd Mitchell was a big, husky, red-faced man with curly hair—handsome in a way, but with a big belly—and I knew only that he worked for the Red Cross, and that my mother was a friend of his wife's, and maybe of his, and that they played cards when my father was gone.

My father looked at my mother in a way I knew was angry. "Why have you got these people over here now, Dorothy? They don't have any business here."

"Maybe that's right," Penny Mitchell said, and she put down her hand of cards and stood up at the table. My mother looked around the room as though an odd noise had occurred inside of it and she couldn't find the source.

"Somebody definitely should've done something," Boyd Mitchell said, and he leaned forward on the table toward my father. "That's all there is to say." He was shaking his head *no*. "That man didn't have to die." Boyd Mitchell clasped his big hands on top of his playing cards and stared at my father. "The unions'll cover this up, too, I guess, won't they? That's what happens in these things."

My father stood up then, and his face looked wide, though it looked young, still. He looked like a young man who had been scolded and wasn't sure how he should act. "You get out of here," he said in a loud voice. "My God. What a thing to say. I don't even know you."

"I know you, though," Boyd Mitchell said angrily. "You're another featherbedder. You aren't good to do anything. You can't even help a dying man. You're bad for this country, and you won't last."

"Boyd, my goodness," Penny Mitchell said. "Don't say that. Don't say that to him."

Boyd Mitchell glared up at his wife. "I'll say anything I want to," he said. "And he'll listen, because he's helpless. He can't do anything."

"Stand up," my father said. "Just stand up on your feet." His fists were clenched again.

"All right, I will," Boyd Mitchell said. He glanced up at his wife. And I realized that Boyd Mitchell was drunk, and it was possible that he did not even know what he was saying, or what had happened, and that words just got loose from him this way, and anybody who knew him knew it. Only my father didn't. He only knew what had been said.

Boyd Mitchell stood up and put his hands in his pockets. He was much taller than my father. He had on a white Western shirt and whipcords and cowboy boots and was wearing a big silver wristwatch. "All right," he said. "Now I'm standing up. What's supposed to happen?" He weaved a little. I saw that.

And my father hit Boyd Mitchell then, hit him from across the card table—hit him with his right hand, square into the chest, not a lunging blow, just a hard, hitting blow that threw my father off balance and made him make a *chuffing* sound with his mouth. Boyd Mitchell groaned, "Oh," and fell down immediately, his big, thick, heavy body hitting the floor already doubled over. And the sound of him hitting the floor in our house was like no sound I had ever heard before.

It was the sound of a man's body hitting a floor, and it was only that. In my life I have heard it other places, in hotel rooms and in bars, and it is one you do not want to hear.

You can hit a man in a lot of ways, I know that, and I knew that then, because my father had told me. You can hit a man to insult him, or you can hit a man to bloody him, or to knock him down, or lay him out. Or you can hit a man to kill him. Hit him that hard. And that is how my father hit Boyd Mitchell—as hard as he could, in the chest and not in the face, the way someone might think who didn't know about it.

"Oh my God," Penny Mitchell said. Boyd Mitchell was lying on his side in front of the TV, and she had gotten down on her knees beside him. "Boyd," she said. "Are you hurt? Oh, look at this. Stay where you are, Boyd. Stay on the floor."

"Now then. All right," my father said. "Now. All right." He was standing against the wall, over to the side of where he had been when he hit Boyd Mitchell from across the card table. Light was bright in the room, and my father's eyes were wide and touring around. He seemed out of breath and both his fists were clenched, and I could feel his heart beating in my own chest. "All right, now, you son of a bitch," my father said, and loudly. I don't think he was even talking to Boyd Mitchell. He was just saying words that came out of him.

"Roy," my mother said calmly. "Boyd's hurt now. He's hurt." She was just looking down at Boyd Mitchell. I don't think she knew what to do.

"Oh, no," Penny Mitchell said in an excited voice. "Look up, Boyd. Look up at Penny. You've been hurt." She had her hands flat on Boyd Mitchell's chest, and her skinny shoulders close to him. She wasn't crying, but I think she was hysterical and couldn't cry.

All this had taken only five minutes, maybe even less time. I had never even left the kitchen door. And for that reason I walked out into the room where my father and mother were, and where Boyd and Penny Mitchell were both of them on the floor. I looked down at Boyd Mitchell, at his face. I wanted to see what had happened to him. His eyes had cast back up into their sockets. His mouth was open, and I could see his big pink tongue inside. He was breathing heavy breaths, and his fingers—the fingers on both his hands—were moving, moving in the way a man would move them if he was nervous or anxious about something. I think he was dead then, and I think even Penny Mitchell knew he was dead, because she was saying, "Oh please, please, please, Boyd."

That is when my mother called the police, and I think it is when my father opened the front door and stepped out into the night.

All that happened next is what you would expect to happen. Boyd Mitchell's chest quit breathing in a minute, and he turned pale and cold and began to look dead right on our living-room floor. He made a noise in his throat once, and Penny Mitchell cried out, and my mother got down on her knees and held Penny's shoulders while she cried. Then my mother made Penny get up and go into the bedroom—hers and my father's—and lie on the bed. Then she and I sat in the brightly lit living room, with Boyd Mitchell dead on the floor, and simply looked at each other— maybe for ten minutes, maybe for twenty. I don't know what my mother could've been thinking during that time, because she did not say. She did not ask about my father. She did not tell me to leave the room. Maybe she thought about the rest of her life then and what that might be like after tonight. Or maybe she thought this: that people can do the worst things they are capable of doing and in the end the world comes back to normal. Possibly, she was just waiting for something normal to begin to happen again. That would make sense, given her particular character.

Though what I thought myself, sitting in that room with Boyd Mitchell dead, I remember very well, because I have thought it other times, and to a degree I began to date my real life from that moment and that thought. It is this: that situations have possibilities in them, and we have only to be present to be involved. Tonight was a very bad one. But how were we to know it would turn out this way until it was too late and we had all been changed forever? I realized though, that trouble, real trouble, was something to be avoided, inasmuch as once it has passed by, you have only yourself to answer to, even if, as I was, you are the cause of nothing.

In a little while the police arrived to our house. First one and then two more cars with their red lights turning in the street. Lights were on in the neighbors' houses—people came out and stood in the cold in their front yards watching, people I didn't know and who didn't know us. "It's a circus now," my mother said to me when we looked through the window. "We'll have to move somewhere else. They won't let us alone."

An ambulance came, and Boyd Mitchell was taken away on a stretcher, under a sheet. Penny Mitchell came out of the bedroom and went with them, though she did not say anything to my mother, or to anybody, just got in a police car and left into the dark.

Two policemen came inside, and one asked my mother some questions in the living room, while the other one asked me questions in the kitchen. He wanted to know what I had seen, and I told him. I said Boyd Mitchell had cursed at my father for some reason I didn't know, then had stood up and tried to hit him, and that my father had pushed Boyd, and that was all. He asked me if my father was a violent man, and I said no. He asked if my father had a girlfriend, and I said no. He asked if my mother and father had ever fought, and I said no.

He asked me if I loved my mother and father, and I said I did. And then that was all.

I went out into the living room then, and my mother was there, and when the police left we stood at the front door, and there was my father outside, standing by the open door of a police car. He had on handcuffs. And for some reason he wasn't wearing a shirt or his corduroy jacket but was bare-chested in the cold night, holding his shirt behind him. His hair looked wet to me. I heard a policeman say, "Roy, you're going to catch cold," and then my father say, "I wish I was a long way from here right now. China maybe." He smiled at the policeman. I don't think he ever saw us watching, or if he did he didn't want to admit it. And neither of us did anything, because the police had him, and when that is the case, there is nothing you can do to help.

All this happened by ten o'clock. At midnight my mother and I drove down to the city jail and got my father out. I stayed in the car while my mother went in—sat and watched the high windows of the jail, which were behind wire mesh and bars. Yellow lights were on there, and I could hear voices and see figures move past the lights, and twice someone called out, "Hello, hello. Marie, are you with me?" And then it was quiet, except for the cars that drove slowly past ours.

On the ride home, my mother drove and my father sat and stared out at the big electrical stacks by the river, and the lights of houses on the other side, in Black Eagle. He had on a checked shirt someone inside had given him, and his hair was neatly combed. No one said anything, but I did not understand why the police would put anyone in jail because he had killed a man and in two hours let him out again. It was a mystery to me, even though I wanted him to be out and for our life to resume, and even though I did not see any way it could and, in fact, knew it never would.

Inside our house, all the lights were burning when we got back. It was one o'clock and there were still lights in some neighbors' houses. I could see a man at the window across the street, both his hands to the glass, watching out, watching us.

My mother went into the kitchen, and I could hear her running water for coffee and taking down cups. My father stood in the middle of the living room and looked around, looking at the chairs, at the card table with cards still on it, at the open doorways to the other rooms. It was as if he had forgotten his own house and now saw it again and didn't like it.

"I don't feel I know what he had against me," my father said. He said this to me, but he said it to anyone, too. "You'd think you'd know what a man had against you, wouldn't you, Frank?"

"Yes," I said. "I would." We were both just standing together, my father and I, in the lighted room there. We were not about to do anything.

"I want us to be happy here now," my father said. "I want us to enjoy life. I don't hold anything against anybody. Do you believe that?"

"I believe that," I said. My father looked at me with his dark blue eyes and frowned. And for the first time I wished my father had not done what he did but had gone about things differently. I saw him as a man who made mistakes, as a man who could hurt people, ruin lives, risk their happiness. A man who did not understand enough. He was like a gambler, though I did not even know what it meant to be a gambler then.

"It's such a quickly changing time now," my father said. My mother, who had come into the kitchen doorway, stood looking at us. She had on a flowered pink apron, and was standing where I had stood earlier that night. She was looking at my father and at me as if we were one person. "Don't you think it is, Dorothy?" he said. "All this turmoil. Everything just flying by. Look what's happened here."

My mother seemed very certain about things then, very precise. "You should've controlled yourself more," she said. "That's all."

"I know that," my father said. "I'm sorry. I lost control over my mind. I didn't expect to ruin things, but now I think I have. It was all wrong." My father picked up the vodka bottle, unscrewed the cap and took a big swallow, then put the bottle back down. He had seen two men killed tonight. Who could've blamed him?

"When I was in jail tonight," he said, staring at a picture on the wall, a picture by the door to the hallway. He was just talking again. "There was a man in the cell with me. And I've never been in jail before, not even when I was a kid. But this man said to me tonight, 'I can tell you've never been in jail before just by the way you stand up straight. Other people don't stand that way. They stoop. You don't belong in jail. You stand up too straight.'" My father looked back at the vodka bottle as if he wanted to drink more out of it, but he only looked at it. "Bad things happen," he said, and he let his open hands tap against his legs like clappers against a bell. "Maybe he was in love with you, Dorothy," he said. "Maybe that's what the trouble was."

And what I did then was stare at the picture on the wall, the picture my father had been staring at, a picture I had seen every day. Probably I had seen it a thousand times. It was two people with a baby on a beach. A man and a woman sitting in the sand with an ocean behind. They were smiling at the camera, wearing bathing suits. In all the times I had seen it I'd thought that it was a picture in which I was the baby, and the two people were my parents. But I realized as I stood there, that it was not me at all; it was my father who was the child in the picture, and the parents there were his parents—two people I'd never known, and who were dead—and the picture was so much older than I had thought it was. I wondered why I hadn't known that before, hadn't understood it for myself, hadn't always known it. Not even that it mattered. What mattered was, I felt, that my father had fallen down now, as much as the man he had watched fall beneath the train just hours before. And I was as helpless to do anything as he had been. I wanted to tell him that I loved him, but for some reason I did not.

Later in the night I lay in my bed with the radio playing, listening to news that was far away, in Calgary and in Saskatoon, and even farther, in Regina and Winnipeg—cold, dark cities I knew I would never see in my life. My window was raised above the sill, and for a long time I had sat and looked out, hearing my parents talk softly down below, hearing their footsteps, hearing my father's steel-toed boots strike the floor, and then their bedsprings squeeze and then be quiet. From out across the sliding river I could hear trucks—stock trucks and grain trucks heading toward Idaho, or down toward Helena, or into the train yards where my father hostled engines. The neighborhood houses were dark again. My father's motorcycle sat in the yard, and out in the night air I felt I could hear even the falls themselves, could hear every sound of them, sounds that found me and whirled and filled my room—could even feel them, cold and wintry, so that warmth seemed like a possibility I would never know again.

After a time my mother came in my room. The light fell on my bed, and she set a chair inside. I could see that she was looking at me. She closed the door, came and turned off my radio, then took her chair to the window, closed it, and sat so that I could see her face silhouetted against the streetlight. She lit a cigarette and did not look at me, still cold under the covers of my bed.

"How do you feel, Frank," she said, smoking her cigarette.

"I feel all right," I said.

"Do you think your house is a terrible house now?"

"No," I said.

"I hope not," my mother said. "Don't feel it is. Don't hold anything against anyone. Poor Boyd. He's gone."

"Why do you think that happened?" I said, though I didn't think she would answer, and wondered if I even wanted to know.

My mother blew smoke against the window glass, then sat and breathed. "He must've seen something in your father he just hated. I don't know what it was. Who knows? Maybe your father felt the same way." She shook her head and looked out into the streetlamp light. "I remember once," she said. "I was still in Havre, in the thirties. We were living in a motel my father part-owned out Highway Two, and my mother was around then, but wasn't having any of us. My father had this big woman named Judy Belknap as his girlfriend. She was an Assiniboin. Just some squaw. But we used to go on nature tours when he couldn't put up with me anymore. She'd take me. Way up above the Milk River. All this stuff she knew about animals and plants and ferns—she'd tell me all that. And once we were sitting watching some gadwall ducks on the ice where a creek had made a little turn-out. It was getting colder, just like now. And Judy just all at once stood up and clapped. Just clapped her hands. And all these ducks got up, all except for one that stayed on the ice, where its feet were frozen, I guess. It didn't even try to fly. It just sat. And Judy said to me, 'It's just a coincidence, Dottie. It's wildlife. Some always get left back.' And that seemed to leave her satisfied for some reason. We walked back to the car after that. So," my mother said. "Maybe that's what this is. Just a coincidence."

She raised the window again, dropped her cigarette out, blew the last smoke from her throat, and said, "Go to sleep, Frank. You'll be all right. We'll all survive this. Be an optimist."

When I was asleep that night, I dreamed. And what I dreamed was of a plane crashing, a bomber, dropping out of the frozen sky, bouncing as it hit the icy river, sliding and turning on the ice, its wings like knives, and coming into our house where we were sleeping, leveling everything. And when I sat up in bed I could hear a dog in the yard, its collar jingling, and I could hear my father crying, "Boo-hoo-hoo, boo-hoo-hoo,"—like that, quietly—though afterward I could never be sure if I had heard him crying in just that way, or if all of it was a dream, a dream I wished I had never had.

The most important things of your life can change so suddenly, so unrecoverably, that you can forget even the most important of them and their connections, you are so taken up by the chanciness of all that's happened and by all that could and will happen next. I now no longer remember the exact year of my father's birth, or how old he was when I last saw him, or even when that last time took place. When you're young, these things seem unforgettable and at the heart of everything. But they slide away and are gone when you are not so young.

My father went to Deer Lodge Prison and stayed five months for killing Boyd Mitchell by accident, for using too much force to hit him. In Montana you cannot simply kill a man in your living room and walk off free from it, and what I remember is that my father pleaded no contest, the same as guilty.

My mother and I lived in our house for the months he was gone. But when he came out and went back on the railroad as a switchman the two of them argued about things, about her wanting us to go someplace else to live—California or Seattle were mentioned. And then they separated, and she moved out. And after that I moved out by joining the Army and adding years to my age, which was sixteen.

I know about my father only that after a time he began to live a life he himself would never have believed. He fell off the railroad, divorced my mother, who would now and then resurface in his life. Drinking was involved in that, and gambling, embezzling money, even carrying a pistol, is what I heard. I was apart from all of it. And when you are the age I was then, and loose on the world and alone, you can get along better than at almost any other time, because it's a novelty, and you can act for what you want, and you can think that being alone will not last forever. All I know of my father, finally, is that he was once in Laramie, Wyoming, and not in good shape, and then he simply disappeared from view.

A month ago I saw my mother. I was buying groceries at a drive-in store by the interstate in Anaconda, Montana, not far from Deer Lodge itself, where my father had been. It had been fifteen years, I think, since I had seen her, though I am forty-three years old now, and possibly it was longer. But when I saw her I walked across the store to where she was and I said, "Hello, Dorothy. It's Frank."

She looked at me and smiled and said, "Oh, Frank. How are you? I haven't seen you in a long time. I'm glad to see you now, though." She was dressed in blue jeans and boots and a Western shirt, and she looked like a woman who could be sixty years old. Her hair was tied back and she looked pretty, though I think she had been drinking. It was ten o'clock in the morning.

There was a man standing near her, holding a basket of groceries, and she turned to him and said, "Dick, come here and meet my son, Frank. We haven't seen each other in a long time. This is Dick Spivey, Frank."

I shook hands with Dick Spivey, who was a man younger than my mother but older than me—a tall, thin-faced man with coarse blue-black hair—and who was wearing Western boots like hers. "Let me say a word to Frank, Dick," my mother said, and she put her hand on Dick's wrist and squeezed it and smiled at him. And he walked up toward the checkout to pay for his groceries.

"So. What are you doing now, Frank," my mother asked, and put her hand on my wrist the way she had on Dick Spivey's, but held it there. "These years," she said.

"I've been down in Rock Springs, on the coal boom," I said. "I'll probably go back down there."

"And I guess you're married, too."

"I was," I said. "But not right now."

"That's fine," she said. "You look fine." She smiled at me. "You'll never get anything fixed just right. That's your mother's word. Your father and I had a marriage made in Havre—that was our joke about us. We used to laugh about it. You didn't know that, of course. You were too young. A lot of it was just wrong."

"It's a long time ago," I said. "I don't know about that."

"I remember those times very well," my mother said. "They were happy enough times. I guess something *was* in the air, wasn't there? Your father was so jumpy. And Boyd got so mad, just all of a sudden. There was some hopelessness to it, I suppose. All that union business. We were the last to understand any of it, of course. We were trying to be decent people."

"That's right," I said. And I believed that was true of them.

"I still like to swim," my mother said. She ran her fingers back through her hair as if it were wet. She smiled at me again. "It still makes me feel freer."

"Good," I said. "I'm happy to hear that."

"Do you ever see your dad?"

"No," I said. "I never do."

"I don't either," my mother said. "You just reminded me of him." She looked at Dick Spivey, who was standing at the front window, holding a sack of groceries, looking out at the parking lot. It was March, and some small bits of snow were falling onto the cars in the lot. He didn't seem in any hurry. "Maybe I didn't appreciate your father enough," she said. "Who knows? Maybe we weren't even made for each other. Losing your love is the worst thing, and that's what we did." I didn't answer her, but I knew what she meant, and that it was true. "I wish we knew each other better, Frank," my mother said to me. She looked down, and I think she may have blushed. "We have our deep feelings, though, don't we? Both of us."

"Yes," I said. "We do."

"So. I'm going out now," my mother said. "Frank." She squeezed my wrist, and walked away through the checkout and into the parking lot, with Dick Spivey carrying their groceries beside her.

But when I had bought my own groceries and paid, and gone out to my car and started up, I saw Dick Spivey's green Chevrolet drive back into the lot and stop, and watched my mother get out and hurry across the snow to where I was, so that for a moment we faced each other through the open window.

"Did you ever think," my mother said, snow freezing in her hair. "Did you ever think back then that I was in love with Boyd Mitchell? Anything like that? Did you ever?"

"No," I said. "I didn't."

"No, well, I wasn't," she said. "Boyd was in love with Penny. I was in love with Roy. That's how things were. I want you to know it. You have to believe that. Do you?"

"Yes," I said. "I believe you."

And she bent down and kissed my cheek through the open window and touched my face with both her hands, held me for a moment that seemed like a long time before she turned away, finally, and left me there alone.

FIREWORKS

Eddie Starling sat at the kitchen table at noon reading through the newspaper. Outside in the street some neighborhood kids were shooting off firecrackers. The Fourth of July was a day away, and every few minutes there was a lot of noisy popping followed by a hiss, then a huge boom loud enough to bring down an airplane. It was giving him the jitters, and he wished some parent would go out and haul the kids inside.

Starling had been out of work six months—one entire selling season and part of the next. He had sold real estate, and had never been off work any length of time in his life. Though he had begun to wonder, after a certain period of not working, if you couldn't simply forget *how* to work, forget the particulars, lose the reasons for it. And once that happened, it could become possible never to hold another job as long as you lived. To become a statistic: the chronically unemployed. The thought worried him.

Outside in the street he heard what sounded like kids' noises again. They were up to something suspicious, and he stood up to look out just when the phone rang.

"What's new on the home front?" Lois's voice said. Lois had gone back to work tending bar near the airport and always tried to call up in good spirits.

"Status quo. Hot." Starling walked to the window, holding the receiver, and peered out. In the middle of the street some kids he'd never seen before were getting ready to blow up a tin can using an enormous firecracker. "Some kids are outside blowing up something."

"Anything good in the paper?"

"Nothing promising."

"Well," Lois said. "Just be patient, hon. I know it's hot. Listen, Eddie, do you remember those priests who were always setting fire to themselves on TV? Exactly when were they? We were trying to remember here. Was it '68 or '72? Nobody could remember to save their life."

"Sixty-eight was Kennedy," Starling said. "They weren't just setting themselves on fire for TV, though. They were in Asia."

"Okay. But when was Vietnam exactly?"

The kids lit the firecracker under the can and went running away down the street, laughing. For a moment Starling stared directly at the can, but just then a young woman came out of the house across the street. As she stepped into her yard the can went *boom*, and the woman leaped back and put her hands into her hair.

"Christ, what was that!" Lois said. "It sounded like a bomb."

"It was those kids."

"The scamps," Lois said. "I guess they're hot, too, though."

The woman was very thin—too thin to be healthy, Starling thought. She was in her twenties and had on dull yellow shorts and no shoes. She walked out into the street and yelled something vicious at the kids, who were far down the street now. Starling knew nothing more about her than he did about anybody else in the neighborhood. The name on the mailbox had been taped over before he and Lois had moved in. A man lived with the woman and worked on his car in the garage late at night.

The woman walked slowly back across her little yard to her house. At the top step she turned and looked at Starling's house. He stared at her, and the woman went inside and closed the door.

"Eddie, take a guess who's here," Lois said.

"Who's where?"

"In the bar. One wild guess."

"Arthur Godfrey," Starling said.

"Arthur Godfrey. That's great," Lois said. "No, it's Louie. He just waltzed in the door. Isn't that amazing?"

Louie Reiner was Lois's previous husband. Starling and Reiner had been business acquaintances of a sort before Lois came along, and had co-brokered some office property at the tail end of the boom.

Reiner had been in real estate then, along with everybody else. Reiner and Lois had stayed married six weeks, then they had gone over to Reno and gotten an annulment. A year later, Lois married Starling. That had all been in '76, and Lois didn't talk about it or about Reiner anymore. Louie had disappeared somewhere—he'd heard Europe. He didn't feel like he had anything against Louie now, though he wasn't particularly happy he was around.

"Just take a guess what Louie's doing?" Lois said. Water had started to run where Lois was.

"Who knows. Washing dishes. How should I know?"

Lois repeated what Starling said and some people laughed. He heard Louie's voice saying, "Well *excuuuse* me."

"Seriously, Ed. Louie's an extraditer." Lois laughed. Hah.

"What's that mean?" Starling said.

"It means he travels the breadth of the country bringing people back here so they can go to jail. He just brought a man back from Montana who'd done nothing more than pass a forty-seven-dollar bad check, which doesn't seem worth it to me. Louie isn't in uniform, but he's got a gun and a little beeper."

"What's he doing there?" Starling said.

"His girlfriend's coming in at the airport from Florida," Lois said. "He's a lot fatter than he used to be, too, though he wouldn't like me to say that, would you, Louie?" Starling heard Reiner say "*Excuuuse* me" again. "Do you want to talk to him?"

"I'm busy right now."

"Busy doing what, eating lunch? You're not busy."

"I'm fixing dinner," Starling lied.

"Talk to Louie, Eddie."

Starling wanted to hang up. He wished Reiner would go back to wherever he came from.

"*Helloooo dere,*" Reiner said.

"Who left your cage open, Reiner?"

"Come on down here and have a drink, Starling, and I'll tell you all about it. I've seen the world since I saw you. Italy, France, the islands. You know what an Italian girl puts behind her ears to make herself more attractive?"

"I don't want to know," Starling said.

"That's not what Lois says." Reiner laughed a horse laugh.

"I'm busy. Some other time, maybe."

"Sure you are," Reiner said. "Listen, Eddie, get off your face and come down here. I'll tell you how we can both retire in six months. Honest to God. This is not real estate."

"I already retired," Starling said. "Didn't Lois tell you?"

"Yeah, she told me a lot of things," Reiner said.

He could hear Lois say, "Please don't be a nerd, Eddie. Who needs nerds?" Some people laughed again.

"I shouldn't even be talking about this on the phone. It's that hot." Reiner's voice fell to a whisper. He was covering the mouthpiece of the receiver, Starling thought. "These are Italian rugs, Starling. I swear to God. From the neck of the sheep, the neck only. You only get tips on things like this in law enforcement."

"I told you. I'm retired. I retired early," Starling said.

"Eddie, am I going to have to come out there and arrest you?"

"Try it," Starling said. "I'll beat the shit out of you, then laugh about it."

He heard Reiner put the phone down and say something he couldn't make out. Then he heard Reiner shout, "Stay on your face then, cluck!"

Lois came on the line again. "Baby, why don't you come down here?" A blender started in the background, and a big cheer went up. "We're all adults. Have a Tanqueray on Louie. He's on all-expenses. There might be something to this. Louie's always got ideas."

"Reiner's just got ideas about you. Not me." He heard Reiner say to Lois to tell him—Starling—to forget it. "Tell Reiner to piss up a rope."

"Try to be nice," Lois said. "Louie's being nice. Eddie—"

Starling hung up.

When he worked, Starling had sold business properties—commercial lots and office buildings. He had studied that in college, and when he got out he was offered a good job. People would always need a place to go to work, was his thinking. He liked the professional environment, the atmosphere of money being made, and for a while he had done very well. He and Lois had rented a nice, sunny apartment in an older part of town by a park. They bought furniture and didn't save money. While Starling worked, Lois kept house, took care of plants and fish and attended a night class for her degree in history. They had no children, and didn't expect any. They liked the size of the town and the stores, knew shopkeepers' names and where the streets led. It was a life they could like, and better than they both could've guessed would come their way.

Then interest rates had gone sky-high, and suddenly no one wanted commercial property. Everything was rent. Starling rented space in malls and in professional buildings and in empty shops downtown where older businesses had moved out and leather stores, health-food and copy shops moved in. It was a holding action, Starling thought, until people wanted to spend again.

Then he had lost his job. One morning, his boss at the agency asked him back to his private office along with a fat woman named Beverley who'd been there longer than Starling had. His boss told them he was closing down and wanted to tell them first because they'd been there the longest, and he wanted them to have a chance for the other jobs. Starling remembered feeling dazed when he heard the bad news, but he remembered thanking the boss, wishing him good luck, then comforting Beverley, who went to pieces in the outer office. He had gone home and told Lois, and they had gone out to dinner at a Greek restaurant that night, and gotten good and drunk.

As it turned out, though, there weren't any other jobs to get. He visited the other agencies and talked to salesmen he knew, but all of his friends were terrified of being laid off themselves and wouldn't say much. After a month, he heard that his boss hadn't closed the agency down, but had simply hired two new people to take his and Beverley's places. When he called to ask about it the boss apologized, then claimed to have an important call on another line.

In six weeks Starling had still not found a job, and when the money ran out and they couldn't pay the rent, he and Lois sublet the apartment to two nurses who worked at a hospital, and got out. Lois found an ad in the *Pennysaver* that said, "No Rent for Responsible Couple—House Sit Opportunity." And they moved in that day.

The house was a ranchette in a tract of small, insignificant houses on fenced-in postage-stamp lots down on the plain of the Sacramento River, out from town. The owner was an Air Force sergeant who had been stationed in Japan, and the house was decorated with Oriental tastes: wind chimes and fat, naked women stitched over silk, a red enamel couch in the living room, rice-paper lanterns on the patio. There was an old pony in the back, from when the owner had been married with kids, and a couple of wrecked cars in the carport. All the people who lived on the street, Starling noticed, were younger than the two of them. More than a few were in the Air Force and fought loud, regular arguments, and came and went at all hours. There was always a door slamming after midnight, then a car starting up and racing away into the night. Starling had never thought he'd find himself living in such a place.

He stacked the dishes, put the grounds in the newspaper and emptied all the wastebaskets into a plastic bag. He intended to take the garbage for a ride. Everybody in the subdivision either drove their garbage to a dump several miles away or toured the convenience stores and shopping malls until they found a dumpster no one was watching. Once a black woman had run out of a convenience store and cursed at him for ditching his garbage in her dumpster, and since then he'd waited till dark. This afternoon, though, he needed to get out of the house, as though with the heat and talking to Reiner there wasn't enough air inside to breathe.

He had the garbage set out the back door when the phone rang again. Sometimes car dealers called during lunch, wanting to talk to the Air Force sergeant, and Starling had learned not to answer until after one, when car salesmen all left for lunch. This time it might be Lois again, wanting him to come by the bar to see Reiner, and he didn't want to answer. Only he didn't want Lois going off somewhere, and he didn't want Reiner coming over. Reiner would think the house with the pony was a comedy act.

Starling picked up the phone. "All right, what is it?"

An unfamiliar voice said, "Dad? Is that you?"

"No dads here, Reiner," Starling said.

"Dad," the voice said again, "it's Jeff."

A woman's voice came on the line. "I have a collect call to anyone from a Jeff. Will you pay for the call?"

"Wrong number," Starling said. He couldn't be sure it wasn't Reiner still.

"Dad," the voice said. It was a teenager's voice, a worried voice. "We're in awful trouble here, Dad. They've got Margie in jail."

"No, I can't help," Starling said. "I'm sorry. I can't help you."

"This party says you've got the wrong number, Jeff," the operator said.

"I know my own father's voice, don't I? Dad, for God's sake. This is serious. We're in trouble."

"I don't know any Jeffs," Starling said. "It's just the wrong number."

Starling could hear whoever was on the line hit something against the phone very hard, then say, "Shit! This isn't happening, I can't believe this is happening." The voice said something to someone else who was wherever he was. Possibly a policeman.

"It's the wrong number," the operator said. "I'm very sorry."

"Me too," Starling said. "I'm sorry."

"Would you like to try another number now, Jeff?" the operator asked.

"Dad, *please* accept. Please, my God. *Please*."

"Excuse the ring, sir," the operator said, and the line was disconnected.

Starling put down the phone and stared out the window. The three boys who had blown up the tin can were walking past, eyeing his house. They were going for more fireworks. The torn can lay in the street, and the woman across the way was watching them from her picture window, pointing them out to a man in an undershirt who didn't look like the man who worked on his car at night. He wondered if the woman was married or divorced. If she had children, where were they? He wondered who it was who had called—the sergeant's kids were all too young. He wondered what kind of trouble Jeff was in, and where was he? He should've accepted the charges, said a word of consolation, or given some advice since the kid had seemed at wit's end. He'd been in trouble in his life. He was in trouble now, in fact, but he hadn't been any help.

He drove toward town and cruised the lot at the King's Hat Drive-Inn, took a look in at the Super-Duper, then drove behind a truck stop. The garbage was with him in the hot front seat and already smelled bad despite the plastic. It was at the Super-Duper that the black woman had yelled at him and threatened to turn his garbage over to the police. Starling stopped back at the Super-Duper, parked at the side of the lot by the dumpster and went inside, leaving the garbage in the driver's seat. A different black woman was inside. He bought some breakfast cereal, a bag of frozen macaroni and a bottle of hot sauce, then went back out to the car. Another car had driven in and parked beside his, and the driver, a woman, was sitting in view of the dumpster, waiting for someone who had gone inside. The woman might be another Super-Duper employee, Starling thought, or possibly the wife of someone in the back he hadn't noticed.

He got in his car and drove straight out to a campground beside the Sacramento River, less than a mile from the house. He had come here and picnicked once with Lois, though the campground was empty now, all the loops and tables deserted. He pulled up beside a big green campground dumpster and heaved his garbage in without getting out of the car. Beyond the dumpster, through some eucalyptus trees, he could see the big brown river sliding swiftly by, pieces of yellow foam swirling in and out of the dark eddies. It was a treacherous river, he thought, full of perils. Each year someone drowned, and there were currents running deep beneath the surface. No one in his right mind would think of swimming in it, no matter how hot it got.

As he drove out he passed two motorcycles with Oregon plates, parked at the far end of the campground, and two hippies with long hair sitting on a rock, smoking. The hippies watched him when he drove by and didn't bother hiding their dope. Two young women were coming out of the bushes nearby, wearing bathing suits, and one of the hippies gave Starling the black power salute and grinned. Starling drove back out to the highway.

The hippies reminded him of San Francisco. His mother, Irma, had lived there with her last husband, Rex, who'd had money. When he was in community college Starling had lived there with them for six months, before moving with his first wife across the bay to Alameda near the airport. They had been hippies of a certain kind themselves then and had smoked dope occasionally. Jan, his first wife, had had an abortion in a student apartment right on the campus. Abortions were not easy to get then, and they'd had to call Honolulu to get a name out in Castroville. They had been married six months, and Starling's mother had had to lend them money she'd gotten from Rex.

When the abortionist came, he brought a little metal box with him, like a fishing-tackle box. They sat in the living room of the student apartment and talked about this and that, and drank beer. The man was named Dr. Carson. He told them he was being prosecuted at that very moment and was losing his license for doing this very thing—performing abortions—but that people needed help. He had three children of his own, he said, and Starling wondered if he ever performed abortions on his own wife. Dr. Carson said it would cost $400, and he could do it the next night, but needed all cash. Before he left he opened his metal box. There was nothing in it but fishing gear: a Pflueger reel, some monofilament line, several red-and-white Jitterbug lures. They had all three laughed. You couldn't be too cautious, Dr. Carson said. They all liked each other and acted like they could be friends in happier days.

The next night Dr. Carson came with a metal box that looked exactly the same as the one before, green with a silver handle. He went into the bedroom with Jan and closed the door while Starling sat in the living room, watched TV and drank beer. It was Christmastime and Andy Williams was on, singing carols with a man in a bear suit. After a while a loud whirring noise, like an expensive blender, came out of the bedroom. It continued for a while, then stopped, then started. Starling became nervous. Dr. Carson, he knew, was mixing up his little baby, and Jan was feeling excruciating pain but wasn't making noise. Starling felt sick then with fear and guilt and helplessness. And with love. It was the first time he knew he knew what real love was, his love for his wife and for all the things he valued in his life but could so easily lose.

Later, Dr. Carson came out and said everything would be fine. He smiled and shook Starling's hand and called him Ted, which was the phony name Starling had given him. Starling paid him the money in hundreds, and when Dr. Carson drove off, Starling stood out on the tiny balcony and waved. The doctor blinked his headlights, and in the distance Starling could see a small private plane settling down to the airport in the dark, its red taillight blinking like a wishing star.

Starling wondered where the hell Jan was now, or Dr. Carson, fifteen years later. Jan had gotten peritonitis and almost died after that, and when she got well she wasn't interested in being married to Eddie Starling anymore. She seemed very disappointed. Three months later she had gone to Japan, where she'd had a pen pal since high school, someone named Haruki. For a while she wrote Starling letters, then stopped. Maybe, he thought, she had moved back down to L.A. with her mother. He wished his own mother was alive still, and he could call her up. He was thirty-nine years old, though, and he knew it wouldn't help.

Starling drove along the river for a few miles until the wide vegetable and cantaloupe fields opened out, and the horizon extended a long way in the heat to a hazy wind line of Lombardy poplars. High, slat-sided trucks sat stationed against the white skyline, and men were picking in the near fields and beyond in long, dense crews. Mexicans, Starling thought, transients who worked for nothing. It was a depressing thought. There was nothing they could do to help themselves, but it was still depressing, and Starling pulled across the road and turned back toward town.

He drove out toward the airport, along the strip where it was mostly franchises and consignment lots and little shopping plazas, some of which he had once found the tenants for. All along the way, people had put up fireworks stands for the Fourth of July, red-white-and-blue banners fluttering on the hot breeze. Some of these people undoubtedly lived out where he and Lois lived now, in the same subdivision. That would mean something, he thought, if one day you found yourself looking out at the world going past from inside a fireworks stand. Things would've gotten far out of hand when that time came, there was no arguing it.

He thought about driving past the apartment to see if the nurses who sublet it were keeping up the little yard. The nurses, Jeri and Madeline, were two big dykes with men's haircuts and baggy clothes. They were friendly types, and in the real estate business dykes were considered A-1s—good tenants. They paid their rent, kept quiet, maintained property in good order, and held a firm stake in the status quo. They were like a married couple, was the business reasoning. Thinking about Jeri and Madeline, he drove past the light where their turn was, then just decided to keep driving.

There was nothing to do now, Starling thought, but drive out to the bar. The afternoon shift meant no one came in until Lois was almost ready to leave, and sometimes they could have the bar to themselves. Reiner would be gone by now and it would be cool inside, and he and Lois could have a quiet drink together, toast better cards on the next deal. They had had good times doing nothing but sitting talking.

Lois was leaning over the juke-box across from the bar when Starling came in. Mel, the owner, took afternoons off, and the place was empty. A dark-green bar light shone over everything, and the room was cool.

He was glad to see Lois. She had on tight black slacks and a frilly white top and looked jaunty. Lois was a jaunty woman to begin with, and he was happy he'd come.

He had met Lois in a bar called the AmVets down in Rio Vista. It was before she and Louie Reiner became a twosome, and when he saw her in a bar now it always made him think of things then. That had been a high time, and when they talked about it Lois liked to say, "Some people are just meant to experience the highest moments of their lives in bars."

Starling sat on a bar stool.

"I hope you came down here to dance with your wife," Lois said, still leaning over the jukebox. She punched a selection and turned around, smiling. "I figured you'd waltz in here pretty soon." Lois came by and patted him on the cheek. "I went ahead and punched in all your favorites."

"Let's have a drink first," Starling said. "I've got an edge that needs a drink."

"Drink first, dance second," Lois said and went behind the bar and got down the bottle of Tanqueray.

"Mel wouldn't mind," Starling said.

"Mary-had-a-little-lamb," Lois said while she poured a glassful. She looked up at Starling and smiled. "It's five o'clock someplace on the planet. Here's to old Mel."

216

"And some better luck," Starling said, taking a big first drink of gin and letting it trickle down his throat as slowly as he could.

Lois had been drinking already, he was sure, with Reiner. That wasn't the best he could have hoped for, but it could be worse. She and Reiner could be shacked up in a motel, or on their way to Reno or the Bahamas. Reiner was gone, and that was a blessing, and he wasn't going to let Reiner cast a shadow on things.

"Poor old Lou," Lois said and came around the bar with a pink drink she'd poured out of the blender.

"Poor Lou what?" Starling said.

Lois sat down beside him on a bar stool and lit a cigarette. "Oh, his stomach's all shot and he's got an ulcer. He said he worries too much." She blew out the match and stared at it. "You want to hear what he drinks?"

"Who cares what a dope like Reiner drinks out of a glass," Starling said.

Lois looked at him, then stared at the mirror behind the bar. The smoky mirror showed two people sitting at a bar alone. A slow country tune started to play, a tune Starling liked, and he liked the way—with the gin around it—it seemed to ease him away from his own troubles. "So tell me what Reiner drinks," he said.

"Wodka," Lois said matter-of-factly. "That's the way he says it. Wodka. Like Russian. Wodka with coconut milk—a Hawiian Russian. He say it's for his stomach, which he says is better though it's still a wreck. He's a walking pharmacy. And he's gotten a lot fatter, too, and his eyes bulge, and he wears a full Cleveland now. I don't know." Lois shook her head and smoked her cigarette. "He's got a cute girlfriend, though, this Jackie, from Del Rio Beach. She looks like Little Bo Peep."

Starling tried to picture Reiner. Louie Reiner had been a large, handsome man at one time, with thick eyebrows and penetrating black eyes. A sharp dresser. He was sorry to hear Reiner was fat and bug-eyed and wore a leisure suit. It was bad luck if that was the way you looked to the world.

"How was it, seeing Louie? Was it nice?" He stared at himself in the smoky mirror. He hadn't gotten fat, thank God.

"No," Lois said and dragged on her cigarette. "*He* was nice. Grown-up and what have you. But *it* wasn't nice. He didn't look healthy, and he still talked the same baloney, which was all before Jackie arrived, naturally."

"All what baloney?"

"You know that stuff, Eddie. Everybody makes *themselves* happy or unhappy. You don't leave one woman for another woman, you do it for yourself. If you can't make it with one, make it with all of them—that baloney he was always full of. Take the tour. Go big casino. That stuff. Reiner stuff."

"Reiner's big casino, all right," Starling said. "I guess he wanted you to go off with him."

"Oh sure. He said he was off to Miami next week to arrest some poor soul. He said I ought to go, and we could stay at the Fontainebleau or the Eden Roc or one of those sharp places."

"What about me?" Starling said. "Did I come? Or did I stay here? What about little Jackie?"

"Louie didn't mention either one of you, isn't that funny? I guess it slipped his mind." Lois smiled and put her arm on Starling's arm. "It's just baloney, Eddie. Trashy talk."

"I wish he was here now," Starling said. "I'd use a beer bottle on him."

"I know it, hon. But you should've heard what this little girlfriend said. It was a riot. She's a real Ripley's."

"She'd need to be," Starling said.

"Really. She said if Louie ran around on her she was going to sleep with a black man. She said she already had one picked out. She really knew how to work Louie. She said Louie had a house full of these cheap Italian carpets, and nobody to sell them to. That was his big deal he needed a partner for, by the way—not a very big market over here, I guess. She said Louie was thinking of selling them in Idaho. Good luck with that, I said. She said—and this would've made you laugh, Eddie, it would've truly—she said it's a doggy-dog world out there. Doggy-dog. She was real cute. When she said that, Louie got down on the floor and barked like a dog. He dropped his pistol out of his whatever-you-call-it, his scabbard, and his beeper"—Lois was laughing—"he was like a big animal down on the floor of the bar."

"I'm sorry I missed it."

"Louie can be funny," Lois said.

"Maybe you should've married him, then."

"I *did* marry him."

"Too bad you didn't stay married to him instead of me. I don't have a beeper."

"I like what you have got, though, sweetheart." She squeezed his arm. "Nobody would love me like you do, you know I think that. Reiner was just my mistake, but I can laugh at him today because I don't have to live with him. You're such a big mamma's boy, you don't want anybody to have any fun."

"I'd like to have a little fun," Starling said. "Let's go where there's some fun."

Lois leaned and kissed him on the cheek. "You smell awfully nice." She smiled at him. "Come on and dance with me, Ed. Justice demands that you dance with me. You have that light step. It's nice when you do."

Lois walked out onto the little dance floor and took Starling's hand. He stood close to her and they danced to the slow music on the jukebox, holding together the way they had when he'd first known her. He felt a little drunk. A buzz improved a thing, he thought, made a good moment out of nothing.

"You're a natural dancer, Eddie," Lois said softly. "Remember us dancing at Powell's on the beach, with everybody watching us?"

"You like having men think about you?" Starling said.

"Oh, sure. I guess." Lois's cheek was against his cheek. "It makes me feel like I'm in a movie, sometimes, you know? Everybody does that, don't they?"

"I never do."

"Don't you ever wonder what your ex thinks about you? Old Jan. That was a long time ago, I guess."

"Bygones are bygones to me," Starling said. "I don't think about it."

"You're such a literal, Eddie. You get lost in the lonely crowd, I think sometimes. That's why I want to be nice and make you happy." She held him close to her so that her hard, flat hips were next to his. "Isn't this nice? It's nice to dance with you."

Starling saw now that the bar was decorated with red, white, and blue crêpe paper—features he'd missed. Little curlicues and ribbons and stars hung from the dark rafters and down off the shaded green bar lights and the beer signs and the framed pictures behind the back bar. This was festive, he thought. Lois had fixed it, it showed her hand. Before long a crowd would be in, the lights would go up and shine out, the music would be turned up loud. It would be a good time. "That's nice," Starling said.

"I just love this," Lois said. Her head was on his shoulder. "I just love this so much."

On the highway toward home, Starling passed the hippies he had seen at the campground. They were heading in now, the women on the rear seats, the men driving fast, leaning as if the wind blew them back.

In town, a big fireworks display staged by a shopping

220

mall was beginning. Catherine wheels and star bursts and blue-and-pink sprays were going off in the twilight. Cars were stopped along the road, and people with children sat on their hoods, drinking beer and watching the sky. It was nearly dark and rain had begun to threaten.

"Everything's moved out to the malls now," Lois said, "including the fireworks." She had been dozing and now she leaned against her door, staring back toward the lights.

"I wouldn't care to work in one," Starling said, driving.

Lois said nothing.

"You know what I was just thinking about?" she said after a while.

"Tell me," Starling said.

"Your mother," Lois said. "Your mother was a sweet old lady, you know that? I liked her very much. I remember she and I would go to the mall and buy her a blouse. Just some blouse she could've bought in Bullock's in San Francisco, but she wanted to buy it here to be sweet and special." Lois smiled about it. "Remember when we bought fireworks?"

Starling's mother had liked fireworks. She liked to hear them pop so she could laugh. Starling remembered having fireworks one year in the time since he'd been married to Lois. When was that? he thought. A time lost now.

"Remember she held the little teenies right in her fingers and let them go off? That tickled her so much."

"That was her trick," Eddie said. "Rex taught her that."

"I guess he did," Lois said. "But you know, I don't blame you, really, for being such a mamma's boy, Eddie. Not with *your* mamma—unlike mine, for instance. She's why you're as nice as you are."

"I'm selfish," Starling said. "I always have been. I'm capable of lying, stealing, cheating."

Lois patted him on the shoulder. "You're generous, though, too."

Rain was starting in big drops that looked like snow on

221

the windshield. Lights from their subdivision glowed out under the lowered sky ahead.

"This weird thing happened today," Starling said. "I can't quit thinking about it."

Lois slid over by him. She put her head on his shoulder and her hand inside his thigh. "I knew something had happened, Eddie. You can't hide anything. The truth is just on you."

"There's no truth to *this*," Starling said. "Just the phone rang when I was leaving, and it was this kid, Jeff. He was in some kind of mess. I didn't know who he was, but he thought I was his father. He wanted me to accept charges."

"You didn't, did you?"

Starling looked toward the subdivision. "No. I should have, though. It's on my mind now that I should've helped him. I'd just finished talking to Reiner."

"He might've been in Rangoon, for Christ's sake," Lois said. "Or Helsinki. You don't know where he was. It could've cost you five hundred dollars, then you couldn't have helped him anyway. You were smart, is what I think."

"It wouldn't matter, though. I could've given him some advice. He said somebody was in jail. It's just on my mind now, it'll go away."

"Get a good job and then accept charges from Istanbul," Lois said and smiled.

"I just wonder who he was," Starling said. "For some reason I thought he was over in Reno—isn't that odd? Just a voice."

"It'd be worse if he *was* in Reno," Lois said. "Are you sorry you don't have one of your own?" Lois looked over at him strangely.

"One what?"

"A son. Or, you know. Didn't you tell me you almost had one? There was something about that, with Jan."

"That was a long time ago," Starling said. "We were idiots."

"Some people claim they make your life hold together better, though," Lois said. "You know?"

"Not if you're broke they don't," Starling said. "All they do is make you sorry."

"Well, we'll just float on through life together, then, how's that?" Lois put her hand high on his leg. "No blues today, hon, okay?"

They were at the little dirt street where the ranchette was, at the far end. A fireworks hut had been built in the front yard of the first small house, a chain of bright yellow bulbs strung across the front. An elderly woman was standing in the hut, her face expressionless. She had on a sweater and was holding a little black poodle. All the fireworks but a few Roman candles had been sold off the shelves.

"I never thought I'd live where people sold fireworks right in their front yards," Lois said and faced front. Starling peered into the lighted hut. The rain was coming down in a slow drizzle, and water shone off the oiled street. He felt the urge to gesture to the woman, but didn't. "You could just about say we lived in a place where you wouldn't want to live if you could help it. Funny, isn't it? That just happens to you." Lois laughed.

"I guess it's funny," Starling said. "It's true."

"What'd you dream up for dinner, Eddie? I've built up a hunger all of a sudden."

"I forgot about it," Starling said. "There's some macaroni."

"Whatever," Lois said. "It's fine."

Starling pulled into the gravel driveway. He could see the pony standing out in the dark where the fenced weed lot extended to the side of the house. The pony looked like a ghost, its white eyes unmoving in the rain.

"Tell me something," Starling said. "If I ask you something, will you tell me?"

"If there's something to tell," Lois said. "Sometimes there isn't anything, you know. But go ahead."

"What happened with you and Reiner?" he said. "All that Reno stuff. I never asked you about that. But I want to know."

"That's easy," Lois said and smiled at him in the dark car. "I just realized I didn't love Reiner, that's all. Period. I realized I loved you, and I didn't want to be married to somebody I didn't love. I wanted to be married to you. It isn't all that complicated or important." Lois put her arms around his neck and hugged him hard. "Don't be cloudy now, sweet. You've just had some odd luck is all. Things'll get better. You'll get back. Let me make you happy. Let me show you something to be happy, baby doll." Lois slid across the seat against the door and went down into her purse. Starling could hear wind chimes in the rain. "Let me just show you," Lois said.

Starling couldn't see. Lois opened the door out into the drizzle, turned her back to him and struck a match. He could see it brighten. And then there was a sparkling and hissing, and then a brighter one, and Starling smelled the harsh burning and the smell of rain together. Then Lois closed the door and danced out before the car into the rain with the sparklers, waving her arms round in the air, smiling widely and making swirls and patterns and star-falls for him that were brilliant and illuminated the night and the bright rain and the little dark house behind her and, for a moment, caught the world and stopped it, as though something sudden and perfect had come to earth in a furious glowing for him and for him alone—Eddie Starling—and only he could watch and listen. And only he would be there, waiting, when the light was finally gone.

COMMUNIST

My mother once had a boyfriend named Glen Baxter. This was in 1961. We—my mother and I—were living in the little house my father had left her up the Sun River, near Victory, Montana, west of Great Falls. My mother was thirty-two at the time. I was sixteen. Glen Baxter was somewhere in the middle, between us, though I cannot be exact about it.

We were living then off the proceeds of my father's life insurance policies, with my mother doing some part-time waitressing work up in Great Falls and going to the bars in the evenings, which I know is where she met Glen Baxter. Sometimes he would come back with her and stay in her room at night, or she would call up from town and explain that she was staying with him in his little place on Lewis Street by the GN yards. She gave me his number every time, but I never called it. I think she probably thought that what she was doing was terrible, but simply couldn't help herself. I thought it was all right, though. Regular life it seemed, and still does. She was young, and I knew that even then.

Glen Baxter was a Communist and liked hunting, which he talked about a lot. Pheasants. Ducks. Deer. He killed all of them, he said. He had been to Vietnam as far back as then, and when he was in our house he often talked about shooting the animals over there—monkeys and beautiful parrots—using military guns just for sport. We did not know what Vietnam was then, and Glen, when he talked about that, referred to it only as "the Far East." I think now he must've been in the CIA and been disillusioned by something he saw or found out about and been thrown out, but that kind of thing did not matter to us. He was a tall, dark-eyed man with short black hair, and was usually in a good humor. He had gone halfway through college in Peoria, Illinois, he said, where he grew up. But when he was around our life he worked wheat farms as a ditcher, and stayed out of work winters and in the bars drinking with women like my mother, who had work and some money. It is not an uncommon life to lead in Montana.

What I want to explain happened in November. We had not been seeing Glen Baxter for some time. Two months had gone by. My mother knew other men, but she came home most days from work and stayed inside watching television in her bedroom and drinking beers. I asked about Glen once, and she said only that she didn't know where he was, and I assumed they had had a fight and that he was gone off on a flyer back to Illinois or Massachusetts, where he said he had relatives. I'll admit that I liked him. He had something on his mind always. He was a labor man as well as a Communist, and liked to say that the country was poisoned by the rich, and strong men would need to bring it to life again, and I liked that because my father had been a labor man, which was why we had a house to live in and money coming through. It was also true that I'd had a few boxing bouts by then—just with town boys and one with an Indian from Choteau—and there were some girlfriends I knew from that. I did not like my mother being around the house so much at night, and I wished Glen Baxter would come back, or that another man would come along and entertain her somewhere else.

At two o'clock on a Saturday, Glen drove up into our yard in a car. He had had a big brown Harley-Davidson that he rode most of the year, in his black-and-red irrigators and a baseball cap turned backwards. But this time he had a car, a blue Nash Ambassador. My mother and I went out on the porch when he stopped inside the olive trees my father had planted as a shelter belt, and my mother had a look on her face of not much pleasure. It was starting to be cold in earnest by then. Snow was down already onto the Fairfield Bench, though on this day a chinook was blowing, and it could as easily have been spring, though the sky above the Divide was turning over in silver and blue clouds of winter.

"We haven't seen you in a long time, I guess," my mother said coldly.

"My little retarded sister died," Glen said, standing at the door of his old car. He was wearing his orange VFW jacket and canvas shoes we called wino shoes, something I had never seen him wear before. He seemed to be in a good humor. "We buried her in Florida near the home."

"That's a good place," my mother said in a voice that meant she was a wronged party in something.

"I want to take this boy hunting today, Aileen," Glen said. "There're snow geese down now. But we have to go right away, or they'll be gone to Idaho by tomorrow."

"He doesn't care to go," my mother said.

"Yes I do," I said, and looked at her.

My mother frowned at me. "Why do you?"

"Why does he need a reason?" Glen Baxter said and grinned.

"I want him to have one, that's why." She looked at me oddly. "I think Glen's drunk, Les."

"No, I'm not drinking," Glen said, which was hardly ever true. He looked at both of us, and my mother bit down on the side of her lower lip and stared at me in a way to make you think she thought something was being put over on her and she didn't like you for it. She was very pretty, though when she was mad her features were sharpened and less pretty by a long way. "All right, then I don't care," she said to no one in particular. "Hunt, kill, maim. Your father did that too." She turned to go back inside.

"Why don't you come with us, Aileen?" Glen was smiling still, pleased.

"To do what?" my mother said. She stopped and pulled a package of cigarettes out of her dress pocket and put one in her mouth.

"It's worth seeing."

"See dead animals?" my mother said.

"These geese are from Siberia, Aileen," Glen said. "They're not like a lot of geese. Maybe I'll buy us dinner later. What do you say?"

"Buy what with?" my mother said. To tell the truth, I didn't know why she was so mad at him. I would've thought she'd be glad to see him. But she just suddenly seemed to hate everything about him.

"I've got some money," Glen said. "Let me spend it on a pretty girl tonight."

"Find one of those and you're lucky," my mother said, turning away toward the front door.

"I already found one," Glen Baxter said. But the door slammed behind her, and he looked at me then with a look I think now was helplessness, though I could not see a way to change anything.

M‌y mother sat in the backseat of Glen's Nash and looked out the window while we drove. My double gun was in the seat between us beside Glen's Belgian pump, which he kept loaded with five shells in case, he said, he saw something beside the road he wanted to shoot. I had hunted rabbits before, and had ground-sluiced pheasants and other birds, but I had never been on an actual hunt before, one where you drove out to some special place and did it formally. And I was excited. I had a feeling that something important was about to happen to me, and that this would be a day I would always remember.

My mother did not say anything for a long time, and neither did I. We drove up through Great Falls and out the other side toward Fort Benton, which was on the benchland where wheat was grown.

"Geese mate for life," my mother said, just out of the blue, as we were driving. "I hope you know that. They're special birds."

"I know that," Glen said in the front seat. "I have every respect for them."

"So where were you for three months?" she said. "I'm only curious."

"I was in the Big Hole for a while," Glen said, "and after that I went over to Douglas, Wyoming."

"What were you planning to do there?" my mother asked.

"I wanted to find a job, but it didn't work out."

"I'm going to college," she said suddenly, and this was something I had never heard about before. I turned to look at her, but she was staring out her window and wouldn't see me.

"I knew French once," Glen said. "*Rosé*'s pink. *Rouge*'s red." He glanced at me and smiled. "I think that's a wise idea, Aileen. When are you going to start?"

"I don't want Les to think he was raised by crazy people all his life," my mother said.

"Les ought to go himself," Glen said.

"After I go, he will."

"What do you say about that, Les?" Glen said, grinning.

"He says it's just fine," my mother said.

"It's just fine," I said.

Where Glen Baxter took us was out onto the high flat prairie that was disked for wheat and had high, high mountains out to the east, with lower heartbreak hills in between. It was, I remember, a day for blues in the sky, and down in the distance we could see the small town of Floweree, and the state highway running past it toward Fort Benton and the Hi-line. We drove out on top of the prairie on a muddy dirt road fenced on both sides, until we had gone about three miles, which is where Glen stopped.

"All right," he said, looking up in the rearview mirror at my mother. "You wouldn't think there was anything here, would you?"

"*We're* here," my mother said. "You brought us here."

"You'll be glad though," Glen said, and seemed confident to me. I had looked around myself but could not see anything. No water or trees, nothing that seemed like a good place to hunt anything. Just wasted land. "There's a big lake out there, Les," Glen said. "You can't see it now from here because it's low. But the geese are there. You'll see."

"It's like the moon out here, I recognize that," my mother said, "only it's worse." She was staring out at the flat wheatland as if she could actually see something in particular, and wanted to know more about it. "How'd you find this place?"

"I came once on the wheat push," Glen said.

"And I'm sure the owner told you just to come back and hunt anytime you like and bring anybody you wanted. Come one, come all. Is that it?"

"People shouldn't own land anyway," Glen said. "Anybody should be able to use it."

"Les, Glen's going to poach here," my mother said. "I just want you to know that, because that's a crime and the law will get you for it. If you're a man now, you're going to have to face the consequences."

"That's not true," Glen Baxter said, and looked gloomily out over the steering wheel down the muddy road toward the mountains. Though for myself I believed it was true, and didn't care. I didn't care about anything at that moment except seeing geese fly over me and shooting them down.

"Well, I'm certainly not going out there," my mother said. "I like towns better, and I already have enough trouble."

"That's okay," Glen said. "When the geese lift up you'll get to see them. That's all I wanted. Les and me'll go shoot them, won't we, Les?"

"Yes," I said, and I put my hand on my shotgun, which had been my father's and was heavy as rocks.

"Then we should go on," Glen said, "or we'll waste our light."

We got out of the car with our guns. Glen took off his canvas shoes and put on his pair of black irrigators out of the trunk. Then we crossed the barbed wire fence, and walked out into the high, tilled field toward nothing. I looked back at my mother when we were still not so far away, but I could only see the small, dark top of her head, low in the backseat of the Nash, staring out and thinking what I could not then begin to say.

On the walk toward the lake, Glen began talking to me. I had never been alone with him, and knew little about him except what my mother said—that he drank too much, or other times that he was the nicest man she had ever known in the world and that someday a woman would marry him, though she didn't think it would be her. Glen told me as we walked that he wished he had finished college, but that it was too late now, that his mind was too old. He said he had liked the Far East very much, and that people there knew how to treat each other, and that he would go back some day but couldn't go now. He said also that he would like to live in Russia for a while and mentioned the names of people who had gone there, names I didn't know. He said it would be hard at first, because it was so different, but that pretty soon anyone would learn to like it and wouldn't want to live anywhere else, and that Russians treated Americans who came to live there like kings. There were Communists everywhere now, he said. You didn't know them, but they were there. Montana had a large number, and he was in touch with all of them. He said that Communists were always in danger and that he had to protect himself all the time. And when he said that he pulled back his VFW jacket and showed me the butt of a pistol he had stuck under his shirt against his bare skin. "There are people who want to kill me right now," he said, "and I would kill a man myself if I thought I had to." And we kept walking. Though in a while he said, "I don't think I know much about you, Les. But I'd like to. What do you like to do?"

"I like to box," I said. "My father did it. It's a good thing to know."

"I suppose you have to protect yourself too," Glen said.

"I know how to," I said.

"Do you like to watch TV," Glen asked, and smiled.

"Not much."

"I love to," Glen said. "I could watch it instead of eating if I had one."

I looked out straight ahead over the green tops of sage that grew to the edge of the disked field, hoping to see the lake Glen said was there. There was an airishness and a sweet smell that I thought might be the place we were going, but I couldn't see it. "How will we hunt these geese?" I said.

"It won't be hard," Glen said. "Most hunting isn't even hunting. It's only shooting. And that's what this will be. In Illinois you would dig holes in the ground and hide and set out your decoys. Then the geese come to you, over and over again. But we don't have time for that here." He glanced at me. "You have to be sure the first time here."

"How do you know they're here now," I asked. And I looked toward the Highwood Mountains twenty miles away, half in snow and half dark blue at the bottom. I could see the little town of Floweree then, looking shabby and dimly lighted in the distance. A red bar sign shone. A car moved slowly away from the scattered buildings.

"They always come November first," Glen said.

"Are we going to poach them?"

"Does it make any difference to you," Glen asked.

"No, it doesn't."

"Well then, we aren't," he said.

We walked then for a while without talking. I looked back once to see the Nash far and small in the flat distance. I couldn't see my mother, and I thought that she must've turned on the radio and gone to sleep, which she always did, letting it play all night in her bedroom. Behind the car the sun was nearing the rounded mountains southwest of us, and I knew that when the sun was gone it would be cold. I wished my mother had decided to come along with us, and I thought for a moment of how little I really knew her at all.

Glen walked with me another quarter-mile, crossed another barbed wire fence where sage was growing, then went a hundred yards through wheatgrass and spurge until the ground went up and formed a kind of long hillock bunker built by a farmer against the wind. And I realized the lake was just beyond us. I could hear the sound of a car horn blowing and a dog barking all the way down in the town, then the wind seemed to move and all I could hear then and after then were geese. So many geese, from the sound of them, though I still could not see even one. I stood and listened to the high-pitched shouting sound, a sound I had never heard so close, a sound with size to it—though it was not loud. A sound that meant great numbers and that made your chest rise and your shoulders tighten with expectancy. It was a sound to make you feel separate from it and everything else, as if you were of no importance in the grand scheme of things.

"Do you hear them singing," Glen asked. He held his hand up to make me stand still. And we both listened. "How many do you think, Les, just hearing?"

"A hundred," I said. "More than a hundred."

"Five thousand," Glen said. "More than you can believe when you see them. Go see."

I put down my gun and on my hands and knees crawled up the earthwork through the wheatgrass and thistle, until I could see down to the lake and see the geese. And they were there, like a white bandage laid on the water, wide and long and continuous, a white expanse of snow geese, seventy yards from me, on the bank, but stretching far onto the lake, which was large itself—a half-mile across, with thick tules on the far side and wild plums farther and the blue mountain behind them.

"Do you see the big raft?" Glen said from below me, in a whisper.

"I see it," I said, still looking. It was such a thing to see, a view I had never seen and have not since.

234

"Are any on the land?" he said.

"Some are in the wheatgrass," I said, "but most are swimming."

"Good," Glen said. "They'll have to fly. But we can't wait for that now."

And I crawled backwards down the heel of land to where Glen was, and my gun. We were losing our light, and the air was purplish and cooling. I looked toward the car but couldn't see it, and I was no longer sure where it was below the lighted sky.

"Where do they fly to?" I said in a whisper, since I did not want anything to be ruined because of what I did or said. It was important to Glen to shoot the geese, and it was important to me.

"To the wheat," he said. "Or else they leave for good. I wish your mother had come, Les. Now she'll be sorry."

I could hear the geese quarreling and shouting on the lake surface. And I wondered if they knew we were here now. "She might be," I said with my heart pounding, but I didn't think she would be much.

It was a simple plan he had. I would stay behind the bunker, and he would crawl on his belly with his gun through the wheatgrass as near to the geese as he could. Then he would simply stand up and shoot all the ones he could close up, both in the air and on the ground. And when all the others flew up, with luck some would turn toward me as they came into the wind, and then I could shoot them and turn them back to him, and he would shoot them again. He could kill ten, he said, if he was lucky, and I might kill four. It didn't seem hard.

"Don't show them your face," Glen said. "Wait till you think you can touch them, then stand up and shoot. To hesitate is lost in this."

"All right," I said. "I'll try it."

"Shoot one in the head, and then shoot another one," Glen said. "It won't be hard." He patted me on the arm and smiled. Then he took off his VFW jacket and put it on the ground, climbed up the side of the bunker, cradling his shotgun in his arms, and slid on his belly into the dry stalks of yellow grass out of my sight.

Then, for the first time in that entire day, I was alone. And I didn't mind it. I sat squat down in the grass, loaded my double gun and took my other two shells out of my pocket to hold. I pushed the safety off and on to see that it was right. The wind rose a little, scuffed the grass and made me shiver. It was not the warm chinook now, but a wind out of the north, the one geese flew away from if they could.

Then I thought about my mother, in the car alone, and how much longer I would stay with her, and what it might mean to her for me to leave. And I wondered when Glen Baxter would die and if someone would kill him, or whether my mother would marry him and how I would feel about it. And though I didn't know why, it occurred to me that Glen Baxter and I would not be friends when all was said and done, since I didn't care if he ever married my mother or didn't.

Then I thought about boxing and what my father had taught me about it. To tighten your fists hard. To strike out straight from the shoulder and never punch backing up. How to cut a punch by snapping your fist inwards, how to carry your chin low, and to step toward a man when he is falling so you can hit him again. And most important, to keep your eyes open when you are hitting in the face and causing damage, because you need to see what you're doing to encourage yourself, and because it is when you close your eyes that you stop hitting and get hurt badly. "Fly all over your man, Les," my father said. "When you see your chance, fly on him and hit him till he falls." That, I thought, would always be my attitude in things.

And then I heard the geese again, their voices in unison, louder and shouting, as if the wind had changed again and put all new sounds in the cold air. And then a *boom*. And I knew Glen was in among them and had stood up to shoot. The noise of geese rose and grew worse, and my fingers burned where I held my gun too tight to the metal, and I put it down and opened my fist to make the burning stop so I could feel the trigger when the moment came. *Boom*, Glen shot again, and I heard him shuck a shell, and all the sounds out beyond the bunker seemed to be rising—the geese, the shots, the air itself going up. *Boom*, Glen shot another time, and I knew he was taking his careful time to make his shots good. And I held my gun and started to crawl up the bunker so as not to be surprised when the geese came over me and I could shoot.

From the top I saw Glen Baxter alone in the wheatgrass field, shooting at a white goose with black tips of wings that was on the ground not far from him, but trying to run and pull into the air. He shot it once more, and it fell over dead with its wings flapping.

Glen looked back at me and his face was distorted and strange. The air around him was full of white rising geese and he seemed to want them all. "Behind you, Les," he yelled at me and pointed. "They're all behind you now." I looked behind me, and there were geese in the air as far as I could see, more than I knew how many, moving so slowly, their wings wide out and working calmly and filling the air with noise, though their voices were not as loud or as shrill as I had thought they would be. And they were so close! Forty feet, some of them. The air around me vibrated and I could feel the wind from their wings and it seemed to me I could kill as many as the times I could shoot—a hundred or a thousand—and I raised my gun, put the muzzle on the head of a white goose, and fired. It shuddered in the air, its wide feet sank below its belly, its wings cradled out to hold back air, and it fell straight down and landed with an awful sound, a noise a human would make, a thick, soft, *hump* noise. I looked up again and shot another goose, could hear the pellets hit its chest, but it didn't fall or even break its pattern for flying. *Boom,* Glen shot again. And then again. "Hey," I heard him shout, "Hey, hey." And there were geese flying over me, flying in line after line. I broke my gun and reloaded, and thought to myself as I did: I need confidence here, I need to be sure with this. I pointed at another goose and shot it in the head, and it fell the way the first one had, wings out, its belly down, and with the same thick noise of hitting. Then I sat down in the grass on the bunker and let geese fly over me.

By now the whole raft was in the air, all of it moving in a slow swirl above me and the lake and everywhere, finding the wind and heading out south in long wavering lines that caught the last sun and turned to silver as they gained a distance. It was a thing to see, I will tell you now. Five thousand white geese all in the air around you, making a noise like you have never heard before. And I thought to myself then: this is something I will never see again. I will never forget this. And I was right.

Glen Baxter shot twice more. One he missed, but with the other he hit a goose flying away from him, and knocked it half falling and flying into the empty lake not far from shore, where it began to swim as though it was fine and make its noise.

Glen stood in the stubby grass, looking out at the goose, his gun lowered. "I didn't need to shoot that one, did I, Les?"

"I don't know," I said, sitting on the little knoll of land, looking at the goose swimming in the water.

"I don't know why I shoot 'em. They're so beautiful." He looked at me.

"I don't know either," I said.

"Maybe there's nothing else to do with them." Glen

stared at the goose again and shook his head. "Maybe this is exactly what they're put on earth for."

I did not know what to say because I did not know what he could mean by that, though what I felt was embarrassment at the great numbers of geese there were, and a dulled feeling like a hunger because the shooting had stopped and it was over for me now.

Glen began to pick up his geese, and I walked down to my two that had fallen close together and were dead. One had hit with such an impact that its stomach had split and some of its inward parts were knocked out. Though the other looked unhurt, its soft white belly turned up like a pillow, its head and jagged bill-teeth, its tiny black eyes looking as they would if they were alive.

"What's happened to the hunters out here?" I heard a voice speak. It was my mother, standing in her pink dress on the knoll above us, hugging her arms. She was smiling though she was cold. And I realized that I had lost all thought of her in the shooting. "Who did all this shooting? Is this your work, Les?"

"No," I said.

"Les is a hunter, though, Aileen," Glen said. "He takes his time." He was holding two white geese by their necks, one in each hand, and he was smiling. He and my mother seemed pleased.

"I see you didn't miss too many," my mother said and smiled. I could tell she admired Glen for his geese, and that she had done some thinking in the car alone. "It *was* wonderful, Glen," she said. "I've never seen anything like that. They were like snow."

"It's worth seeing once, isn't it?" Glen said. "I should've killed more, but I got excited."

My mother looked at me then. "Where's yours, Les?"

"Here," I said and pointed to my two geese on the ground beside me.

My mother nodded in a nice way, and I think she liked everything then and wanted the day to turn out right and for all of us to be happy. "Six, then. You've got six in all."

"One's still out there," I said, and motioned where the one goose was swimming in circles on the water.

"Okay," my mother said and put her hand over her eyes to look. "Where is it?"

Glen Baxter looked at me then with a strange smile, a smile that said he wished I had never mentioned anything about the other goose. And I wished I hadn't either. I looked up in the sky and could see the lines of geese by the thousands shining silver in the light, and I wished we could just leave and go home.

"That one's my mistake there," Glen Baxter said and grinned. "I shouldn't have shot that one, Aileen. I got too excited."

My mother looked out on the lake for a minute, then looked at Glen and back again. "Poor goose." She shook her head. "How will you get it, Glen?"

"I can't get that one now," Glen said.

My mother looked at him. "What do you mean?"

"I'm going to leave that one," Glen said.

"Well, no. You can't leave one," my mother said. "You shot it. You have to get it. Isn't that a rule?"

"No," Glen said.

And my mother looked from Glen to me. "Wade out and get it, Glen," she said in a sweet way, and my mother looked young then, like a young girl, in her flimsy short-sleeved waitress dress and her skinny, bare legs in the wheatgrass.

"No." Glen Baxter looked down at his gun and shook his head. And I didn't know why he wouldn't go, because it would've been easy. The lake was shallow. And you could tell that anyone could've walked out a long way before it got deep, and Glen had on his boots.

My mother looked at the white goose, which was not more than thirty yards from the shore, its head up, moving in slow circles, its wings settled and relaxed so you could see the black tips. "Wade out and get it, Glenny, won't you, please?" she said. "They're special things."

"You don't understand the world, Aileen," Glen said. "This can happen. It doesn't matter."

"But that's so cruel, Glen," she said, and a sweet smile came on her lips.

"Raise up your own arms, 'Leeny," Glen said. "I can't see any angel's wings, can you, Les?" He looked at me, but I looked away.

"Then you go on and get it, Les," my mother said. "You weren't raised by crazy people." I started to go, but Glen Baxter suddenly grabbed me by my shoulder and pulled me back hard, so hard his fingers made bruises in my skin that I saw later.

"Nobody's going," he said. "This is over with now."

And my mother gave Glen a cold look then. "You don't have a heart, Glen," she said. "There's nothing to love in you. You're just a son of a bitch, that's all."

And Glen Baxter nodded at my mother, then, as if he understood something he had not understood before, but something that he was willing to know. "Fine," he said, "that's fine." And he took his big pistol out from against his belly, the big blue revolver I had only seen part of before and that he said protected him, and he pointed it out at the goose on the water, his arm straight away from him, and shot and missed. And then he shot and missed again. The goose made its noise once. And then he hit it dead, because there was no splash. And then he shot it three times more until the gun was empty and the goose's head was down and it was floating toward the middle of the lake where it was empty and dark blue. "Now who has a heart?" Glen said. But my mother was not there when he turned around. She had already started back to the car and was almost lost from sight in the darkness. And Glen smiled at me then and his face had a wild look on it. "Okay, Les?" he said.

"Okay," I said.

"There're limits to everything, right?"

"I guess so," I said.

"Your mother's a beautiful woman, but she's not the only beautiful woman in Montana." And I did not say anything. And Glen Baxter suddenly said, "Here," and he held the pistol out at me. "Don't you want this? Don't you want to shoot me? Nobody thinks they'll die. But I'm ready for it right now." And I did not know what to do then. Though it is true that what I wanted to do was to hit him, hit him as hard in the face as I could, and see him on the ground bleeding and crying and pleading for me to stop. Only at that moment he looked scared to me, and I had never seen a grown man scared before—though I have seen one since—and I felt sorry for him, as though he was already a dead man. And I did not end up hitting him at all.

A light can go out in the heart. All of this happened years ago, but I still can feel now how sad and remote the world was to me. Glen Baxter, I think now, was not a bad man, only a man scared of something he'd never seen before—something soft in himself—his life going a way he didn't like. A woman with a son. Who could blame him there? I don't know what makes people do what they do, or call themselves what they call themselves, only that you have to live someone's life to be the expert.

My mother had tried to see the good side of things, tried to be hopeful in the situation she was handed, tried to look out for us both, and it hadn't worked. It was a strange time in her life then and after that, a time when she had to adjust to being an adult just when she was on the thin edge of things. Too much awareness too early in life was her problem, I think.

And what I felt was only that I had somehow been pushed out into the world, into the real life then, the one I hadn't lived yet. In a year I was gone to hard-rock mining and no-paycheck jobs and not to college. And I have thought more than once about my mother saying that I had not been raised by crazy people, and I don't know what that could mean or what difference it could make, unless it means that love is a reliable commodity, and even that is not always true, as I have found out.

Late on the night that all this took place I was in bed when I heard my mother say, "Come outside, Les. Come and hear this." And I went out onto the front porch barefoot and in my underwear, where it was warm like spring, and there was a spring mist in the air. I could see the lights of the Fairfield Coach in the distance, on its way up to Great Falls.

And I could hear geese, white birds in the sky, flying. They made their high-pitched sound like angry yells, and though I couldn't see them high up, it seemed to me they were everywhere. And my mother looked up and said, "Hear them?" I could smell her hair wet from the shower. "They leave with the moon," she said. "It's still half wild out here."

And I said, "I hear them," and I felt a chill come over my bare chest, and the hair stood up on my arms the way it does before a storm. And for a while we listened.

"When I first married your father, you know, we lived

on a street called Bluebird Canyon, in California. And I thought that was the prettiest street and the prettiest name. I suppose no one brings you up like your first love. You don't mind if I say that, do you?" She looked at me hopefully.

"No," I said.

"We have to keep civilization alive somehow." And she pulled her little housecoat together because there was a cold vein in the air, a part of the cold that would be on us the next day. "I don't feel part of things tonight, I guess."

"It's all right," I said.

"Do you know where I'd like to go?"

"No," I said. And I suppose I knew she was angry then, angry with life, but did not want to show me that.

"To the Straits of Juan de Fuca. Wouldn't that be something? Would you like that?"

"I'd like it," I said. And my mother looked off for a minute, as if she could see the Straits of Juan de Fuca out against the line of mountains, see the lights of things alive and a whole new world.

"I know you liked him," she said after a moment. "You and I both suffer fools too well."

"I didn't like him too much," I said. "I didn't really care."

"He'll fall on his face. I'm sure of that," she said. And I didn't say anything because I didn't care about Glen Baxter anymore, and was happy not to talk about him. "Would you tell me something if I asked you? Would you tell me the truth?"

"Yes," I said.

And my mother did not look at me. "Just tell the truth," she said.

"All right," I said.

"Do you think I'm still very feminine? I'm thirty-two years old now. You don't know what that means. But do you think I am?"

And I stood at the edge of the porch, with the olive trees before me, looking straight up into the mist where I could not see geese but could still hear them flying, could almost feel the air move below their white wings. And I felt the way you feel when you are on a trestle all alone and the train is coming, and you know you have to decide. And I said, "Yes, I do." Because that was the truth. And I tried to think of something else then and did not hear what my mother said after that.

And how old was I then? Sixteen. Sixteen is young, but it can also be a grown man. I am forty-one years old now, and I think about that time without regret, though my mother and I never talked in that way again, and I have not heard her voice now in a long, long time.

RICHARD FORD

The Sportswriter

The end and the aftermath of a marriage, the emotional dislocation and the discovery of a new life while in the embrace of troubled memories of the old, have seldom been more harrowingly plotted.

'. . . an outstanding novel' CHRISTOPHER WORDSWORTH, *The Guardian*

'. . . a magnificent voyage of self-discovery through the Waste Land of suburban New Jersey which sets [Ford] alongside Philip Roth and Saul Bellow' JONATHAN RABAN, Books of the Year, *The Observer*

A Piece of My Heart

The vicious, yet moving and funny, story of two men, one pursuing a woman, the other searching for his own self.

'A modern book of great power. Mr Ford writes with a stark brilliance that imprints descriptions of the land and people deeply into one's consciousness' *Daily Telegraph*

'Here is clarity, sharpness and originality. The dialogue is immaculate. The storytelling and plotting are confident and rich in texture. This is quality writing in the highest American traditions of Faulkner, Hemingway and Steinbeck' *The Times*

Rock Springs

Stories about ordinary people trying to make sense of their lives.

'Every detail has a kind of tough rightness; where people work, what they eat, what they listen to on the car radio. Behind precisely accurate dialogue, Ford lets us make out the vulnerability of people whose tenderness rarely finds expression . . . Alongside *The Sportwriter*, *Rock Springs* confirms Ford's place among our finest writers' *The Times*

Flamingo

ADELAIDA GARCIA MORALES

The Silence of the Sirens

In a timeless, dark hillside village in southern Spain, two
women, one deeply, obsessively in love, become entangled
in a fantasy dreamworld where fear and hope are poised in
precarious balance.

'a beautiful, sincere book, one of those books that are
thought up, felt and written with such simple mastery that
the author's "talent" is transparent, indefinable – you are
simply left with the passionate interest of reading on.'

Le Figaro

'. . . sings with insane magic. This book is like the script of
a strangely silent opera, disconcerting but convincing.'

Kate Cruise O'Brien, *The Sunday Times*

Flamingo

HELEN DIXON

Playing Foxes

'A beautifully written first novel of bereaved young housewife, Anna, who takes in a Japanese student for extra funds and to cheer up her children.' *Company*

'. . . a delicately described domestic clash between two cultures.' *Books*

'. . . a perceptive study of contrasting cultures.' *The Scotsman*

Flamingo

MARGUERITE DURAS

La Douleur

'The work cuts to the bone: distressing and illuminating as the texts are about the nature of war and the self, and the eroticism of grief and violence. How rare and valuable is this account of the last wild, hurtful, murderous days of Hitler's Reich in Paris. Enough to make you change your view of history.'   Fay Weldon

The Lover

Rarely have I read a novel so flawlessly written, so intensely felt that the usual veil between the reader and the writing dissolves. The reality of the fiction is, very nearly, unbearable.'   *Spectator*

Outside
Selected Writings

Drawn from magazine and newspaper articles written over a twenty-year period, *Outside* is an unforgettable chronicle of Duras's involvement with the world around her, an involvement fuelled by an overwhelming urge to denounce injustice, and an irresistible curiosity about love, crime, art, passion and politics.

Flamingo

ANTHONY STORR

Solitude

In this brilliant and acclaimed book, the eminent psychoanalyst Dr Anthony Storr challenges the widely held view that success in personal relationships is the only key to happiness. He argues persuasively that we pay far too little attention to some of the other great satisfactions of life – work and creativity. In a series of skilful biographical sketches, he demonstrates how many of the creative geniuses of our civilisation have been solitary, by temperament or circumstance, and how the capacity to be alone is, even for those who are not creative, a sign of maturity.

'This is a short book, but so rich in ideas, and presented with such a telling combination of gentleness and authority, that it is also exceptionally absorbing and thought-provoking.'

Claire Tomalin, *Observer*

Flamingo

Flamingo

Flamingo is a quality imprint publishing both fiction and non-fiction. Below are some recent titles.

Fiction
☐ The Shadow Bride *Roy Heath* £4.95
☐ Family Mashber *Der Nister* £5.95
☐ The Idle Hill of Summer *Julia Hamilton* £3.95
☐ Night Night *Sharman MacDonald* £3.95
☐ Stephen and Violet *Susan Barrett* £3.95
☐ The Beginning of Spring *Penelope Fitzgerald* £3.95
☐ Ghosts *Eva Figes* £3.95
☐ My Friend Matt and Hena the Whore *Adam Zameenzad* £3.95

Non-fiction
☐ Uncommon Wisdom *Fritjof Capra* £4.95
☐ Feeding the Rat *Al Alvarez* £3.95
☐ A Pike in the Basement *Simon Loftus* £3.95
☐ The Book of Five Rings *Miyamoto Musashi* £3.95
☐ The Dancing Wu Li Masters *Gary Zukav* £4.95
☐ More Home Life *Alice Thomas Ellis* £3.95
☐ In the Ditch *Buchi Emecheta* £3.95

You can buy Flamingo paperbacks at your local bookshop or newsagent. Or you can order them from Fontana Paperbacks, Cash Sales Department, Box 29, Douglas, Isle of Man. Please send a cheque, postal or money order (not currency) worth the purchase price plus 22p per book (or plus 22p per book if outside the UK).

NAME (Block letters) _____

ADDRESS_____

_____

_____

While every effort is made to keep prices low, it is sometimes necessary to increase them at short notice. Fontana Paperbacks reserve the right to show new retail prices on covers which may differ from those previously advertised in the text or elsewhere.